AMERICAN
NATURE
WRITING
2002

Selected by John A. Murray

Fulcrum Publishing
Golden, Colorado

To my son, Steven

Library of Congress Cataloging-in-Publication Data

American nature writing 2002 / selected by John A. Murray.
    p. cm.
ISBN 1-55591-315-6
1. Nature—Literary collections. 2. American literature—21st century. I. Murray, John A., 1954–
PS509.N3 A46 2001
810.8'036—dc21   2001002330

Printed in the United States of America
0 9 8 7 6 5 4 3 2 1

Editorial: Daniel Forrest-Bank, Mindy Keskinen
Cover and interior design: Alice Merrill
Typesetting: Pro Production
Cover painting: *High Clouds,* oil on canvas, 18" x 24".
    Copyright © 1998 John A. Murray.

Fulcrum Publishing
16100 Table Mountain Parkway, Suite 300
Golden, Colorado 80403
(800) 992-2908 • (303) 277-1623
www.fulcrum-books.com

CONTENTS

3

CONTENTS

INTRODUCTION

by John A. Murray

My truths, three in number, are the following: first, humanity is ultimately the product of biological evolution; second, the diversity of life is the cradle and greatest natural heritage of the human species; and third, philosophy and religion make little sense without taking into account these first two conceptions.

—E. O. Wilson, from *Naturalist*

As the *American Nature Writing* annual enters its ninth volume and begins a fresh association with a new publisher, it is well to pause and reflect on the changes that have transformed our country since the series was created. In the past decade the country has, among other things, established the largest number of national parks, monuments, and historic sites since the passage of the comprehensive Alaska Lands Bill of 1980. These spectacular natural areas include the 1.9-million-acre Grand Staircase–Canyons of the Escalante National Monument (Utah), the million-acre Grand Canyon–Parashant National Monument (Arizona), Great Sand Dunes National Park (Colorado), the Missouri Breaks National Monument (Montana), and the Northern Pacific Marine Reserve (Hawaii), to name just a few. The publishing world, too, underwent unprecedented changes in the 1990s, as editors and readers witnessed the meteoric rise of Amazon.com and other Internet book providers, the proliferation of retail book "superstores" by such companies as Barnes & Noble and Borders, and an era of deep book discounting (with a commensurate effect on literacy, as well as on publishing).

Nine years is both a small and a large period of time. In terms of the Grand Canyon or the Grand Teton, of course, it is only a moment, but in terms of human society, it represents an almost generational epoch. This is especially true when a civilization is crossing the threshold into a new century and millennium. In large part because of these signal changes, the recent past has been particularly rich for writing about nature. One thinks of Peter Matthiessen's pioneering work in Asia (*Tigers in the Snow*), E. O. Wilson's influential leadership in biodiversity (*The Ants*, winner of the Pulitzer Prize), and David Quammen's compelling inquiry into island biogeography (*Song of the Dodo*). To a writer whose mature period of productivity is ordinarily limited to one or two decades, nine years is a virtual lifetime. In that span Darwin sailed around the world on the HMS *Beagle* and wrote four of his most important books, as well as the scientific essay that anticipated *The Origin of Species.* Thoreau lived for fifteen months at Walden and went on to compose all of his historic essays ("Civil Disobedience," "A Plea for Captain John Brown," "Walking") and his one immortal creation, *Walden.* Rachel Carson produced the central body of work for which she will be forever remembered: *The Edge of the Sea, The Sea Around Us, Under the Sea Wind,* and *Silent Spring.* Looking forward to the next decade, it is clear we can expect further positive developments for nature and literature.

Through it all—the computer revolution, the lingering twilight of the twentieth century, the fireworks attending the birth of the third millennium—this modest collection has faithfully appeared every year. To date, over 170 authors have been featured in this series. Some are established writers, while others are just emerging. Most fall somewhere in between. When I look back over the past nine volumes, I think of a forest, and of the individual writers as trees in that forest. Canopy after canopy, branch after branch, these diverse talents rise all around. The young, the old, the middle-aged. Grand patriarchs and eager upstarts. Flourishing writers whose hard work has brought them good luck, and those with yet-fulfilled careers handicapped by unexpected misfortune. Looming behemoths with enough books in them to build a small library, and fragile seedlings with a single essay to their credit. Males and females, withered bachelors and venerable matriarchs, reclusive cabin dwellers and gregarious city folk, the whole aswarm with struggle and color, darkness and radiance, silence and noise, altruism and avarice, fertility and decay—an ancient, ever-green ecosystem that is forever producing new niches for new writers to fill.

———————

What I have most tried to do in this series is to nurture emerging talent, especially women writers (whose work is disproportionately represented on our shelves). Why? Because when I started out writing there was no one to render such assistance. Like most people entering the guild, I was a self-sufficient entity, and this Cervantes-like period persisted for some time. The experience, of course, made me a stronger person and a better writer, but I always vowed that if I ever reached a position where I could help emerging authors, I would do everything I could for them (i.e., the lessons learned over ten years can just as well be absorbed in two or three years). Other than watching my young son grow, nothing gives me more happiness than to know that I have, as an editor, helped an emerging writer in some practical way—to improve their vision and craft, to liberate their imagination, to sharpen their critical sense, to deepen their ethical awareness, to validate their dreams, to assist concretely in publishing their essays or books.

My approach with this annual has been to make the selection process entirely democratic. When someone submits a piece of writing, it doesn't matter to me who they are or what they have done in the past. I have rejected lackluster works from famous writers who live on Penshurst-like estates and I have accepted brilliant essays by seasonal rangers who live most of the year in leaky backpacking tents. I have published works by colleagues and critics, friends and strangers, a president and a prison inmate alike, and always with equal enthusiasm. To each submission I apply the same editorial standards of excellence. I always hope for the best, and commence reading in that optimistic frame of mind. Above all, I try to remain editorially neutral—to include those works for which I am personally enthused, as well as those for which I feel less personal affection, but which I know will find an appreciative constituency. For this literary task, I have often thought that my upbringing contributes a unique advantage—I was born the middle son of a middle-class family in the middle of the country in the middle of the last century. As a result of my origins and my journey, and as an inherent part of who I am, I naturally bring the open-minded perspective of an Everyman to the job of editing.

Some might lament that this egalitarian philosophy will inevitably increase the number of writers and make matters more challenging for some. I take the contrary view. The one thing that nature has taught me is that active competition is a desired state of affairs. For three billion years the free and open contest for resources has driven natural selection and evolution on this planet. The process has, among other things, functioned well enough to produce and shape the human race, as well as to foster some measure of social progress. Literary history demonstrates that the periods of most spirited competition and experimentation—the annual dramatic contests of Aeschylus, Sophocles, and Euripedes; the literary horseraces of Marlowe, Jonson, and Shakespeare; the informal competitions of Hemingway, Fitzgerald, Faulkner, and Steinbeck—have consistently produced the works of greatest excellence. Mediocrity prevails only when competition is stifled, standards are lowered, and conformity imposed. The sometimes raucous but always lively marketplace of ideas ensures that innovation flourishes over imitation.

With this in mind I am, with this year's collection, instituting the William O. Douglas Nature Writing Award. It carries with it no wooden plaque or gilded trophy, no sheepskin certificate, no monetary compensation—for the authentic writer does not write for payment, but rather from the happiness that derives from pursuing truth and beauty. The award carries with it only the knowledge that this editor, for whatever it is worth, found a particular work to be the best that crossed his desk in the previous year (not the "best" of that year, but the "best to cross his desk"—there is a difference). It is named in honor of one of the seminal figures in the environmental movement. William O. Douglas served on the Supreme Court from 1939 to 1975. During his tenure Douglas, among other things, authored the "Wilderness Bill of Rights" (1965) and wrote the 1972 court opinion stating that wilderness has a right to legal standing in the courts (*Sierra Club v. Morton*). Douglas was also an ardent environmentalist, helping to form what is now the Arctic National Wildlife Refuge, and a distinguished nature writer (*Farewell to Texas: A Vanishing Wilderness, My Wilderness: East to Katahdin, My Wilderness: The Pacific West*). The award is meant to set the literary bar as high as possible, to encourage writers to always tell the truth, to remind us of the importance of making a difference, and to honor work well done.

This year's award goes to the poems by the distinguished New Mexican poet and essayist Penny Harter, whose work has appeared in previous *American Nature Writing* anthologies (1999, 2000, 2001). Many of the diverse themes and points-of-view present in this 2002 collection are evident in her work, as she thoughtfully explores the importance of place to the human spirit and to the creative artist. The geography of the imagination, the confluence of choice, the vagaries of wild and human nature—all are given consideration in her poems. In the poem "Pelvis With Moon, 1943," inspired by the well-known oil painting by Georgia O'Keeffe, Harter writes of a bone in the desert that had "fallen from some female" and that had once "cradled her young." In her poem, as in the painting, the bone becomes a powerful symbol, inspiring an epiphany that evokes both the myth of Mother Earth and the interdependence of all life.

In an earlier poem, "In the Distance," Harter writes: "We are all moving/toward the same horizon." This perspective—an overwhelming sense of a shared mission in guarding that which has saved us—pervades the other selections in this year's volume, from Glenn Vanstrum's look at the faraway wild of the Arctic Brooks Range to Penelope Grenoble O'Malley's examination of suburban life in the Santa Monica Mountains north of Los Angeles. Each contributor, regardless of style or approach, pays quiet homage to this same universal principle of reverence and duty. In the end, we are left with the sense that each author is part of a larger movement determined to leave the world a better place. Each no doubt fervently believes that words have power and that books can slowly but significantly change the world, if only one reader at a time.

As always, I invite my readers to send me their work (P.O. Box 102345, Denver, Colorado 80250). I am especially interested in writing from underrepresented regions of the country (the Northeast, the Midwest, the Deep South), from those who write about nature in the urban or suburban context, from those known only locally or regionally (or perhaps not at all) but with national potential, and from those with writings inspired by travel abroad. The selections do not have to be strictly natural. I invite essays, stories, and poems in which nature is on the margins as well as those in which it is the focal point. Chiefly, I am attracted to writing that is original in voice and perspective and that evidences excellence in craft. The best way for a potential contributor to achieve a sense of my editorial approach is to review the selections in the nine volumes to date.

Thank you, dear friends, for having lovingly nurtured this series with your bookstore choices, kind submissions, and welcome inquiries. Your warm and friendly cards, letters, and packages are truly cherished—I always open them first, and an unexpected salutation is a wonderful way to start the morning. Working together—readers, writers, and editors—we can keep the *American Nature Writing* series alive and well in this challenging new century. This effort, we can be sure, will be as beneficial for literature and nature as it will be for the society that is sustained by literature and nature.

EAGLES, SOUTH RONALDSAY, ORKNEY

Suzanne Ross

We walk, my friend and I, to the Isbister chambered tomb, the Tomb of the Eagles, along a farm track sloping uphill toward the flagstone cliffs at the sea's edge. Like much of the land on the Orkney Islands, the Liddle Farm on South Ronaldsay is treeless, windy pasture. But close to the ground along the track, flowers bloom. We search for the small white blossoms of grass of Parnassus and easily find the purple globes of sheep's bit. The thin, tilted sheets of flagstone surface only as we near the cliffs.

Here rock pipits flutter between the jutting angles of the sandstone boulders. A ringed plover gleans insects in the rock litter; its piping call audible, its body melts from moment to moment against the gray and honey-brown stone. The wind sharpens, and the soft inland sounds fade. Fulmars glide and bank over the cliffs and above the sea just past my reach. Here at the cliff edge the land falls abruptly away into the sea below, and we hear the steady wash of waves on rock.

Some 5,000 years ago, people began to build this tomb. They chose this high cliff with the tilted and broken flagstone and the endless sound of the sea. For eight, even ten generations, perhaps 200 years, they worked. They maintained access to the tomb for more than 1,500 years, generations beyond counting. We stand here now at the cliff edge, the entrance of the tomb behind us as the fulmars ride the

11

constant wind and the sea climbs and then falls away from the rock face below us.

———

The setting of the Tomb of the Eagles is dramatic. The entrance looks out upon a flagstone forecourt created by the partial remains of a wall—called a hornwork—to the north, and the raised ground level—probably also once a wall—to the south. Beyond the forecourt, the cliffs fall to the sea.

The encompassing walls of the forecourt and the thick walls of the tomb itself are constructed of layered flagstone slabs. A heavy lintel stone above the doorway forces us down upon hands and knees for a five- or six-foot crawl along the tight entrance passage into the interior of the tomb. We stand up in the long narrow main chamber, some eight feet in height at the center and divided into three stalls by vertical slabs of flagstone, each four or five feet tall, that thrust out of the walls. Two small raised compartments are built into the walls opposite the entrance, another in the wall just on our right. Two more chambers are formed by additional vertical flagstones at either end of the main chamber.

Inside it is dark, even with a good flashlight, and damp. It is impossible to get a sense of the size and shape of the small raised compartments without crawling in. I can't bring myself to crawl in.

———

The Tomb of the Eagles is but one of many such chambered cairn tombs associated with the neolithic people who lived in the north of Scotland. The stark and wind-whipped Orkneys, as well as the Shetlands still farther north, are rich in these ancient structures. The earliest tombs, dating from the beginning of the fourth millennium B.C., were probably built by the first settlers to cross the Pentland Firth from Caithness, the northeasternmost region of Scotland, perhaps to South Ronaldsay, the nearest landfall, less than ten miles distant. Today, if the day is clear, the nearest of the Orkneys—South Ronaldsay and Hoy, are just visible on the horizon from the cliffs at John O'Groats.

The tomb at Isbister was first excavated in 1958 by Ronald Simison, who, along with his family, still works the Liddle Farm. They continue today as the custodians of the tomb itself and of the small "museum."

————

We arrive well before ten o'clock, when the site is opened to visitors. It's a gray-on-gray day in mid-August, all color and sound muted and subdued. The air is still, neither warm nor cool, and shadowless. As we walk toward the gate, a white nanny goat hurries towards us, bright in the quiet that surrounds her. Her cool golden eyes with their horizontal pupils are steady, confident, unrevealing as she takes my fingers into her mouth, testing and tasting. A woman calls out to us, inviting us in.

The museum is really only three narrow acrylic cases arranged along the window wall of an enclosed porch at the front of the main house on the farm. Not all of the contents of the tomb remain here on the farm, but what does remain is taken from the cases piece by piece by Mr. Simison's young granddaughter, working in the museum this summer for the first time.

She takes out stone implements, some crudely fashioned, others delicate and crafted with skill and care. A graceful mace-head of a dark, white-veined stone, three small axe heads, a slim, oval knife of the palest green, and a polished jet button, smooth to slickness and deep black as the eye of a fulmar. I am surprised by the tactile pleasure of these stone objects in my hands.

Three human skulls rest in the second case, the skulls of two men and a woman. Time has rubbed the bone of each to the same warm, honey-brown of the flagstone on this side of South Ronaldsay. Mr. Simison's granddaughter takes each skull out in turn, speaks about its notable features, and offers each to us to hold. I have never held any human skull before; these are nearly 5,000 years old. The matter-of-factness of the proceedings is eerie, unnerving.

All three of these people died early, well before the age of thirty, as it seems was common. The wisdom teeth of one young man had not yet descended but remain forever embedded in the bones of his jaws. Across the top of the woman's skull runs a depression, a groove pressed into the bone. Probably she carried heavy loads by means of a tumpline or band round her head.

Before she closes this case, Mr. Simison's granddaughter lifts out the last of the remains she will tell us about today. She places in our hands the talons of white-tailed sea eagles, themselves also nearly 5,000 years old. The talons, about the length of my curved index finger, as well as other bones of sea eagles, were found mixed with the human bones in the tomb.

––––––––––

It was about 2,400 B.C., more than 4,000 years ago, that archae-ologists believe the builders sealed the tomb after some 800 years of use. At that time, they lifted off the flagstone lintels of the roof and filled the main chamber with stones laid horizontally. Included in this infill were disarticulated human bones and the skeletal remains of at least ten white-tailed sea eagles.

As the modern excavation worked backward through time, down through the infill to the floor of the main chamber and into the small side compartments, the tomb gave up its contents but not its wonder. Within the main chamber, the builders placed masses of human bones, not as complete skeletons but certainly in a pattern of sorts, with skulls arranged along the walls, each with a pile of bones before it. In one of the small side compartments, they laid more bones, unaccompanied by skulls; the remaining two side compartments, however, they filled with human skulls. These were the bones of more than 300 people, placed in the tomb at various times over the 200 years of its earliest use. And mixed with all of these bones were the bones of white-tailed sea eagles.

At last, at the most ancient level of the tomb, the space below the flagstone floor of one of the side compartments, excavators came to the foundation deposit. Here too they found not complete skele-tons but the disarticulated and partial remains of fifteen men and women, and again, the disarticulated and partial remains of white-tailed sea eagles.

————

What can we say about fragments of lives glimpsed across time in this way? What can we know of beliefs and motivations? Archaeologists do agree that tombs such as this one must have functioned more complexly than as mere burial vaults for a community's dead. For while the Tomb of the Eagles held more than 16,000 human bones, the partial remains of 342 people, the complete skeleton of not even one person was found. Present in the tomb instead are samples of the bones of community members spanning the 800 years of its most active use.

The archaeologist who has written most extensively about the Tomb of the Eagles, John W. Hedges, suggests that what was needed was a store of ancestral remains in this, the spiritual focal point of the community. He believes that the people who built this tomb must have practiced "excarnation." In other words, the bodies of the dead were exposed to scavengers, likely on platforms in the curving flagstone forecourt outside the entrance of the tomb. Once the bodies were rid of flesh, a sampling of bones was taken into the tomb and placed on the floor of the main chamber. Over the years, bones and skulls were separated and moved to the compartments in the side walls of the end chambers. As they could not in life, the members of this community mingled with one another across the years, generation with generation, in death.

But what of the bones of generations of white-tailed sea eagles mixed with these human bones at every level of the tomb across the centuries of its use? Only one conclusion seems plausible: the sea eagle was the totem of the people who built this tomb. Human being and white-tailed sea eagle, linked here in death as they were linked in life. And so the name of the tomb at Isbister is doubly accurate. It *is* the Tomb of the Eagles.

————

Yet what did the builders of the tomb know of the bird whose bones they mingled with their own in this necessary repository of ancestral remains? They knew the physical actualities. The wingspan of the eagle, roughly 6 feet, exceeded their own heights on average by at least a foot. The archaeologist Anna Ritchie even suggests that the people of this community would have been aware that the sea eagles tended to live longer than they did themselves, perhaps thirty years or more. And, I must say it now, it would have been the sea eagles that cleaned the flesh away from the bones of their dead.

We can only speculate about the meanings the builders of the tomb constructed around these physical actualities. Even so, it does not seem idle to imagine that for them the white-tailed sea eagle was of encompassing importance. Their bodies enclosed within the bird's wingspan. Their lives encircled by the bird's life span. Their flesh consumed at the end in the first sacred act of preparation for internment within the tomb.

They soar above us. Their shadows pass over us and engulf us. They consume us. We are in them. We are here together where the land ends and falls away to the sea.

———

We stand near the cliff edge beyond the tomb and the flagstone forecourt, watching the fulmars as they bank and glide. A young arctic skua, a dull mottled brown, passes. Gull-heavy, head tilting, it is watchful, ready, aware that the ledges here may yet hold fulmar chicks. Surely this too is where the sea eagles, like the skua, once passed. Large and imposing birds, their wings spread expansively, they too must have soared and then descended to ride the firm updrafts here along these jagged flagstone cliffs—watchful, ready, aware.

We see no eagles today although in the past they were a common sight. They disappeared from Orkney some 150 years ago. Persecuted throughout the eighteenth and nineteenth centuries by gamekeepers on the vast Highland estates, their numbers in all of Scotland fell to near-extinction levels. The last active nest was reported in 1916 on the Isle of Skye, at one time a stronghold. But the severest persecutions occurred at the times of the Highland Clearances, when people were turned out of their crofts and off their lands to make way for sheep. Lamb-killers, the eagles were called. They were themselves easy to kill. As willing consumers of carrion, they readily took the poisoned bait.

In 1975 the long process of reintroduction and recovery began with young birds taken from the still-viable Norwegian population and, after a time, released on the island of Rhum in the Inner Hebrides. Susceptible to the falconer's training, these young sea eagles are capable as well of "hacking back," that is, returning over time to a wild state, recovering as it were wild knowledge. And because of their willingness to take carrion meat, these young birds can be supported in the early days of their recolonization.

Slowly, their numbers in Scotland are growing as a result of the regular introduction of young birds from Norway and the increasing experience and nesting success of the birds already present in the refounded Scottish population. Although in recent years several birds thought to have come from the west of Scotland have been sighted in Orkney, these islands still await the sea eagles' permanent return.

All I know of the white-tailed sea eagle I must take from books. I stand now on this angled flagstone cliff, dizzy at the sight of the waves below me, longing to feel the shadow of those wings pass over me. This longing feels like an emptiness, and my fear is that it is a permanent absence. Such an absence as this can only be felt where once there was a real and palpable presence, a presence in the bones. The necessity of this bird, I realize, is what we share with the people who built this tomb.

Ours is a longing, a hunger not easily sated. For it is a hunger of the spirit. Yet pulsing at the center of the sea eagle's absence is the hope that lingers of another presence.

We see no eagles today. They are gone, perhaps forever.

———

We walk away from the tomb to our right along the cliff edge path toward Ham Geo. A geo (pronounced "gyo") is an inlet or cove steeply cut into the rock. We sit on one side of the geo on up-slanted rocks covered by lichens the color of the absent sun and softened by tufts of grass.

I sit, troubled, aware that I am not present, that my time is not this time, aware of an emptiness down to the bone that I cannot name.

Fulmars course past a few feet in front of us and at eye level, marking the position of the cliff edge that we cannot see. Their gray-tinged wings are stiff, unerring; only their white heads shift. From time to time, one bird passes very close, and I hear wings slice air. On this gray day, the deep glow of their jet eyes startles.

On the opposite side of the geo, a sharply angled shelf of rock stretches away from the cliff and into the sea. A single black-backed gull and three cormorants, the strength of color drained from their black feathers, have come up onto the shelf to rest and watch. They stand, facing seaward. In the sea beyond the point of the flagstone shelf, other cormorants dive, then surface again to float, dipping their heads from time to time to scan for fish. One rises briefly, chest above the sea, head and neck extended, beating its wings to dry them.

Behind the rock shelf, a raft of eider ducks, females and young of the year, rise and subside in the gray-green swell and wash. They drift around to the inlet side of the shelf, their communal intention discernible only in its result. Waves heave them toward the rock, their swimming flight visible beneath the water as it rises against the shelf. But they ride and dive, fearless, untroubled.

A female grey seal breaks the surface in the bay between the flagstone shelf and the cliff edge where we sit. She bottles, gazing round her for a time, before she slides again below the dark sea. Then comes a snorting and blowing of air below us and to our left. Two seals, a bull and a cow, float away from the rock wall, one before the other, bodies fully extended, gray on gray, along the surface of the sea. First one, now the other, they too slide beneath the dull water.

I sit, facing seaward, present for a time—watchful, ready, aware. For a time, in this place, we are together.

———

The cliff-edge world fades as we walk away from Ham Geo and inland again along another farm track. Meadow pipits dart above the dried husks of seathrift, no longer pink. Rock gives way to pasture, and we see the buildings of the Liddle Farm hazy in the distance before us.

Then, without warning, here, the empty gray sky breaks open. A flock of fifteen or twenty black-headed gulls billows like blown thistle seeds above, behind, around a hen harrier, cool-eyed and resolute. Her flight is the pulsing presence at the center, filling the emptiness. Time slows, and my hungry eyes consume her. She arcs upward, the white patch of feathers just above her long tail and her ruddy shoulders visible only for a moment. She extends her legs as if to stoop, talons reaching down to clasp a fence post. But she veers left and recedes away from us, flowing on with measured wing beats, head held low and level in concentration. Seeing deep into the upthrust blades of grass, between the white capillary-veined petals of the grass of Parnassus, through the narrow passage to the nest of the meadow vole, across generations beyond counting, she sees into time itself.

The hen harrier, although rare, holds on in Orkney.

ABOVE THE CHUKCHI SEA

Glenn Vanstrum

"The sea begins in the mountains."

—Chinese proverb

Black lava scree and basalt spires loom above us, ramparts and turrets of a dark mountain castle in Alaska's Brooks Range. We have been climbing since dawn, or what passes for dawn here at 68 degrees north latitude. Our feet crunch and slide on sunlit black lava chips. The ridge to the summit hangs unchanged overhead, no matter how far we climb. There is something about the clear, hard light of the Arctic—distant boulders turn to pebbles under your nose, and outcroppings just above take hours to approach.

To the east and south, barren, snow-laced peaks stretch to a crystalline, purple-blue horizon. To the north and west, hidden by the mountain, plains of permafrost greet the thawing Chukchi Sea. Only rich, green tundra 2,000 feet beneath our boots betrays the otherworldly feel of the landscape and reassures us we are still on planet Earth.

My knee joints, cold and stiff in the sleeping bag when an early bird shook the tent at 2 A.M., are now warm and well-oiled with pain. The blister on my left big toe, a real honey I've been working on for a fortnight, has become a searing point of agony.

Steve, a taciturn Pennsylvania mountain man, has never once complained on our long trek across the Lisburne Peninsula into the DeLong Mountains. His beard is wet with sweat and melted frost, his usually sparkling blue eyes are now dull and lined with fatigue. He bails suddenly, echoing what my feet long to hear:

"I'm turning back. Can't go on. Meet you at the tussocks."

Dennis Schmitt, our leader, pauses. Dennis knows the Brooks Range better than just about anyone. He has spent every summer here for decades, speaks Inuit, and has climbed dozens of nameless peaks. Now his lined weathered face grimaces. A long, wiry arm, sleeved by an ancient, faded-blue, oft-mended parka, reaches to scratch behind thinning hair where it doesn't itch.

To split a party in the middle of nowhere is not a good idea. In case of injury, we have only a small line-of-sight radio to flag down a passing plane, and the device lies eight miles back at camp. Trouble is, in the last month we have yet to see an airplane, a road, or a building. Here in northwest Alaska, at the divide between the Kokolik and Noatak Rivers, there is no civilization—only tundra, mountains, caribou, and the odd barren-ground grizzly.

Dennis is too dedicated a mountaineer to quit, too conscientious a leader to feel good about continuing. But Steve is tough. Dennis figures he'll be okay.

"Be careful," is all he says. My feet and I watch longingly as Steve glissades down a snow chute. Foolish pride keeps me climbing.

———

We have come here to taste the essence of true wilderness. Two weeks ago a Cessna with oversize tundra tires brought our bodies and packs to an abandoned oil-exploration strip on the remote northern slope of the Lisburne. Jutting into the Arctic Ocean, this northwest corner of Alaska contains the DeLong Mountains, part of the Brooks Range, a collection of peaks above the Arctic Circle that stretches 600 miles across northern Alaska.

All told, the area of the Brooks and neighboring North Slope, gentle tundra hills falling down to the icy sea, contains 120,000 square miles of territory. With the exception of a dozen or so Inuit hamlets and the Prudhoe Bay oil development, this is uninhabited, raw land.

Climb one of the nameless peaks in the DeLongs, the Endicotts, the Bairds, the Romanzofs, or any of the other mountains that make up the Brooks, and you can be fairly sure that no human footsteps have preceded you. Although the summits range from 4,000 to 8,000 feet, the treeless nature of this high-latitude region, with its razor-sharp, extraterrestrial vistas, leaves you with the impression that you are above treeline in the Himalayas. And in a sense, high here above the Arctic Circle, you do stand on top of the world.

As with most land in Alaska, there is no agreement among humans as to who exactly owns what, or what can be done there. The National Park Service has carved out great swaths: Noatak National Preserve, Kobuk Valley National Park, Gates of the Arctic National Park. The National Petroleum Reserve claims virtually all of the North Slope and much of the Brooks. And local Inuit have historical tribal claims to the region, with the money and lawyers to back them up. All three groups have different agendas, and all three meet in court regularly.

With harsh and unforgiving weather, polar bears, grizzlies, and waves of bloodthirsty insects, few people visit the Brooks; only a handful live here. But a journey to this corner of the United States is a guaranteed adventure, a tour into the heart of wilderness. The Sierra Club leads a half-dozen backpack trips to the Brooks and North Slope every year. Private outfitters in Fairbanks lead other expeditions. With the exception of traveling on the brutal oil-truck highway from Fairbanks to Barrow, all journeys here have one thing in common: A small plane brings you in, and, with luck, that small plane will take you out.

The pilot, hefting my backpack, chuckled.

"Shit," he said. "Must be eighty pounds. When I go into the bush, mine weighs only twenty-five pounds."

I thought of telling him about my thirty pounds of cameras and film, or the fact that we weren't hunting and were carrying all our food, but I decide to let him gloat. You want a bush pilot in Alaska to be on your side, especially when you depend on the guy to bring you back out.

Bush pilots are Alaska legends, right up there with Itidarod winners and Denali rescue mountaineers. Only a few months earlier, bad weather delayed for days one well-known charter pilot with twenty years' experience, a veritable Mr. Brooks Range, from picking up a group of stranded hunters. When a break in the clouds finally appeared, up he went.

One member of the search and rescue team told me later the bush pilot wore a high-tech metallic survival suit. It didn't help him much when he smacked his single-engine plane into the cumulo-granite, but it did make finding his body easier. Rumor had it he'd been unable to buy life insurance for his wife and kids. I was especially nice to our pilot.

We left Kotzebue, a little Inuit settlement just above Alaska's Seward peninsula, and flew due north over the breakup of the Noatak River. The spring arctic sun warmed us, casting a golden glow to mountains, rivers, and tundra. I felt giddy with adventure—until the pilot and Dennis began to argue.

"This is the Kugururok River basin," the pilot yelled over the Cessna's roar. He waved his arm in an expansive gesture, as if he owned the place. From Texas, he works six months a year here in Alaska, then snowbirds back to the Amarillo panhandle.

"No, it's not," said Dennis. "We're two basins east of that, this is the Nimiuktuk." Dennis had just spent two months fishing and rafting on the Noatak River with Inuit friends. He does not suffer fools gladly.

"The hell it is," continued the pilot. "Look. There's Misheguk Mountain."

"Look there," shouted Dennis. "*That's* Misheguk. You're looking at Amaktukvik Pass."

The lurching of the small plane and vastness of the scenery made my stomach reel. How could a landscape be so barren and wild that two experts could not agree on even the proper river valley? The argument made me recall writer John McPhee's take on this Great Land: "If one could do something so improbable as to steal Italy, the place to hide it would be Alaska."

At last we saw a defining landmark, a black lava mountain with jagged spires that stood out from the pale limestone of the rest of the

DeLongs. Copter Peak. Named, we wondered, for a helicopter crash site? It was the massif we are now climbing.

Viewing the weather-worn volcano from the air, it occurred to me that the mountain, sheltered by bitter winters and inaccessability, could hide many metallic secrets, for acidic magma can mix with basic limestone to precipitate rich ores. Geologists look for such anomalies, hoping to find veins of gold, platinum, nickel, and iron. And under the adjoining limestone peaks surely lay the heritage of an early Earth, an Earth with unrecognizable continents like the huge Pangaea, an Earth with dense, oil-producing tropical vegetation.

We landed on a gravel strip built by a mining exploration team some fifty miles from the black mountain. After stretching cramped muscles, we unloaded our gear. Bob, a slight biologist in his forties with a deep tan and a long blond ponytail, claimed to have made a pile of money selling rare Colombian rain forest plants to a drug company. Now retired, he still knew a lot of botany. He showed me how to appreciate the tundra: "Lie down on your belly and look closely."

From an ant's perspective, the tundra was bursting with biodiversity. Flowers and sedges, some only a millimeter across, jumped into view. One sedge formed a hood, like a cobra, with a strange green spike growing within. A yellow flower, Ross avens, unfurled five delicate, lacquered petals. A small pool of water swarmed with mosquito larvae. A purple, woolly lousewort wrapped its stem with soft, pale fur. On a chunk of limestone, algae-bacterial symbiosis, the same symbiosis found in corals, gave strength to ancient yellow lichen struggling against the north wind.

Bob talked Steve and me into climbing a low mountain that looked to be a quick two-hour hike. If I had checked my topo, I would have known it was Tingmerkpuk Mountain, elevation 3,787 feet. If I had been on the North Slope before, I would have known what a tussock is. But with mountaineering skills rusted by years of surfing and diving, I didn't know better, and off we strolled.

Shouldering cameras and a snack, we soon found ourselves slipping and sliding on small mounds of grass, each about a foot wide and a foot high, surrounded by puddles of water. Permafrost below, and constant freezing and refreezing, turns the arctic soil into billions of slippery miniature hillocks. A hiker can either hop from tussock to tussock, risking a sprained or broken ankle if he slips off, or slosh along in the water, lifting tired limbs and cold, wet boots without respite over the nasty mounds of tundra.

Tussocks! They made a mile into a two-hour journey, fraught with peril and exhaustion. Walking on them was like walking on wet basketballs. How we grew to hate them! And so it was with great envy that we saw our first herd of caribou glide by, only fifty yards away, cows with six-inch horns and newborn calves. Caribou have wide, splayed hooves like snowshoes. Broad, flat and deeply cleft, the hooves can make soft clicking noises, sounds produced by a tendon slipping over a bone in the foot. To them a tussock is a natural springboard. Seeing us, they galloped off, never once stumbling or breaking stride.

Both male and females caribou are antlered; they are the only genus of the deer family possessing this trait, although the female antlers are much smaller than the magnificent racks of the males. Weighing up to 250 pounds, males look even bigger due to their heavy coats of woolly underfur and stiff, straight, tubular outer guard hairs, a layer that enables them to survive in the Arctic. Brown or gray above, both sexes have whitish bellies. And they are more than caribou, of course: they are Santa's reindeer.

As we struggled up to a wide plain beneath Tingmerkpuk, we encountered a newborn calf, still wet with amniotic fluid, lying patiently on a pile of tussocks. Her pale-white fur glistened in the low sunlight, her almond eyes stared imploringly at the human intruders. Her mother darted nearby, nervous at our presence.

"Let's get out of here," I cautioned. With growing apprehension I watched Bob stumble up to within a yard of the calf. He ground away with his video camera, then took still photos with his fancy Leica.

"Leave her alone!" I yelled, but Bob was determined. He reached to touch her. The mother caribou fled, speeding off across the plain.

Steve and I marched on up the mountain in silence. I looked back but saw no sign of the mother caribou.

"Oh, it's all right," said Bob later. "The mother learned the baby's scent, I'm sure of it." Steve and I said nothing.

After long hours of climbing we reached the peak of Tingmerk-puk. Bob scratched his name and the date with a piece of limestone chalk, first on one boulder, then on another. Somehow, this second desecration of perfect wilderness failed to surprise us. Bob, for all his biologic wisdom, just didn't get it.

I wanted to tell him what Teddy Roosevelt had said: "Leave it as it is. The ages have been at work on it and man can only mar it . . ."

Wilderness. We flew out here to find it, far from the madding crowd. No phone wires. No phones. Nature. We came here to witness her majesty, both as beautiful scenery and as implacable, unpredictable force.

I realized "wilderness" could be a slippery and relative concept. *Webster's New World Dictionary* defines the word in various ways:

1. a region uncultivated and uninhabited; a waste; a wild.
2. a barren, empty, or open area of nature. 3. a portion of a garden set apart for things to grow wild. 4. a large, confused mass or tangle of persons or things. 5. a wild condition or quality.

Bob, I thought, preferred definition number four. He was, I felt, part of a large confused tangle. On the way down we found the calf where we had left her, alone, unable to stand, sans mother. She was doomed if she did not nurse soon. There was nothing for us to do. I wanted to strangle Bob.

Ten hours later, still short of the camp, we paused for a silent snack. Bob picked up a pair of caribou antlers to carry home. When we finally reached the tents on Eagle Creek, he realized he had lost his precious Leica. He must have set it down carelessly at a rest stop.

I found myself throttling a burst of wicked glee. Karma. A small price to pay for the life of a baby caribou, I thought, but better than nothing.

All this passes through my tired brain as I look up at Copter Peak, at Steve's departing glissade tracks, at Dennis, and at Bob. To distract myself from pain and fatigue, I keep reviewing events from the past few weeks.

The rest of us grew to view Bob, in spite of his botanical knowledge, as a real enfant terrible. However you defined wilderness, his definition, and his relationship to nature, was different from ours.

————

The first day out we spied a pair of adult wolverines and their twin offspring one hundred yards away. The North Slope is honest country. You can see clearly for miles and the vegetation is knee-high at best. There is no deception, no hiding, no lying about who or what you are. The adult wolverines, pound for pound among the fiercest meat-eaters on the planet, left their yearling offspring behind at what Dr. Maurice Hornecker, an expert on large carnivores, calls a rendezvous site. They marched up a low hill out of sight. For two hours we watched through binoculars as the heavily furred black and brown adolescents gamboled in and out of a large snowdrift.

Wolverines, the largest members of the weasel family, can weigh up to 70 pounds. Blessed with unbelievable ferocity, they have poor eyesight and indifferent hearing and use their keen sense of smell to find carrion, eggs of ground-nesting birds like ptarmigan, lemmings, and berries. In winter, when they can move faster over the snow than their prey, they can overcome caribou and Dall sheep. There are reliable reports of wolverines driving grizzlies and cougars from their kills, and they are infamous for stripping trap lines and breaking into cabins to ravage food caches.

Because the fur of the animal accumulates less frost than other furs, it is the favored trim for parka hoods in the arctic region. That fact, in addition to persecution for raiding cabins and killing caribou, has led to widespread trapping and hunting and a classification as vulnerable by international conservation organizations. And so we were happy to see this rare carnivore, more than content to sit and watch from a distance.

Bob, bored with all the waiting, decided to march off after them to get a better photo. As he approached the snowdrift, the wolverines took one look and scampered in a wide circle, first toward the rest of us, then up and after their parents. I wondered if the family would reunite successfully and recalled an interview I'd done earlier with Dr. Hornecker, who had performed one of the few field studies of the mysterious animal. "In general, wolverines do not do well with man's intrusion," he said. "Wide-ranging, solo hunters except when raising young, they tend to be found only in true wilderness."

———

After two days of brutal tussock hiking, I found myself in a tent, exhausted, lying in a down bag. To sleep on permafrost is to sleep on a giant block of ice. The sedges and flowers insulate your body at first, but then the cold wins out, thickening and slowing your blood to sluggish reptile consistency.

"Hey, photographer man," yelled Steve, shaking my tent.

"Get up. We got a bear here."

I grabbed my camera and long lens and leaped out of the tent, nude, into the chill morning. Barren-ground grizzlies eat a mostly vegetarian tundra diet and are smaller than their huge salmon-fed southern cousins. For them, the low-lying plant life of the tundra is one great smorgasbord. Grasses, sedges, roots, moss, bulbs and forbs—it is a springtime vegetarian's delight, and these brown bears revel in ranging and grazing over what to them is an infinite salad bowl. They remain substantial predators, and they will eat meat. This particular bear, a stout male weighing probably 600 pounds, lumbered straight into camp. The 3 A.M. sun backlit his cinnamon fur. Huge muscles rippled as his great head bobbed up and down.

There is nothing like staring into the deep, curious eyes of a brown bear, your adrenaline surging, the arctic wind caressing your bare goose-skin flesh. I started tripping the shutter, careful not to aim the lens at the bear for more than a second at a time, lest he determine the baleful glass eye to be a threat.

With a snort, the grizzly turned and strode by our tents, 50 feet away. As my heart slowed to the speed of maybe a frightened sparrow, I gradually became aware of hysterical laughter and giggling. It dawned on me, after diving back into my warm bag, that I made a ludicrous sight standing there in the cold, unadorned but for a 300-mm lens.

———————

Several long days later, after a brief snowstorm, we arrived at a bluff overlooking a vast river that poured north from the cordillera of the Brooks to the Chukchi Sea. The Kokolik. Standing on the edge, we could see all of creation.

At our feet flowed snowmelt, rushing, singing. Here and there bobbing heads with small antlers charged across the river. On the far bank, small groups gathered, dipping their hooves in the water, searching for a shallow passage. On green hills in the distance, as far as the eye could see, small white specks were grazing, moving. Caribou. By the thousands, by the tens of thousands, caribou spread over a vast tableau.

Struck speechless by the scene, we heard a soft thunder, the sound of a summer storm approaching. Twenty cows and calves scurried up a well-worn game trail and crossed in front of us, only yards away.

Comparable only to the migrations of the wildebeest in the Serengeti, huge herds of caribou make great sweeps across northern Alaska and Canada. Estimates vary, but this herd, the Western, together with the eastern herd, the Porcupine, number close to 500,000 animals. After wintering in the mountains, sheltered from the wind and giving birth, the cows leave to graze their way across the nutrition-rich tundra, always one step ahead of their archenemy. They run, but not from brown bears, although a bear will take a caribou when it gets the chance. They flee, but not from wolves, although wolves, too, love the taste of caribou meat. No, their enemy is the lowly mosquito. We are too early to find more than larvae in the cold, clear water that surrounds the tussocks, but the North Slope clouds with mosquitoes every summer. Although precipitation is scant, on the order of 10 inches or less per year, there is nowhere for the water to go—permafrost prevents any soaking into the ground. And so, although rivers run strong, every depression around every tussock is a perfect breeding ground. Tundra flowers provide nectar for the male mosquitoes, but the females can only reproduce with a blood meal. Caribou provide it, as much as a half-pint or more per week.

A wrong turn and a caribou can die from anemia. And so they migrate.

For days we camped on the high bluff and studied the restless beasts. Lying in photographic ambush on an island covered with felt-leaf willows, I captured a small group crossing the river. On reaching the cut-bank on the far side, the driven animals struggled to regain solid ground. A female helped her calf, nudging mightily from behind. The calf, bawl-ing, fell and was swept off by the current. Her mother swam after it to help again. Each crossing was a drama, each calf that made it a victory.

After our rest on the Kokolik, we trekked up into the DeLongs, where herds of male caribou sporting great racks came down to follow the females to the North Slope. Hiking along the river bank in light snow, following a fresh set of enormous wolf tracks, we saw a brown blob in the distance. It was a grizzly, I thought, but Dennis was not so sure. We approached and saw that the grizzly had horns.

Musk ox. A brute of a 1,000-pound animal, bearing long guard hairs and dense underfur, *kiviat,* the warmest in the world, eight times warmer than sheep's wool. The lone beast, ruminating on willow shoots, ignored us as we inched closer. Dennis made it clear that peo-ple do get impaled by the bayonet-like horns, but we had the security of a steep river cutbank on our left.

"Should he charge," he whispered, "jump in the river." The Kokolik looked cold and deep, not a good place to swim.

Driven to extinction in Alaska, a few breeding pairs of this rela-tive of the sheep/goat takin of Tibet, reintroduced from Greenland and the Canadian High Arctic, have grown back to a thousand animals. This one, a lone bull, driven off from its harem of females by younger, stronger males in a great, head-butting battle, would no doubt fall prey to predators in the coming year or two. Musk oxen are legendary for protecting themselves from wolves in a circle like African cape buffalo, their substantial horns at the perimeter. Good as this defense was for ursine and lupine attackers, it failed miserably against modern firearms wielded by humans, who dispatched entire herds with ease. Foolishly then, perhaps, allowing us to make a portrait, the musk ox turned, unhurried, and marched off, its skirtlike, brown guard hairs sashaying in the wind.

———

Endless scree-sliding footsteps later, we reach the rocky ridge that leads to the Copter Peak summit. My thoughts, still with musk ox and caribou, shift to sheep. Dall sheep. As in the creatures who have reached this ridge well ahead of us humans and made a game trail that leads to the summit in twenty minutes. Along the way we see nests, smooth spots some three feet or so in diameter, worn in the rocks where the herbivores rest. Why do they climb so high, far above any vegetation? To avoid predators? We can only surmise.

Approximately 110,000 of these animals remain in North America, with most making their home here in Alaska. Like bighorns, Dall sheep live in high-altitude mountain habitat and do not readily cross intervening areas without guidance from older, dominant males. They depend on the knowledge of their elders to learn the seasonal negotiations of complex migratory paths and ranges. As with many wild sheep, then, the hunting of prime, large-horned males can be devastating to the young, who rely on education, not just instinct, for survival. We suspect there is little hunting here, although we see only beds and no other ovine sign.

Cheated of our first ascent, we don't mind that the sheep have gotten here first. Even Bob refrains, unbidden, from carving his name on a rock. The actual summit requires deft footwork and use of handholds. It ends on a rocky turret with 2,000 feet of exposure over most points of the compass and room for only one climber. One by one we ascend and descend the spire, each knowing a false move would be fatal. On all sides, the mountain drops away to reveal a vast, untouched panorama of nameless peaks and valleys draped in lavender, indigo, and velvet green.

We share chocolate bars and a few crumbs of cheese. I toss down some Copter Peak runoff collected hours before—cool, sweet water spiced with mosquito larvae. The food and drink taste better than any five-star restaurant cuisine.

There is something anticlimactic in the descent from a successful climb. There is joy in glissade, swooping down over snow fields, skiing on one's boots. There is sweet release in seconds of effortless rappelling down a vertical cliff that took hours to ascend. But you are covering ground you know, you have journeyed to the unknown, and now you are back-tracking. Anticlimax. It is no accident that most climbing accidents occur on the descent. Climbers are tired, their guard is down, and the terrain, once so foreboding, now seems familiar and contemptible.

Knowing this, we are careful. There is no one to call for help. The arctic sun lowers to the northwest. It is 10 P.M. We have been on the mountain for twenty hours.

At last we reach tundra and water at the base of Copter Peak. No more lava, just tussocks. Their verdant hue makes up for the indignity they inflict on the human gait. I stop at a rivulet lit golden by the fading light to photograph a still life of wildflowers: phlox, moss campion, bell heather.

The snows above trickle crystalline music, each melting note building into a crescendo at my knees. Wild bebop riffs trickle downward around me toward the sea. Water, the jazz that makes life dance, water, singing, gurgling, melodic, filling the still, evening arctic with harmony and joy.

The aquatic cycle appears before my tired eyes, a vision born of exhaustion and climbing victory. First the moisture steaming into the air off the chill Chukchi, clouds billowing over the Brooks, the gentle fall of myriad, crystalline snowflakes, each a work of art, their melting under the noon sun. Then drops rappelling down the mountain like climbers, joining, building to the rill in front of me, diving inexorably down with a thousand other streams and brooks to form the mighty Kokolik, roaring, heedless of caribou and musk ox, rushing to the salty brine universe that washes far tropical shores, the whole loop only to begin once again.

How like water life is, rising up from the earth in its humble beginnings, growing into roaring youth and powerful adulthood, then the slow, riverine slide into the sea of death, the egalitarian decomposition, the merging and blending with soil and sand, worm and microbe, until a new spiral, a new mortal coil, appears once again. Water and life: two winding strands of pearls, changing yet repeating, separate yet intertwined . . .

A shout from the others draws me back.

"Bear," I hear. Philosophic musings shattered, I rush madly over tussocks, changing lenses at a run, trying not to lose balance, ignoring blisters, taking in the almost midnight sun, the perfect light.

Reaching the others, I see a mother brown bear and her cub. The mother bounds forward at us, a full-on charge. Too tired to react, we stand, dumb, frozen. She halts for a moment at twenty paces, perplexed, and then dives down the mountain into a clump of willows. The cub is left, lonely, lost.

"Wurp, wurp, wurp," the cub cries, coming toward us. A more plaintive cry I have never heard. "Wurp, wurp." What is it doing? We hike up the hill, pushing our exhausted limbs. Our great fear is to find ourselves between the cub and its 400-pound mother. No matter how high we climb, the cub stays with us.

I raise my lens for a shot. Everything is perfect, the cub darting its head up, the willows backlit by the glowing rays of dusk. Just as I press the shutter, Bob backs into me, knocking the lens.

I try again, but now the cub is bobbing, weaving. It knows we are not its mother, yet the big she-bear refuses to leave her refuge, and the cub follows us.

Finally, a good hundred yards above the willows, we decide to cut across.

"We will only draw the cub away from its mother if we go higher," says Dennis. Off we go between bears, breaking the cardinal rule of every bear-encounter book I have read. We march quickly, imagining a mighty paw swat slamming into our necks with each step on the tussocky tamarac. At last we are past, and we see the cub heading down toward momma bear. "Wurp, wurp . . ." It is a sound I will never forget. It hangs in my head as we clump the last miles to camp. A motionless blue patch on the mountain slope above catches my attention. I ask Dennis what he thinks it is. He says, tiredly, "Oh, it must be some kind of trash."

Dully, my exhausted mind thinks this over. Trash. Trash. We have seen no litter all month. No people. No cars. Wait a minute.

As if one, we reach the same conclusion together. The blue patch—it must be Steve. We race up the slope, yelling his name, fearing deep in our hearts what we will find. I have seen many things in hospitals, but I have yet to see the victim of a bear mauling, and harden my heart, preparing for the worst.

"Steve, Steve!" we shout, hysterical. His motionless body lies splayed over the tundra, arms, legs akimbo.

"Steve, Steve!" we sob, getting closer.

The corpse starts to move. First a hand, then a head pops up. Steve is alive. He hugs each one of us. His relief is palpable. Waiting for us, he had made himself comfortable and dozed off in the sun. Fast asleep on his tundra bed, he was awakened by a strong odor, something like a wet, unwashed dog. He opened his eyes to stare at the female grizzly nuzzling through his parka, her great muzzle wet and cool on his skin, her bear breath hot across his belly. Feigning death, petrified by fear, he has held motionless ever since.

Later, over a willow fire, Steve and I share a last slug of cognac. Always a quiet soul, he stares into the flames with a deep, luminous glow, some sort of primeval understanding. It occurs to me that his meeting with she-bear forms the acid test of wilderness. True wilderness is a place untouched by humans. It is a place where the forces of nature prevail, where humans must be humble, where large, dangerous animals—animals that can eat you—roam in a state of freedom.

The next morning, we break camp early and race for the patch of tundra that, we hope, our bush pilot will find. The day is clear and cool, a fine day for flying. A herd of caribou, males with proud antlers, grazes on what passes for a strip. A drone reaches us from the south. It is the first motor noise we have heard in a month. The caribou, ignorant of its meaning, ignore the sound, sprinting out of the way only at the last second in front of the landing Cessna.

Our presence has not gone unnoticed here. As Heisenberg proved with his Uncertainty Principle, any observer interacts with, and affects, the thing observed. I wonder, then, if humans can ever get to know true wilderness. Is "wilderness experience" an oxymoron? By visiting this place, do we not make what is wild somehow . . . civilized?

Aldo Leopold agreed: "All conservation of wildness is self-defeating, for to cherish we must see and fondle, and when enough have seen and fondled, there is no wilderness left to cherish . . ."

I stare across the pilot's instruments, through the windshield, down across miles of brilliant, diamond-sharp mountains, shining silver rivers, endless, glacial valleys. Somewhere below a bear cub calls for its mother: "Wurp, wurp." Two young wolverines wait patiently for their parents to return; a Dall sheep nestles into its nest, high atop a lava ridge. Scrambling up a cutbank, a caribou calf struggles to keep up with its mother. In this far corner of North America, these things and more carry on, whether or not people are there to witness them.

A new revelation dawns. We humans are, in our own imperfect way, as wild as the bear and caribou. Myself, Steve, Dennis, the pilot, even, I think grudgingly, Bob. Man is not separate from nature. Pride and arrogance may keep us aloof from musk ox and barren-ground grizzly. But there is no escaping parallel evolution, near-identical DNA, shared mitochondria, and mortality.

John Muir wrote, as if he anticipating Leopold's thoughts: "Bears are made of the same dust as we, and breathe the same winds and drink of the same waters. A bear's days are warmed by the same sun, his dwellings are overdomed by the same blue sky . . ."

Like an arctic tern, migrating from one pole to the next, our Cessna cuts south under those sparkling rays, knifing through those cobalt heavens. Lost in thought, silent in the face of overwhelming grandeur, we swoop over a vast valley the size of Italy, no different from a dozen valleys to the east, no different from a dozen valleys to the south and west.

TO COLE COLE

Vicki Lindner

She knew she would not reach Cole Cole even before she started to walk, knew she could not do twenty-five kilometers in the sand with this pack. These new boots, she had learned on her last hike with Freyda, were a half size too short, had bruised her big toenails on the Towers of Paine in wind that tossed her body against rocks. Worse than the bruises was the raw blister that oozed into grit trapped beneath its loose moleskin plaster. She was determined to do a minimum of fifteen kilometers, but how far was that? Eons dispersed into the sky's opaque membrane—she had not worn her watch—and she had no idea how long she'd been walking, or if darkness would strand her on this wild beach overnight.

Just a few days ago she was camped in a filthy trekker's refugio, still stuck with Freyda, hundreds of miles south. There, far from the blue ice leaves of the unattainable Gray Glacier, a thin French guide had drawn her a map. At what then seemed a turning point in a meaningless journey, he had advised her to go to the Free Zone, buy a cheap mochila, then take the ferry to this insular island from Puerto Montt. The line penciled from a dot he had labeled "Cucao" ran up her notebook to "Cole Cole," representing, she'd imagined, a short uphill hike. He had said "six kilometers," she was fairly certain, not six hours; but *seis horas caminando,* six hours walking, was what all the locals, including Pedro, and the bored guard at the CONAF kiosk, had told her, their arms flung indifferently north.

She'd informed the French guide that she had left her own knapsack at home because she was traveling with Freyda, who'd once ruptured disks heaving sacks in Africa, and couldn't carry 10 pounds, much less a pack. He'd stared at her acutely, as if to imply that this, as well as other shortfalls, could still be remedied. "Next time you must come here with someone who can carry fifty-five kilos," he said, his voice private, intense, like the muffled bird call of an Andean flute. He pointed to the Japanese woman he had guided on a ten-day tour of the Circuit, cheerfully inhaling a bowl of steaming four-grain porridge. "She is carrying thirty-five kilos and she is fifty-four years old," he exclaimed. How old does he think I am, she wondered hopefully. Despite Freyda's compliment about her "good aging genes" she no longer deceived herself about looking younger. After that, the apotheosis of Cole Cole, "next time," and what could still be changed was a secret that she shared with him, this guru of the International Female Midlife Crisis, whoever he was. (He revealed only that he'd come to visit this country and stayed forever.)

"Good luck," he whispered as Freyda clumped down the stairs. Even her footsteps managed to sound pissed. She wore a pancaked safari hat, a leftover from Kenya, and a purple rubber wind suit that stuck to her body like a wet plastic bag and made her look fat. Her dry, lipstick-less mouth was ratcheted into an upside-down Y by her anger (about what?). She would ferret out a minor injustice—a different exchange rate than the teller had said—and snap like raw electricity from a cut wire in places like banks. Freyda had asked the French guide if he would donate some of his boiled water for tea, pressing her palms into a praying formation, sing-songing, "Oh thank you thank you," before he agreed. She hated watching her old friend, not fat, but thicker, almost humped, trying to look cute to get a young guy to take care of her. Perhaps Freyda was the same as she had always been—they hadn't seen each other for a couple of years—and it was she who had changed, living with Jack in the unfinished cabin so far from Manhattan. "He's pretty!" Freyda whispered about the French guide honing his Swiss army knife in the window's dusty sunset light. "Hey, remember what's-his-face in Ecuador?"

She instantly recalled (although she'd just as soon not have) an image of a slender, long-haired boy with skin the color of wet bentonite, framed by a ragged stone archway—of what? A ruined convent? She couldn't dredge up his name—it had been twenty years—but oddly the name of the German guy that Freyda had met in Colombia came back. (*Franz.* He'd never joined her in Cuzco as he'd promised he would.) That was the summer she and Freyda had hooked up on a third-class bus to Latacunga, two solitary women adventurers, never married, and discovered that they both lived alone in Lower Manhattan, free spirits more or less, who traveled abroad whenever they could. In Latacunga, they had bought a pile of sugary pastries heaped in baskets at a market bakery, and had eaten them all as they obsessed about love, or in their cases, lack of it.

This was supposed to have been the anniversary return to South America, a celebration of a twenty-year friendship forged in wanderlust, a difficult one—they were too much alike, bossy, controlling—but after the scene over the penguins she had been positive that the trip wouldn't work. She should never have come to this country with Freyda, ditching Jack on New Year's Eve, a mistake. Freyda had argued that her office closed for the holidays on December twenty-third; why should she cut her vacation short by a week? She had acquiesced, changed her flight to the day after Christmas, succumbing to the memory of a no-strings-attached freedom, when she owed men nothing but desire—not to Freyda's self-centered demands, she thought.

The penguins had turned their relationship tense, but they agreed to be polite, instead of arguing nonstop, and to continue to Torres del Paine National Park together and see how it went. At the garbage-strewn *refugio,* infested with mice, without a shower or electric lights, they learned that the boat that crossed Lake Esmeralda to Gray Glacier had sunk. Their itinerary was shot! Burdened with Freyda's oversized suitcase mounted on wheels, they were unable to go anywhere without public transportation, or at least a horse, and horses cost fifty dollars a day in the national park. Instead, they resolved to store the suitcase, sufficiently massive to qualify as "trunk," and her own aqua duffel in the visitor's center, bungee-cord the two-man Tadpole to her medium-sized daypack, cram it with food, strap their sleeping bags to their belts, and hike to the Gray Glacier; but then a chaotic Patagonian wind had blown up.

The thin French guide had taken her aside, intoned in his lyrical voice, "You cannot walk there with your face in this wind without a good pack." He'd glanced at Freyda, unpinning her faded underwear from the portable clothesline she'd strung over the dirty foam mattress and stuffing it into her king-sized valise. He ought to know, she thought; his tee shirt, baring his sinuous vine arms to the chill, revealed tight muscles shaping his chest. Freyda was right; twenty years ago who could say what might have happened with him, but looking good for your age, she understood, was not the same as looking good to young men. Jack had worried that she might "take up" with someone—touchingly, he saw her as universally attractive. She'd located a Lacdel phone booth on New Year's Day and called him. He wasn't at home at 7 A.M., ominous, as the cabin must be snowed in.

While Freyda futzed with her embarrassing laundry, the Japanese hiker pointed to the black-and-yellow striped suitcase, flung open on the *refugio* floor, revealing its complex stuffing of plastic bags, a heavy, supportive car seat, and a portable umbrella with broken ribs. "You go with all that?" she shouted, grabbing her big round stomach and laughing.

———

The sea at Cucao belonged to an age before the entire world was discovered. Its waves gathered energy from the transparent moon's ghost and blasted forward as if there was no shore to catch them. The relentless curls of white foam that dissipated without changing velocity or shape were making her dizzy, or maybe the Korean-made *mochila,* not as comfortable as her backpack at home, was aggravating nerves in her neck. This iconic dream of a beach, unmarred by resort hotels, thinned to a shiny vibrating tine, then vanished. There would be no way to capture its endlessness in a photograph, but she could imagine eulogizing its unspoiled beauty to her academic colleagues when they asked, without interest, "How was your trip?" or to Freyda, who might not have come to this island after their Air Passes took them in different directions.

Like a petulant child, Freyda had refused to say where she was going, or even to say good-bye, after she lost the coin toss for the laminated map of the south. The next day they'd bumped into one another in an ecclesiastic museum featuring dusty stuffed albatrosses. Freyda was coughing with a severe bronchial cold, holed up in Casa Mochiladero, the same type of seedy, two-dollar youth hostel she'd favored the summer they'd met, sharing a room with six adolescent male rock climbers, all smoking cigarettes and dope. She'd felt sorry for her old friend then, trapped in her miserly concept of youth, despite a decent job and an inheritance. Getting to Cole Cole would prove she'd had a moral imperative to jettison Freyda's moving van of a suitcase, her neurotic fury, her cheapness, and her dowager's back, although she had to admit this no longer seemed a good reason to plod so many kilometers in pain, *agony.*

In the end, Freyda had been the one to suggest that they separate. On their last hike up the steep trail with views of Cambrian granite dikes, she had said, "Let's face it, even when we aren't battling over every little thing this isn't good." They had argued childishly about whose fault it was: *You and your pronouncements!* Freyda exclaimed, and she had retorted, *You're always projecting anger at me. Whatever I may be doing to you, I'm not doing that.* Then Freyda said, sensibly, that if they didn't stop this they really wouldn't be speaking to each other by the end of the hike. They'd agreed never to travel together again, but to keep in touch. At the top of the boulder cascade, where the wind flattened the air into dust-laden sheets that flapped through the gorge, moving the surface of the diaphanous lake that roared beneath the towers' oblique fingers of rock, their resentment did dissipate. Yet as she descended the rough path she secretly planned to take the French guide's advice, buy the Korean *mochila,* and backpack to Cole Cole, transforming the failed reunion into an important adventure she could one day tell Freyda about.

————

Twenty-five kilometers in one day was pushing it, though, she should have known that. *Seis horas?* More like six years, she thought ironically. She wished she had taken a chance on the weather and left the tent in the *residencia.* The mimeographed CONAF map did show a shelter at Cole Cole, as the French guide had said, but none of the trekkers coming from there had seen it. To be on the safe side she had fastened the Tadpole plus metal stakes, $7^{1}/_{2}$ pounds each, under the straps on the front of the pack instead of sticking them under the flap on the top where she had stowed the heavy water bottles. As a result, the tent dragged her backward like a claw hooked into the tendon between her shoulder and neck. There was no point in trying to repack unless she dumped most of the water and drank from the river at Cole Cole, which, according to Pedro, was clean and safe.

The joints in her hips were beginning to ache. Her powers of concentration should enable her to blot the *tavernas,* black horseflies the size of newborn mice, if not the pain, from her consciousness. These whining insects, materializing in the late morning heat, pursued her denim shirt on cool breezes emitted by the surf. They would have eaten Freyda alive, like the fleas in the infested hotel on the beach in Ecuador the summer they'd met. She had refused to give the poor Indian girl who gently bathed the infected bites the blue bandanna she'd begged for. I need it, Freyda kept insisting. At the time she'd believed that her new traveling companion's refusal to bestow a trivial gift signified more than pure selfishness; the girl's maternal tenderness was pressing warped psychic buttons, perhaps. Oh, just give it to her, she'd said. You can buy another in New York for twenty-five cents. The scene over the penguins had reminded her of that long-ago incident; Freyda, the self-acclaimed world traveler, had always viewed the citizens of foreign countries as servants.

She had met the Ecuadoran boy at a drunken carnival in that town on the coast. Within minutes, it seemed, they were fucking on the beach. Twenty years later, the memory of the sex eluded her, but the cans and bottles beneath their bodies, the other couples passing behind a curtain of salt-infused darkness, the music strained through the Pacific's lapping, came back with visceral clarity. She couldn't remember speaking Spanish with him. Surely they spoke? That's right, he had been an exchange student in Canada and learned some English.

When she had returned to the hotel, Freyda was lying on the cold tile floor. Thin, wiry curls propped up on a pillow, she was playing Bach on a recorder, her face still inflamed from the bites. Her back had collapsed again, she said with stoic cheer. She hoped she would still be able to trek to Machu Picchu with Franz. That's really wild! Freyda had exclaimed with admiring wonder when she told her about the boy on the beach. Freyda could always give back the excitement of semicrazed trysts that she herself would too quickly forget.

Before they had flown down to Punta Arenas at the beginning of this trip, they sat in the zócalo in Santiago, watching gypsies, drums attached to their backs, whirling dizzily to their self-imposed beat. "Catching up," as Freyda called it, they had strayed to the risky subject of the future, growing older. Freyda complained about her poor circulation; her legs had always been lumpy with purple varicose veins; now they were worse. They don't see your legs unless they're in bed with you, she had said consolingly, aware, as the words left her mouth, that her own legs were all right. Freyda had rambled on, as she often did, about Hank, her favorite ex, dead of a brain tumor at forty-nine; she imitated his buoyant Swahili greeting when they had traveled in Kenya decades ago, shortly before he went back to his first wife. She continued on to the subject of that fat, crazy lawyer who had crashed at her place when he came down to the city to fight for custody of an illegitimate son. As the loud gypsies danced, Freyda said with a calm acceptance, I think he was the last one; I don't think there will be any more men. Then she exclaimed, with cheerfully exaggerated envy, I want a Jack! This comment, intended to be flattering, made her feel guilty, both for having the man her friend wanted and for abandoning him.

———

If she had known she would end up backpacking without Freyda she would have brought her MSR water filter, her Whisper Lite stove and light freeze-dried food. She wouldn't be shlepping four greasy milpoa, fresh tomatoes, six rolls, cheese, and two weighty cans of *sardinas desmenuzadas.* Few provisions were available in Cucao because the dirt road to the small settlement had been half washed out. Even in dry weather the town was remote. The woman who ran the *residencia* where she had spent the night told her that until last year, when electricity arrived, there was no ice; when one family slaughtered a sheep it shared the meat with other families. There was still no television or hot running water; Pedro heated buckets on the wood stove for baths. He had looked at her, a deliberately neutral expression on his long, sour face, suggested that she take a guide—him—and a horse to Cole Cole. He must have seen the weakness she had hid from herself. Why hadn't she hired him? She had the money.

She stopped to rest—for the second time in half an hour—on a white driftwood log hurled out of the sea. Immediately the horseflies were on her, injecting venom into the back of her neck. Before leaving left the *residencia* this morning she had raised the pack plus herself to a standing position by slipping her arms in the straps and crouching on all fours while bracing her hands on the chair next to the bed. *I'm not going to get there,* she thought. As she trudged toward the wood-slatted suspension bridge, a backlit streamer of evaporating moisture laddered up along the pale sticks of a fence. Pedro's Arabian horses wheeled, snorting, through moon-colored grass and ignited tendrils. Vines rubbed magenta flowers into the blur of fresh sun. She could hear the ocean beating drumrolls on its sliding skin. She followed the broad backs of two Mapuche women, mounted on mules, parading ahead. A small Indian man wearing a formal blue suit, vest, and fedora galloped by on a chestnut gelding, crying to her enthusiastically, *"Cole Cole! Seis horas caminando!"* She felt exhilarated then, glad to be attempting what she believed she should do, and for a little while she felt able to carry the pack.

A male figure emerged from the mica haze of the primordial beach. The young man joined her on the log; his dark eyes, shy yet intently inquiring, followed her finger as it attempted to trace the route on the lousy CONAF map. He said, casually, that he had not arrived at Cole Cole; it was *difícil* to walk in the sand with boots. (His were not Gore-tex, but black leather military cast-offs.) He had camped by the lake instead.

She gestured toward a faraway point extending rocky knobs into the ocean. "To Punta Denai?" she asked him.

"No," he said, squinting at the map. "The place where the trail left the beach was not there, but *mas lejos,* beyond that. You must cross two rivers, using the bridges if you do not miss them, climb a small mountain, thick with jungle; the path is easy to lose because it not marked." They talked for awhile; he was a student from a small town near Temuco.

Solita? Alone? he questioned, like everyone else from this country. She had developed a snappy retort, *Sí, como no?* (Yeah, why not?) She didn't use it with him (his brown eyes, shining with the self-involved sincerity of the idealistic young, deterred her), or mention that she had started the trip with a friend. People from this country reacted negatively, almost with fear, to the revelation that she hadn't gotten along with her traveling companion; perhaps in Spanish she was saying more than she meant. (*No one goes alone here,* a sophisticated woman from the capital had told her.) Now she replied, "Yes, solitude is better sometimes." The student nodded doubtfully; he was alone too, but he was not a middle-aged female American tourist.

She looked at the sun, said *adios,* and struggled to her feet, like a camel unfolding its legs to leverage a burden attached to its hump. Her ankles were killing her. The student worriedly watched her go. As she felt herself disappearing down the beach's platinum funnel, she realized that instead of hurrying on to a place that she wouldn't get to, she could have stayed on the log and talked to him. She could have asked about Temuco, the birthplace of Pablo Neruda.

The Ecuadoran boy had had the same long, dark hair, scraped back in a pony tail, the same receptive eyes and wet clay skin that this student did. She remembered his last name—*Aguilar,* or was it *Aguilar Lanza?*—but not his first. Twenty years ago, she had flown from Cuzco back to Quito, leaving Freyda still waiting for that German shit. The boy had managed to meet her at the airport (she hadn't told him the time of her flight) and carried her duffel to a cheap hotel. That night he led her through a cobblestoned back street to an unsigned rooming house that must have been a brothel where unmarried couples also went to have sex. After twenty years she could picture the bed, a narrow cot, with one thin, gray sheet that bunched up to reveal a blood-stained green mattress. Flimsy partitions concealed the owner of a continual wet cough. Doors banged all night. He had gasped *Dios!* in grateful amazement, then translated, *my Got!,* knowing she spoke enough Spanish to understand *God.* She remembered telling Freyda the story in the Café Dante when they got together for cappuccino in New York. *Do you think you'll ever hear from him?* her friend had asked, interpreting, as she always would, any male–female encounter, however ephemeral, as legitimate romance. She had never imagined she would hear from him, although she had given him her address, watched him read it, sounding out the English words with careful attention, button the paper into his breast pocket, then happily pat the place where it was.

———

All morning she had encountered other hikers, mostly young couples, returning to Cucao from Cole Cole. When the hot sun dried the flare of her shadow, she saw two men and a woman, walking briskly, as if their cumbersome packs were loaded with bubble wrap. "It was beautiful there, all right," one of the men, an American, told her. "Great views of the bay . . . I have no complaints except for the flies." The way to drive them all off for a nanosecond, he said, was to injure one, badly, by bashing it with your hat. He took off his hat, and swiped a buzzing *taverna* to demonstrate, revealing faded red hair, and a lined, freckled forehead.

He looked at her closely, recognizing, she knew, the type she was—an aging hippie like himself—hiking alone with a useless pink backpack. She told him she was headed to Cole Cole . . . probably wouldn't get there though; this Korean pack was junk; she should never have put two liters of water in it. She'd heard you could take water out of the river, but she was a coward. . . . The trekkers at Torres del Paine were using the trail for a bathroom, and that really scared her.

"My Argentinean friends here will drink anything," the sunburned man said, gesturing toward the silent couple that gazed at her curiously, "but the water in that river didn't look too good. The drought has made it awfully muddy. You were supposed to drink on one side of the bridge and bathe downstream on the other. I let it settle, then boiled it."

"See, and I don't have a stove."

He stared at her. "How about a pot?" he asked. "You're alone?"

"Yeah." She explained that she had started the trip with a woman friend, but it hadn't worked out. This guy, a hip American, would understand what she hadn't said; then, inexplicably, she felt as if she were betraying Freyda.

"She left you in the lurch, huh," the American stated. He looked at his watch, noted that they had been walking for four hours. "You could still get to Cole Cole before dark. What time does the sun set? Ten, ten-thirty?"

"Actually, I'm considering bagging it. Cole Cole can't be much better than this," she said, circling her head to encompass the here and now, the Zen of the glittering, undiscovered beach. The American looked at her sorrowfully, and she saw herself through his blue eyes, nested in crow's feet, a crazed hag, limping alone, face clenched in torture. She realized that she wasn't carrying enough food, water, or the right equipment for a four-day trip into the heart of a jungle. "I might camp at the lake instead," she said, remembering that the student from Temuco had mentioned one.

"Lago Cucao. It's about half a mile back, inland a ways. You already passed it," the American informed her.

Had Freyda gotten rid of her? Perhaps, she thought, as she continued on. (She hadn't wanted to give up, turn around, in front of an audience.) She had tried to control her irritation, to be kind, to comprehend that her furious friend must be going through a dark night of the soul she hadn't confided. After the absurd scene over penguins she had lost it, though; rage had dredged her voice in a whisper, *"Ugly American! You made a fool out of yourself and me!"* and immediately regretted the cruel word *ugly*. That night, alone in the room on New Year's Eve, she had written to Jack a letter, it turned out, he never received.

———

She reached the point after circumnavigating an inlet the breadth of a Dead Sea that refused to part. The sand sucked her blistered feet into it. Sobbing feebly, she threw down her pack, picked it up again, howling. She heard her cry waver through the loud air like an imaginary spear and vanish. Now she sat, weary, her shoulder knotted in a painful spasm, on a baklava of shale. Thick ropes of a rubbery orange seaweed plopped over the chewed rocks where hand-shaped fronds gestured, oblivious to the absence of soil. Birds she couldn't name, wings blackened by the late sun into charred silhouettes, cruised overhead. The oasis's flowing tide streams pooled into clear eyes of water on scalloped white shells, a miniature world of extravagant beauty, offering her a truth that her focus on Cole Cole, a destination some French guide had inscribed in her notebook, might have caused her to miss. Could Cole Cole, whatever it was, be more inspiring that this? She knew she lied to console herself, not for failing to reach the goal, but for not having the strength.

She took off her boots and peeled away the waterlogged moleskin. The broken blister had been bleached by wet, wool socks to the color of drowned flesh. *Rene.* The Ecuadoran boy's name was Rene. When he had walked her back to her cheap hotel the following morning, the friendly maid, ironing sheets, had projected a scorn she could feel brushing her face like a spider's web. Then the maid had looked the other way, pointedly, as if she were shunning a prostitute. (That she had not told Freyda about.) A few months later the boy had written a barely literate letter, *Hello, Babe! I am here thinking to you,* and included a flash-bleached photograph of himself, lounging on a sunken blue sofa, wearing an unbuttoned candy-pink shirt. *I want to come for to visit you in United States of America.* He had desired not her, but her prosperous country; from the perspective of her real life in Manhattan, she realized that she'd known this from the start. After that, she had avoided thoughts of their depraved rutting, two dogs on a beach, although only Freyda had known about it and had never judged her. Now she wondered if she had damaged Rene by altering the path of his expectations while forgetting his name.

As she soaked her feet in the opal stream, the ancient Mapuche she'd greeted at the beginning of the journey, still wearing a formal blue suit, galloped up on his horse, leaped off, and cast a homemade reel into the surf. "*Corvina!*" he exclaimed gaily. She watched him with dull amazement; he was a hundred years old, yet his eyes, blinded by the cooked egg whites of cataracts, did not stop him from riding, fishing, recognizing her. "*Cole Cole?*" he shouted again, confident that she was still headed to the same place as the rest of her kind. She nodded dumbly. As he remounted he threw his arm, like a lariat, north. "*Seis horas caminando,*" he cried, and rode off smartly, spurring his steed into the dense, drought-bleached jungle.

Could she be no closer to Cole Cole than she was this morning when she set out? Had she walked all day and gotten nowhere? It was possible. She had never seen the lake, the rivers, or the bridges that were supposed to cross them. She stood up, disoriented. She wanted to call, "Wait! Where is the path?" *Donde está el sendero?* but the monotone thud of the sea, her desolation, swallowed the words before she could speak.

She sat on the point, gazing into the tide pool's eons of layered white shells until the hard pink sun expanded, fraying at the edges, and dropped. When she arose she dumped most of the water and turned back to look for the lake.

————

An animal will steal her food that night. The Mapuche woman, manager of the crude campground near Lago Cucao, will open her mouth wide, laughing, and exclaim, "*Sí! Perros! O gato cholo!*" Before she leaves this country, she will ford a rain-swollen river, risking hypothermia, to get to El Encanto, because she never made it to Cole Cole. There she will eat the *sardinas desmenuzadas* in a water-logged rowboat as multiple waterfalls stream down boulders. On the Esplanade in Puerto Montt she will meet a gypsy woman, *del Norte,* maybe a thief, who knots the hundred pesos she gives her in the ruffled hem of her long flowered skirt, saying, "Because you have given me this coin I will answer one question." After she asks it, the gypsy will reply, flat pale eyes gazing past her face to the port, "You will suffer much sorrow and disappointment in this life." Forest fires will burn underground on the insular island of Chiloe, where in the time of Darwin torrents of rain fell. Blue glaciers in Puerto Natales are melting beneath the ozone hole; she and Freyda had seen that for themselves. Home in the unfinished cabin, she will feel confused and lost, although Jack will be there, resentful about New Year's Eve, but glad she is back. She will tell him the news her lost letter contained: Freyda castigated the driver from the agency they'd booked to take them to the Pinguinera because he was late. *It is New Year's Eve; I meant no harm.* "Freyda, will you shut up!" she interjected. Freyda had cursed her then with a hatred so venomous, so long-stifled, so biblically intense that she had immediately repressed the exact words her friend said. *You know this woman long?* "She can't tolerate schedule changes," she'd apologized to the driver, who understood English, wondering why she was defending this selfish crone, a stranger she barely recognized. Young, coarsely handsome, the driver recited a proverb: *It is better to go alone than badly accompanied.* He offered to give them their money back, but together they traveled to the end of the earth, to an unfrozen bay, where the ancient tuxedoed birds twirled stunted wings and poked their heads out of burrowed nests. When she tells the story of her lonely, dissatisfying, final adventure, as she often does, the scene over a penguin tour seems insignificant, a weak denouement, a poor reason to hike twenty-five kilometers in pain, to abandon an old friend. She will realize she had known she would not get to Cole Cole even before she started to walk. Why did Freyda carry a broken umbrella all the way from New York?

ACROSS THE ISTHMUS OF PANAMA

Tom Zydler

We had become an issue at the evening gatherings of the *congreso* in Mula Tupu, the home village of Florentino. Should they allow us to disappear into their territory, Kuna Yala, until we reached the Pacific side of the Continental Divide? That was the question. Kuna men who see the forest as a source of daily food doubted the purity of our desire to hang out there for the sake of communing with nature. Even Florentino, who would be leading the trek, began asking odd questions obviously prompted by the elders. Looking for gold, minerals, or oil? We could hardly blame them for being suspicious after what had happened to other parts of the Isthmus of Panama, scalped of trees, ravaged by cattle, poisoned by mining. We staked our hopes on support from Florentino who, after all, had known us for a few years, and we waited.

Mula Tupu, the second-largest village in San Blas with a population of about 3,000 (plus uncountable milling children) had a concrete-block guest center. We ate downstairs and slept above the restaurant in hammocks strung between posts that also propped the corrugated iron roof. Open shutters on glassless windows let the breeze whistle through. To the north we looked over a quilt of silvery thatched roofs at the white line of waves breaking on the reefs protecting the village. Farther out and beyond a low-wooded point stood Tup Bak, an island named for its resemblance to a beached whale. To the south, past more thatched roofs, rose the dense green hills. Veiled by low mists, they held a promise of adventure, we hoped. Directly below the windows, at the village wharf, lay *Nueva Graciela,* a sharp-ended Colombian coconut-shipping *canoa,* still propelled only by sail, a rarity among the twenty-six vessels engaged in this trade.

"We are leaving tomorrow morning," announced Florentino when he joined us for the evening meal on our third day in Mula Tupu. To help lug our supplies we would have his brother, Eleucadio, and Livorino, the husband of a cousin from the Urrutias' compound. Livorino, born in the mountain village of Mortí, knew the trails. Once over the hump of the Continental Divide we would walk down to where Río Quadi joins Río Mortí on the way to the Pacific. Since the trail ended at that point Florentino arranged for a Mortí man to paddle a canoe upcurrent to meet us in four days.

As we had already settled down into the Mula Tupu village routine, this sudden efficiency nearly overwhelmed us. How? When? Permission? We have it? "No problema," explained our friend. A man just arrived from Mortí to stock up on cigarettes for his *tienda* up there; Mula Tupu, like other coastal villages, received regular supplies from the port of Colón by Kuna-owned small freighters. He would leave the next day, same as us, but being a Kuna, never mind the load he carried, he was going to get to the canoe pick-up point in one day, drop downriver to his home, rest a few days, and then come back to get us.

First we had to buy Florentino's freedom from village obligations. Seven dollars was the fine for not contributing his share to the pool of food necessary to feed the guests attending the forthcoming General Congreso, the semiannual meeting of *caciques, sahilas,* and other people of importance representing the fifty villages of Kuna Yala. And four dollars for permission to visit Mortí, as well as five dollars for the permit to leave the village and live in Panama City where he hoped to find work after our hike. In Panama City he would join the Mula Tupu village chapter and pay dues to the village purse as all Kunas who live outside the Comarca must do. And we thought the U.S. tax system was too much to bear.

We had no doubt what time we awakened on the morning of our departure. The computer voice trapped in the wall clock downstairs gargled a tune every hour; it was "Waltzing Matilda" at five. Nancy started her day of adventure in the hotel outhouse, which stood over the water like all the others along the island perimeters. As a concession to guest comforts ours had a roof and walls of painted planks instead of heliconia leaves. In the predawn murk she put a flashlight in the corner while taking a shower with half of a coconut shell dipped in a bucket. When she spotted a gigantic spider crawling onto the wall I could hear her scream in our barn upstairs, but it was nothing, just a large land crab projected into a Hollywood monster by the light. And Nancy, like a true daughter of the tidal rivers of Georgia, was weaned on boiled crabs.

In the Urrutias' extended-family compound we said good-bye to Diodelis, Kaira, Rubalino, Areme, Nelesia, Yalyn, Inavale, Manecio, and others and patted a couple of infants smeared black with the juice of *jagua* fruit to make them invisible to bad spirits. They invited us to sit on their 6-inch-high stools because otherwise, every time we moved, our heads knocked off rows of women's *mola* blouses hanging from rafters. The father, Anzelmo, wished us a good trip and we noticed how, below the tanned, long-nosed face, his torso skin was beginning to acquire the pink hue you might expect in an English country squire. Aging Kuna men often suffer from such loss of melanin. We never learned the mother's name; she kept it secret from strangers, as older Kuna women do according to a vanishing custom. Excited about Florentino's departure and the long absence he had planned, she chattered to us in Kuna, imploring us to take good care of him in the city. Florentino, who first had to get us through the forests and over the hills, was raring to go after a night of good dreams—dreams being an important part of Kuna spiritual life.

Going by canoe up Río Ibedi, Eleucadio paddled and Livorino rode on the bow to check out the wildlife. Youngest of the crew, Livorino had borrowed a shotgun from Anzelmo Urrutia to keep us in fresh meat. We secretly hoped that he did not have enough experience to hit anything. In any case, we decided to talk loudly whenever game was around. There was nothing wrong with Livorino's eyesight. At one river bend he pointed out a mottled venomous snake coiled asleep on a branch, several camouflaged birds whose Kuna names he rattled off, a *kio-kio* parrot, a buff and brown raptor that hunted *kio-kios,* gaudy woodpeckers. Even we could see a flock of *quilis,* tiny green parakeets that often end up as pets in Kuna villages.

Florentino divided the loads on the riverbank and I photographed Nancy, five foot eight, towering over the Kunas. At five feet, Eleucadio got to carry a U.S. army duffel bag of food supplies that felt like about 80 pounds to me. Livorino, the hunter, was favored with a slightly lighter bag and Florentino shouldered a Kuna backpack of woven straw with straps of plaited vines, full of pots and pans. My waterproof pack of camera equipment weighed 35 pounds. Nancy had an orange backpack with the first-aid kit, flashlights, drawing paper, board and colored pencils for drawing plants, surprise candy bars, clothes, water bottles. Heavy enough, she needed help to load it on her back.

The portable Global Positioning System unit read 08°56.19' north and 077°46.002' west when we took off through a low land covered by secondary-growth trees mixed with farming plots distinguishable solely by the telltale banana and plantain leaves. Only a large, open communal cornfield was littered with slashed and partially burnt stumps. Constantly on the lookout for a *pifa* palm with fruit now in season, we came upon Esmellin Gonzales, who had just macheted a thicket of high heliconias to get under a thin, tall palm trunk. High bunches of orange fruit were shining in the sun. *Pifa* was such an important staple in Mesoamerica that during the conquest the Spanish cut millions of these trees in order to starve the indigenous peoples into submission. You do not get *pifa* by climbing; for protection against intruders the palm trunk has developed anklets of long spines pointing down at a likely forager. The Kunas, however, cut a few handy vine tendrils and tied them around three loose saplings into a flailing pole long enough to knock the fruit down. We loaded the extra fodder on top of Florentino's light pack.

The trees grew thicker as we increased our distance from the coast. The path narrowed and darkened. Down this green tube we heard voices, first faint, then strong enough for the Kunas to recognize that they belonged to their neighbors, who were busy shaving chunks of a tree into paddles with machetes. The pleasant stroll ended when the land tilted upward. Writhing roots invisible in the forest gloom crisscrossed our way, forcing us to pay attention and occasionally launching us into facedown flights that were only accelerated by the heavy weight of our backpacks.

Livorino was first to spot a large *yoli* tree axed down near the side the trail. The white flesh of the wood, shorn of its bark, already showed the outline of a canoe sculpted into the trunk. After the canoe owner hacked out the boat shape and separated it from the rest of the tree, he would organize twenty or thirty men to drag it to the water's edge. Later, at home, he would work with a scoop adze to hollow the inside and to hew the final curves of the bow and stern. It would take weeks of chipping wood in the evenings after his routine daily trips in search of food on the mainland.

Apart from stockpiling *ob*, corn, after the harvest during *Ob ni*, our month of September, Kunas do not have a tradition of long-term food preservation. Every day at dawn men in canoes paddle through the dark sea on the way to rivers and the mainland to collect plantains and yucca, hunt, or gather firewood. They return home in the early afternoon, bathe, eat, and play with children, in a thousand-year-old rhythm of human life. In the evenings men go to the *congreso,* and boys go fishing. Women sail to rivers to launder clothes and fetch water. At home, in addition to child care and cooking, they stitch and stitch. The reverse-appliqué *mola* patterns they design, cut, and sew probably developed from body painting in the early twentieth century. Ceremonial events, such as a girl's coming of age, require all the women in a family to dress in a new design every morning for three days. In addition, *molas* have become popular outside Panama as a sophisticated form of folk art, making these women serious wage earners. Still, cash is scarce, and jobs are rare and poorly paid; our guides made $6 a day, a good wage by rural Panama standards. The Kunas must grow and catch their food to survive.

Healthy forests contribute water to flowing rivers, which in turn nourish fertile lowlands, and game is abundant. Arturo Navarro, a Mula Tupu man we bumped into on the trail, carried a big bird slumped over his shoulder—a *sigli,* a great curassow, the size of a large turkey. It was a female with clean, cinnamon-colored body feathers, a tail with creamy crossbars, and a crown crest of curls. The sight fired up the killer instinct in Livorino, who promised we would have one before long. Soon enough, a bird flew from behind our left shoulders and began to parallel our course. Before we could even cough, in one smooth motion Livorino slipped out of his pack, raised the gun and *Bam!*—the bird crashed into the trees ahead. This male's black body feathers shimmered with blue, and a bright-yellow bulbous growth sat on top of his beak. The dead bird ended up next to the *pifa* bunch on Florentino's pack, which grew heavier as the day progressed.

We had dreams of sleeping in the thick of the forest, but the Kunas would only camp on open ground. This meant resting on river bars or banks covered with cannonball-sized rocks. Nancy and I tied our rainbow-colored hammocks, woven by an indigenous group in Colombia and sold by the coconut traders, to small trees so flexible that our backsides cleared the rocks by an inch. Within an arm's reach, on the ground, we had plastic tarps in case of rain and fine mesh nets to ward off the mosquitoes that never showed up in this uninhabited, pristine forest. We felt like rich gringos on a safari. Meanwhile, the Kunas, who thought hammocks in the forest were for wimps, only arranged beds of rocks and driftwood. I tried one of those—a true instrument of torture. The Kunas might be short but they were all muscles of cheerful disposition, and tough. We watched in disbelief as Eleucadio, after an entire day of lugging his dead-weight pack uphill, did push-ups.

Livorino and Florentino started two campfires to boil the *pifa* fruit and to roast the bird. After the *pifa* they cooked lentils, added chow mein noodles and then rice. We ate and ate; the great curassow had the flavor of wild goose and chewed like one of those rubber animals sold in The

Nature Store. For dessert the Kunas mixed oatmeal with water and 2 pounds of sugar, which explained why Florentino had wanted 15 pounds of sugar for the trip. Before dark spilled into our little hole in the forest they found large crayfish wiggling in the river; the lack of a net nearly drove the Kunas crazy. They were still splashing in the river with machetes when we fell asleep. They must have done well, for in the morning a ring of crustacean carapaces surrounded the smoldering embers.

We were walking through vines that flowed from trees like streams of toothpaste from giant tubes when Florentino explained that the vines' soft wood was used as medicine for people who saw things that did not exist. The forest became dark and damp, the forest floor covered with flowers like purple violets—good for the eyes. We could use some of such medicine. For us the "trail" disappeared long before we climbed Morbep Yala, the hill of Morbep, Queen Conch in Kuna, and a very tasty Caribbean mollusk. The next hill's name translated as "can see the ocean," a puzzle of a name since the forest closed in on us with the canopy so thick that our GPS could not receive satellite signals. According to old Spanish records the early conquistadors encountered hundreds of thousands of people on the Isthmus, so these hills could once have been bare enough to offer a view of the sea. Perhaps the forest tribes traded for fresh conch here, for we could not have gone very far from the coast on these winding rough slow paths.

Along the way Livorino kept showing us tracks of jaguar and *uebar,* a wild pig, and the spent cartridges he had stuck on twigs to mark his hunting hits.

"This is where I shot two *sainos,* wild hogs. I carried them both back. Over there, see that one? I got a female *ñeke*—she had two male embryos!" he enthused, referring to a Central American rodent.

Kuna hunters dry male embryos as talismans in the belief they bring good hunting luck. At the top of the hill a large white raptor, with a dark stripe across its tail, landed nearby and watched us sliding down before we climbed another hill. By the time we stopped for a midday meal Nancy and I had problems putting one foot in front of the other and thought everybody needed a break. As soon as the packs hit the ground Eleucadio took a bath, then grabbed a boulder and pumped it up and down above his head. Livorino ran into the trees looking for game. It was Florentino's turn to cook a soup of Chinese noodles mixed with corned beef.

Nobody pranced, though, when we hit the steepest trail yet. Even the Kunas took short breaks, everybody breathing hard. Sweat poured down our gringo noses, but the Kunas did not sweat much. Big trees grew there, *baila,* with hard, durable wood used for the main pillars of a hut, and *quibo,* the "quipo" of the Pacific coast of Darién, which bulges out about eight feet above the ground looking as if it grew a beer belly. Kunas collect its sap to fatten domestic pigs and emaciated people who must gain weight. Finally, at the crest, the highest point of the trek, the watershed and the Continental Divide, we stopped to look at *urgukdula,* gray-winged moths with rose-colored bodies that live on *urguk* trees with gray and pink bark—we would have never spotted them without prompting.

"Try to catch them," Livorino said, and the moths jumped from under our palms only to land a couple of inches away, as if teasing us.

Kunas believe that the juice from the mashed bodies of these insects smeared over a boy's arms will infuse him with similar agility and make him a winner in boxing and a *millionario.*

Much of the indigenous forest medicine lore must have begun when people related the physical features of a plant or animal to themselves. When it worked, the healers filed it into tribal memory until it grew into a body of knowledge. What took a few thousand years to create may vanish under the pressure of fast, modern drugs that first reached the indigenous people through missionary clinics set up by various Christian denominations. Florentino, once our teacher of Kuna traditions, now clammed up on the subject. He had found a Christian God and during breaks on the trail read a Bible. He missed the meetings in the two-story Baptist Mission headquarters overlooking the ocean from the north tip of Mula Tupu, the first concrete building in the village. He related, however, how in the 1980s his uncle went missing on a hunting trip for three days and a search party went through this area. Crossing a river they came upon a flat rock covered along the edges with "Kuna crosses," split heliconia leaf stalks with cross twigs in the clefts. They knew he must have spent the night there protecting himself against evil spirits. A few hours later, in a camp of hunters from Uala, a mountain hamlet, they learned the uncle was safe in Mortí. The strong belief in spirits that dwell in trees explained why we camped on hard, rocky river banks at a relatively safe distance from the dense woods. Often, when a man cuts the wrong tree and releases evil spirits, his whole village may suffer an epidemic. To ward off the disaster a powerful *nele*, a spritual interpreter, will work with life-size balsa *uchus*— anthropomorphic carvings—and order men to stay away from women.

A change in minnow species marked our crossing to the other side of the Isthmus. When we washed in the Atlantic rivers, small gray fry with black spots nibbled on our legs only tentatively. Now 3-inch-long fish with red tails mouthed our feet aggressively, making us dance and lose the soap downstream. We still had to climb some hills but most often slithered downhill. Nancy, who, unlike us men in rubber boots, wore running shoes, ended down on her bottom so often that the Kunas began counting her falls as a game. Boulders of all sizes covered in moss or algae bordered the rivers and made the two of us slow down; breaking a leg here would cause serious problems. The Kunas bounced from rock to rock at high speed, believing that if your foot does not stay on the slime long it will not have time to slip. One of the river banks was named *iguana* after the almonds on the ground that *arri*—iguanas in English or Spanish—eat. Since none of the indigenous languages in Panama use the word "iguana" for the animal, some early Spaniard must have misunderstood his guides and his mistake perseveres to this day. A gap in the trees over the Iguana bank allowed our GPS to get a fix, 08°54.39' north and 077°52.92' west. Two days of fording streams and dragging our feet up and down hills had taken us about seven miles west and a couple of miles south.

On the third day we reached the confluence of Río Quadi and Río Mortí, the bank of round stones where the canoe would meet us and take us down to the Mortí village. I was delighted to see nobody waiting. We dropped the packs and threw ourselves into the cool stream, not even peeling off our socks soggy with sweat. Howler monkeys roared all around us but out of sight—Kunas shoot monkeys as game. Blue morphos, after flitting like handkerchiefs in the breeze, dropped down and took off from the pebbly beach. A large butterfly splattered with brown and cream on the back, its bright orange belly brushed with charcoal, spent an hour repeatedly landing on my sweat-drenched shirt. Spiders crawled in and out of the cracks in the rocks and green grasshoppers with eyes like red lanterns cruised from one boulder to another. Quarter-inch-long brown frogs sprang out of our way every time we moved.

Being stuck in one place for twenty-four hours gave us time to walk in the forest freely, not weighed down with packs. The parklike Río Quadi ran through designer-arranged, perfectly squared granite blocks frilled with ferns. We leaned down to look closely at fungi flourishing on a fallen tree that spanned a water trickle like an arching bridge. Nancy reached to touch one of the plants hanging in orderly rows from its shady underside and a cloud of frantic bats exploded past our heads. As we sat quietly a bird landed near. Its orange-yellow chest flowed into a green head and neck which shimmered blue when the bird turned its yellow beak toward us: some kind of trogon. I photographed a succulent leaf which had sprouted a crimson flower from its edge. Nancy found a round, brownish leaf patterned with concentric coils as if a dizzy worm tunneled from the perimeter to the center within its fibers. Florentino explained that Kunas use these leaves as fetishes and that a woman who thought she had good luck might include the concentric motif in a *mola* design.

Whispering waters and quiet bird calls belied the power of these mountain rivers during the season of rains. While the contorted, springy trees on the gravel shoal at the streams' confluence were leafy and green, those further downstream were bent as if knocked by a hurricane. With amazement I examined granite rocks, one the size of an Italian Fiat, stuck in their branches. Downstream from the camp bank, where the two rivers had already merged into one, I looked into dark water perhaps 20 feet deep. I carefully slithered over the steep rocks along the water getting closer to the Pacific by a few hundred yards. From there I began to hear the ominously loud boom of invisible rapids.

In the afternoon of the second day of camping on the shoal, two young men carrying rifles walked into the camp. We had just eaten our daily "bouillabaisse" of rice boiled with bully beef, canned sardines, lentils, Chinese noodles and the last onion—not at all as disgusting as it sounds, hungry as we were after roaming around all morning. They had paddled the canoe from Mortí, tied it up below the rapids, and were in a hurry . . . it would take six hours to get downstream to the village. As we packed up Nancy heard them mention a hundred balboas (dollars) to Florentino. Forewarned, I asked the price for the passage, expecting the ten dollars per head that Florentino had arranged in Mula Tupu. Well, their price had gone up, so I countered halfway—after all here a man works a week to earn thirty dollars. Money-wise Kunas always bargain readily, but these two men spun on their heels and walked away. Vanished for good after paddling upstream for perhaps twelve hours. Somewhat stunned, we squatted down watching the naked carcass of yet another of Livorino's great curassows cure in the smoke from a low fire.

"No trails, Florentino, ha?"

"We could build a raft, but at this height balsa does not grow, only tough heavy trees."

"Could we chop a trail along the river?" I asked Livorino who had done this trip to Mortí many times.

"Very hard to do," he explained. "Because of large rocks we have always used canoes. From here down, the river is deep with high banks."

"I'll pay double wages." They nodded approvingly.

We had already settled into the hammocks for the night when Florentino came to explain they could not do it. The Urrutia household had now been without men to get food for four days, the *congreso* in Mula Tupu and in Mortí would penalize them for going on to another village without permits, and they really did not want to antagonize the people in Mortí. I already thought that for some reason we were given the outrageously high canoe fare to discourage us from coming to Mortí.

"I understand. We'll start back to the coast in the morning," I agreed. Nancy felt crushed with disappointment, but I rationalized that our main goal was to stay in the virgin forest for a while, and so we would.

With almost empty packs and home ahead, Livorino and Eleucadio wanted to rush back; for us, however, going fast would almost certainly end in injury. We plodded on, each step an adventure, especially when descending. At an area with huge granite slabs, Nancy, who was mostly sliding on her seat, put her hand down for support right into a triangle chiseled in the rock. A circle was near it, and more symbols all over the stone face. Only a few nights earlier Florentino had described how his grandfather read ancient Kuna picture writing, but his father could not. Our guides showed total indifference to the discovery, and I felt so intimidated by slowing them down that I did not even dig the camera out of the waterproof backpack.

We could now recognize the places we had passed on the way up, particularly the tree with flowing sap attracting swarms of tiny wasps whose bites had ballooned into huge but painless welts on my hand. Soon after, I slipped, fell hard, and stayed down, removing my straw hat to cool off and rest. A 3-inch frog with wavy yellow lines on its body sat on the hat and stayed hanging onto the brim when I put it on again. I could see its tiny feet every time I looked up—an enterprising male trying to spread his genes far and wide. His tenacity during several more of my spills ended a couple of hours later when, propelled by the weight of my backpack filled with photo equipment, I took a violent header into the leaves and clay soil.

The Kunas kept showing us things. Florentino held up a flowering anthurium, a medicinal flower that smelled like menthol and soap, used to cure stuttering children. We kneeled down to examine orchid blossoms, fallen angels from the high canopy, and pushed our noses in to get the fragrance—instead, hordes of minute ants crawled up our noses and kept us sneezing. The forest scents ranged from scotch and hash browns to sawdust and strong perfume, and quite often, a whiff of skunk. Livorino, leading, spotted the animals first. A silky anteater with golden fur, smaller than a cat, scurried up a tree and watched us from a safe height. The canopy above was so thick that raindrops tapping the leaves above never reached us. Only the river opened a narrow crack to expose clouds traveling across the sky.

I guessed that we essentially followed the run of just one river, now and then taking shortcuts over the mountains between its looping curves. Treacherous mossy rocks lined the straight river reaches. Nancy cautiously slowed down when negotiating the most slippery granite and only rarely landed on her bottom. Like a fool I tried to imitate the flying Kuna leaps and eventually landed on my knee with a resounding thud of bone on stone. To keep the injury warm and the blood circulating I limped on and soon forgot it. As we walked through a curtain of thin vines hanging down to face level Livorino spotted a 6-foot *caiman,* a crocodile, which promptly dove in deep. Through the clear water we could see his outline on the bottom, so Eleucadio lopped off a straight limb from a short tree and threw it, spear fashion, at the croc. The animal shot off like a nuclear submarine toward safer regions.

At our last camp on the lowlands, *chitres*—microscopic gnats— came at dusk to feed on us. Florentino, Eleucadio, and Livorino, brought up in smoky huts, threw some wet wood on the fire and moved in closer, but our eyes itched and wept so badly in the smoke that we finally sprayed ourselves with Off. In the morning the Kunas woke us up excitedly. They had found a cache of iguana eggs and were happy to add them to the great curassow carcass that Livorino smoked each evening to preserve until the return home. After we finished walking for the day we always changed from our wet clothes into a dry set for the night. The last morning on the trail, Nancy, while reluctantly pulling on wet jeans, picked a brown leaf off the cloth. It wiggled just before she flicked it down, where the leaf turned into a brown scorpion and scooted for cover.

By the time we reached Río Ibedi and found the canoe left for Livorino and Eleucadio, everybody was loaded with spoils of the forest.

Nancy carried the violets Florentino had collected to relieve his father's suffering eyes because he himself was festooned with coils of vines for tying together thatch roofs. Each of the guys collected special river rocks that work well as *uchus,* and Eleucadio carried an empty instant-coffee jar full of chopped heliconia shoots mixed with gravel and water, a mixture he drank to gain strength—the *green* steroids!

We paddled out of the river into a hot strong sea breeze. In the distance, several canoes returning home from the outer islands raised palm fronds as sails to scoot before the wind. After the cool evenings in the pure leafy air of the hills it felt clammy and feverish. We longed to go back to where life felt cleaner than anywhere that we had ever lived. I hoped we were turning into forest freaks.

ROAD RUNNER

Alianor True

What is it that draws me out into the desert in the hour before dawn? That causes me to leave the comfort of bed and lingering sleep and confront a landscape in which all that is not rock is light? Is it the violet flush across the eastern sky, or the immaculate silence of an immense place? Is it the marathon I will run in a month? Or the little boy with leukemia for whom my run is raising money? Or is it something larger, born of open spaces and solitude and a deep sense of communion? Whatever it is, I am powerless to resist it. So I find myself here again, as I was yesterday and the day before, running, always running toward a place that is just beyond the next bend in the road.

Oftentimes on these runs I leave myself, in heat and dehydration and fatigue, sitting beside the road to watch a young woman jog toward me, and then pass by, and then fade into the distance. I am a wall of weathered red sandstone, or a scrub-filled wash, or a century-old Joshua tree. Then, other times I am deep inside myself, fighting the pain, pushing onward, feeling the body rebel, and resisting the temptation to stop. There is something about the desert that quietly helps the imagination on these runs. If I were to run beside the sea, or through a forest, or across a grass prairie, it would be different. Here, though, the country is austere and disciplined, and I find myself each day becoming more and more like the desert through which I run: a body and spirit reduced to essentials.

I should tell you that distance running is a pursuit often scorned. I am frequently told that I am not of sound mind, and that such long solitary treks are the mark of one who is young and foolish. Nevertheless, I am here and ready to begin again in the chill of early morning.

As I set out, I am conscious of each step, of the jarring motion of my legs and shoulders, the discord of my limbs. Each breath is rough in my mouth and loud in my ears. My eyes dart back and forth, sweeping the narrow road and the steep reddish banks on either side. I scan upward toward the bluish-gray sky and glance back and forth across the road to the sparse vegetation spotting the desert floor. Shadows of Joshua trees stretch long over the crisp yucca stalks and clumps of rabbitbrush nestled along the roadside. Two burros lift their heads, moist brown eyes tracing my path away from them. My sunglasses nudge the bridge of my nose as I ease into a regular pace. Step, step, breath. Step, step, breath. I cross over the cattle grate and run past the road markers at the edge of the Red Rock Wilderness.

I am lucky to be running here at Red Rock. While the Mojave is not short on two-track roads stretching back into nowhere, few loop around to a main highway, and are as accessible for caching water. This loop of thirteen miles is paved, so I don't worry about twisting an ankle or tripping over rocks buried in sand. The BLM set this canyon and the surrounding area, over 197,000 acres, aside as a National Conservation Area, and has managed it like a park, with an entry fee, a visitor's center, developed roadside stops, and maintained trails. It has become a destination, a point of interest for many in the area and for those passing through.

The first few hills come easy. Gradual swells lift my feet higher as I lean forward, head down. I try not to let myself focus on them, only on the first mile marker, two small rises away. One foot down and one foot up, the running shuffle. I crawl up the hills, sink relieved into the dips and wait for the turns, twisting around the high banks of desert sand, coral-pink in the brief glow of sunrise. The sun begins to heat the air, but the shaded pockets remain cool where the road dips and dives along the Calico sandstone formations. I will miss this dark fresh air later in the day; the chill on my forearms. I ease upward and pass the first parking area on the road. Calico is a place for visitors to stop and walk, read an interpretive sign, embark on the worn trails that lead back into the rocks. It waits, empty and vacant for now. In a few hours, the first of the day's rush of cars will fill the spots and people will crowd the overlooks. Leaving it behind and approaching the two-mile marker, I think briefly that I may be running in place. I could *walk* faster up this slope. I keep my head down until I crest the hill and enjoy a quick flat spell for a moment. My heart rate decreases, and I slowly disappear around the curve and down.

Here is the first challenge—climbing nearly 3,000 feet of elevation in the first five miles, pushing my legs up the next hill, pressing and pulling my way into the desert and away from the city. I love the twists of the first few miles, the way the road drapes the curves of the land, hiding the scenery until I am ready to see it. The smooth glow of sunlight glancing off the rock formations as I round a curve is enough to keep me going. The landscape is far from monotonous as it flies by straight and fast, disappearing before it can even be seen. I am small in the shadow of the road bank as I emerge into the sun, my shadow stretching long and slender before me.

With the radiant energy invading the dense dawn air, ravens circle and shift on the warming thermals above me as I wheel and bank around the two-mile curves. Light and quick, gaining momentum and sustaining speed uphill, I round the corner and descend toward Sandstone Quarry, the three-mile mark and my first water stop. Just past the marker post, my water bottle rests under a black brush plant, unmoved from where I stored it last night. The water is still cool. I slurp as I pace in a tight circle. Thirty seconds later I screw the lid on the bottle and drop it back underneath the shrub. The raven squawks above, prodding me onward.

Ravens may be the most visible of the local birds, but hidden in the scrub are mourning doves, cactus wrens nesting in cholla cacti, and white-throated swifts, which can always be found cruising for insects near seasonal and permanent water sources. I don't hear these birds as much as I've heard others in different parts of the country, where the chatter of tweets and chirps from trees and bushes fills the morning air.

Here the air is hushed. Except for the harsh caw of a raven, it seems comparatively silent, lying in wait for dusk, for water, for rain, waiting to emerge and come alive.

The sun is out in full force now. A trickle of sweat runs down the back of my neck. My lips are dry; my sunglasses slip on the thin sheen of sweat and sunscreen coating my nose. The next two miles track steadily uphill. I know this as I trudge and shuffle, not expecting relief. Below me, small gray pebbles are trapped in weathered asphalt, worn and crumbling at the edge. I glance up every so often, above the slanted pavement at my feet. The High Point overlook is out of sight behind the undulating topography. Reflective yellow road markers measure my progress and watch me pass as I rise above the yucca and brush, leaving Joshua tree territory, head down, arms pumping.

My shadow has shrunk. She struggles, her head mere inches from my feet. Sweat drips from my temples; my hair swings back and forth. A slow gust flows through the wash, refreshing and cool on my damp hair and face. I spy a desert tortoise from the corner of my eye, nibbling the tender bloom of a prickly pear. Her neck strains, wrinkled skin hanging loose, munching, chewing. Her progress around the cactus has taken all morning, stopping to eat, staying in the thin shadows, tracking the path of the sun across the sky.

A flutter of noise and rustling brush bursts into flight on my left, and suddenly a flock of Gambel's quail is clattering up from the scrubby vegetation clustered in the wash. For a few moments, I am flushing quail with every few steps. Two, three, five, and then seven birds rush across the road. Another flock emerges from behind the snakeweed. Puzzled at how anything out here can have such a burst of energy, I wonder if I disturbed their early-morning ritual search for seeds and water. The land itself seems so lethargic. I tread up the hill and turn the corner, still running.

I round the final bends, nearing the High Point. A steep downhill before rushing to the top, the momentum in my legs carrying me through. The expansive panorama of the Red Rock valley stretches across the horizon as I enter the parking area and skirt the perimeter, absorbing the view. The visitor's center rests far below, a tan square nestled behind a small rise. My truck is a tiny red dot and the distant highway a gray ribbon disappearing around the desert formations. Las Vegas is nothing but an alien town in the distance, draped in a veil of smog. I breathe deeply from my perch. I have climbed 3,000 feet, entered the Red Rock high country. I am backed against the base of the mountains. Sandstone cliffs and walls soar above me and step up into the Toiyabe National Forest, up into the peaks through which I will hike on fires later in the season.

I turn back toward the mountains, away from the view, and slip into a small pocket of cool air. The glaring sun hasn't yet penetrated every nook and cranny of the rock walls and the elevation gain helps me escape the rising heat. I wipe my forehead with the palm of my hand. A bead of sweat seeps into the corner of my right eye; sunscreen stings. The biggest hill is at my feet, and I tuck my head down, arms moving me up the mountain. Steady, steady, I climb. This is the last of the significant inclines. Despite the struggle, I don't resent the slope. I know that once I reach the top, it will be over. I will have won. It morphs into a short-term goal: something to strive for, to master, and then to leave behind. This hill, like all the others, will be scaled and then gone in my footsteps, a reminder of my accomplishment. Shuffle, shuffle, exhale. A swish and two cyclists whoosh by. One looks over at me, sporting dark sunglasses, and nods. "Nice pace," he says. "Good job." My heart races: I am a marathoner, I am a runner, I am strong and fast. I smile and whisper thanks as they zoom over the crest, gone.

Close to the top, I push myself through the draw. The road passes over the rise, steep banks on either side. There is a brief moment of shade as I glide through. The maintenance crew has placed small boulders along the road, and I feel like a royal procession of one as I saunter through. My next landmark, the six-mile post and another water bottle, are just ahead. Pacing myself down a smooth hill, down, down. A tall road sign appears, and the dirt road to the White Rock Spring lot stretches to the west. Time for refueling, a gulp of water, pace in a circle. Another group of cyclists whoosh by as I squeeze the last drops of my strawberry-banana Powergel onto my tongue. Sunglasses, bright jerseys, and black spandex. Serious expressions. They don't look at me. The Powergel tastes like frosting, sweet and thick, chalky with vitamins. A quick mouthful of water rinses my throat and I'm off.

The winding road cruises downward. I have mastered the hills; the test of strength is over. Now comes the real challenge, the test of endurance—the long, hot, flat miles through the floor of the Red Rock Valley. I sail down fast, leaning back and trying to slow my pace. I drift onto the flats and think how many times I have seen this road—from a car window, from behind the wheel of my wild-land fire engine, on previous runs. It is no longer fresh and unseen, holding mysteries and discoveries beyond every curve and hill. I know what lies ahead. It is comfortable, and the curves and shapes of the desert fit my body as I run. I am familiar with what I see and smell, with the heat rising from the road and the sun bearing down on my back. I recognize the plants, the turnouts, what mile I am passing, what vista is around the bend. With quiet affection, I run through the wilderness, this desert space I can call my own.

A rattler slithers away from the approaching pounding of my feet. I break for a second, and pause to glance for him inside the sagebrush. I keep running; he is gone. As the road spreads out before me, my attention drifts away from my immediate surroundings as I stare at a faraway point. The creosote and sagebrush transform into vague roadside plants, and the distant horizon becomes my destination. I own this road, running right up the middle. Mile nine, my next water break, rests alongside a straight stretch where the road parallels a dip in the plain. No grand views of the rock formations here, just the plain desert for all it's worth. Scraggly tufts of cheatgrass peek out among the thick juniper shrubs along the disturbed roadside. I begin again, tackling the smooth, flat miles that lead me back to the highway and the heat.

The mountains are behind me now. The cool shade and springs they offer stretch to the north and west, and groves of trees—cottonwoods, mesquite, and a few ponderosa—nestle against the base of the rocks. I am running farther from those verdant spots with every step, into the open floor of the valley. Gradually losing the experience of physical sensation, my arms and neck feel light and open. No longer do my quadriceps rise and fall. The soles of my feet lose contact with the road, and I forget the feel and sound of the *slap, slap, slap* of my sneakers against the pavement. The swish of my nylon shorts is lost into the background. My eyes stare vacantly forward; I don't look around. All is quiet. My breath, the wind, the ravens disappear. I am moving without noticing motion, sound, or thought. I cut through the desert air, sweating, running, a blur of movement across the still arid landscape.

From what I've heard, this is when most people get bored with running, claiming the length of time as too long to look around at the same setting, no matter where it is or how it is shaped. This is when they feel exhausted with the repetitive motion of their legs, unsatisfied with the thousands of footsteps they have taken, knowing they could cover the same distance in a few short minutes were they riding a bike or driving a car. Some dislike the solitude, the independence, the humble method of moving oneself. Some claim they have nothing to engage their mind, their higher faculties, while their body moves continuously. And therein lies the beauty of it. That after running all this time and covering all this ground, there is indeed nothing to think about. Pressing past physical and mental limitations and environmental challenges to a feeling of such inner calm that the outside seems to melt away, and one can become just another element of the desert. A body drifting through the heat, cooled by air currents, searching for water.

I lose touch with everything. The thoughts I turned to earlier in my run, to take my mind off running, have no place here. No images of my distant lover, the fire season unrolling in front of me, the future marathon and the little boy and his cause for which I am raising money. There are no ideas or reasons, just the air and soil and shrubs that stream past me, and the road beneath my feet. I am a desert animal, sensing the most salient features of my surrounding habitat. The temperature, the slope of the hill, the brushing of my forearms against my abdomen, the dry swallow. I seep into the zone, that magical spell of space and time where I can eclipse the present, pushing my body to new limits, unraveling what I know I can achieve, and striving past it.

I am wrapped in the fog of running. My body has become a machine, propelling itself past the ten-mile mark. A sharp flap and flutter from behind startles me into awareness and a roadrunner snaps out of the air and settles into a running pace alongside me. The comedy of the situation, a cartoon figure popping out of the air to keep me company, assures me of the wonder and circumstance given to those who encounter this environment on its own terms. For a moment, I am joined by a comrade, another desert runner, who knows what this landscape has to offer, and how to appreciate it. Dark gray and rather ungroomed, it quickly outpaces me on speedy feet, leaving me to run solo again. Two more bends later, and I see the gate, the juncture of the Loop Road and Highway 159. Here my solitude ends, as the highway jolts me back to human civilization. Two empty horse trailers are parked in the gravel lot across the cattle grate. I cross the highway, running with the traffic, now confined to the shoulder. Motorists zip by. Some are kind enough to scoot over and spare me the brunt of their vehicle's wind and fumes. Others bear down and leave me feeling lucky to escape roadkill status. I surge up the smooth climb to Red Rock lookout, facing the High Point from the south. Groups of Lycra-clad cyclists are prepping for their ride on the same road I have just finished on foot. I rise over the hill and congratulate myself on fourteen miles well done. Two to go.

This last bit of the run completes the loop through Red Rock. Running along the southern edge, I can gaze across the valley and examine from afar the rocks and cliff walls I have just passed. From here, they are rounded protrusions emerging from the desert floor, backed by the higher forested mountains. The vibrant colors capture my gaze. Streaks of ruddy sandstone, rust and maroon, salmon and ruby, layered among limestone beiges, browns, and grays. Lifting in contrast to the sharp azure sky of the springtime Nevada Mojave. And I was just there, witnessing those colors come to life under the rising sun, all alone, the first privileged eyes to see the desert in daylight.

I pull into the Red Rock entrance. My legs are sandy and dusty, crusted salt lines my face and skin. The air around is hot, morning breezes lifting from the southwest as convective heating begins to bake the valley. I look past the highway, into the washes filled with brush and boulders strewn by seasonal floods. For a few hours this morning, I have added my own movement to these elements, my own addition to the scrub and sand and heat.

During tomorrow's run, with confidence gained from today's journey, I'll remember how the roadrunner and tortoise, the rocks and the cacti, compose and define this powerful landscape, offering those who explore the desert an example of the vitality and resilience that rests within each one of us.

HEIRLOOM

Lisa Couturier

Although I knew I could not have it, I asked the falconer for a feather, a brown striped feather from his peregrine falcon tethered beside me to her perch, brushing my arm with her long, outstretched wing.

Possessing any body part of a peregrine falcon is illegal, the falconer, Heinz Meng, reminded me. Even the small, downy feathers that this peregrine he called Janice had shed—and which lay mixed with her sticky droppings below her perch—were off-limits.

Feathers: the ultimate symbols of flight, of lightness, of the unrestricted power of transcendence. "When a feather spirals earthward," writes James Cowan in *Letters From a Wild State*, "it is a signal that [a bird] has acted in accordance with its nature, expelling a quill with which its own flight is assured."

The red breast feathers of robins scattered under leaves in the woods. The yellow feathers of finches in the wild lupine. The blue jay's feather poking through pine needles. The sparrow's feather floating in a rain puddle. I spent my childhood perfecting the art of finding feathers in the way some people concentrate their spare energy finding four-leaf clovers. The primary flight feathers. The main coverts and lesser coverts. The secondary flight feathers. All were available and, once I had lifted them, were stashed away in my small reproduction of a buried treasure box, the kind that children imagine are filled with jewels deep at sea and which I had, in fact, been given as a child. By the time I had asked Meng for the peregrine feather, I'd had the treasure box for twenty-five years and it was nearly full.

As a kid, I took the feathers out of the box periodically, though not with the symbolic or romantic intentions of garnering transcendence or lightness. Life was not yet so weighted. My aim was much more simple-minded and sensual. Through the feather I could stroke a small part of the bird's sleek, streamlined, silky body and imagine not myself but, as Cowan says, the *bird* in flight.

Surely you know of children who have insatiable desires to acquire things: insects, or pictures of the moon, model airplanes, or dolls, or trucks. Maybe you were one of them; we all have something. For me it was simply feathers of suburban birds, a largely indistinct group of avians. Nevertheless, my fascination spread beyond finches and robins to the intelligent crow, the mysterious owl and eventually—during an extended backpacking trip in Vermont's Green Mountains one summer with friends—to the elusive peregrine falcon.

That summer, as I remember it, I approached a cliff at the top of a mountain, where a man appeared from behind the rocks. Amidst the high-pitched, insistent and obstreperous *kek kek kek kek* of birds I could not see, the man said protectively: "We are reintroducing peregrine falcons to these cliffs. You'll have to turn back."

Being young and believing that the world, and at that moment the Green Mountains, belonged to us, my friends and I stood our ground. Until the man, apparently a biologist, sharply said, "You must turn back."

We marched away, unaware that at that time, in the mid-1970s, DDT and other related pesticides had decimated America's population of peregrine falcons. The biologist's captive-bred peregrines were part of an enormous effort to restore the falcon to the eastern United States. I hiked down the mountain scanning the ground for a feather different from all those I'd had at home in my treasure box—a feather that might belong to the peregrine I'd not even seen. And I eavesdropped on the sky, hoping on an off chance to trace the voice I had heard to the flying body of this elusive yet clearly important bird. It would be decades before I again would be this close to a peregrine.

———————

"The feathers are lovely though, aren't they," said Dr. Meng as he walked into his house to do some paperwork and left me sitting on the grass with his peregrine Janice. Secured to her low perch with leather jesses, which were like leashes around her legs, she preened, stretched her wings, and glared into the surrounding trees where sparrows, robins, and house finches darted by, perilously close to her. The small birds seemed to know that wild prey caught on the wing was a nearly impossible delicacy for Janice.

I watched this raptor, not much larger than a crow, flutter her brown, tan, and ivory feathers against the spring grass. If she were to hunt a pigeon, she would spot the prey—with eyesight eight times more powerful than a human's—as far as a mile away before diving after it "like a feathered bomb," Meng had said. She would fold her wings and transform herself into the shape of a bullet traveling up to 200 miles per hour. Gravity adding a terrific power to her skull-splitting blow, she would strike the pigeon with her sharp talons, sounding like a punching fist. The pigeon would fall to the ground. Janice would circle down, land on her prey and jab her razorlike beak into the bird to cut its neck and spinal cord, finishing her kill. A perfect predator.

Oh, to be free of the jesses, to be the brutal poetry of the air— these were Janice's desires, I guessed; and her endlessly shrill and rapid *kek kek kek kek!* was how she alarmed the world to her presence.

———————

Falco peregrinus. Falco comes from the Latin *falx* or "sickle," which describes the bird's sickle-like talons and beak. *Peregrinus* is Latin for "wanderer." Sickles that wander. A partial list of the peregrine's common names shows that they occupy the world: Peregrine, Wanderfalk, Slechtvalk, Pelerin, Pellegrino, Sokol, Shaheen, Kidgavitch, Kiriat. Living on every continent except Antarctica, peregrines have inhabited virtually every language since ancient times. The Egyptians, for example, believed that the peregrine, flying at dawn and dusk, assisted the sun in rising and setting each day.

The summer after I met Meng, I waited through late afternoons for a pair of peregrines to fly the sun down behind the New York Hospital–Cornell Medical Center on Manhattan's Upper East Side, where the birds lived and still do live. The hospital's sky-scraping stone walls resemble the peregrines' ancestral cliff dwellings; the city's resident pigeons, as well as birds who migrate along the Atlantic flyway during spring and fall, are their ample food source. Far below the nest, in the hospital's parking lot, I fixed my binoculars on what I'd come to imagine as an inner-city cliff near the East River, one of fifteen sites that monogamous pairs of wild peregrines occupy within the five boroughs of New York City.

Chris Nadareski, who took me on unofficially as a graduate student assistant, is one of the few who has climbed the heights to each nest site. A wildlife biologist who studied under Heinz Meng in college, Chris is the New York City Department of Environmental Protection (NYCDEP) biologist responsible for the New York City peregrines. He is quick to remark that "the peregrines help maintain an ecological balance in the city, even though it's so far out of whack in so many ways. If, at the top of the food chain, they're successful, we know that the ecosystem is working at the lower levels." His love and enthusiasm for the peregrines are contagious. He's a man who, upon seeing a pair fly into their nest, will immediately explain and imitate their behavior for the curious onlooker: "*Eee-chup, eee-chup* is what they're saying. Now see them bow," he says as he squats and bows. "They're preparing for their courtship rituals." An explanation like this casts a sort of peregrine love-spell over many people who manage the city's famous buildings and bridges where the peregrines nest. They may get the species wrong ("Hey, Chris, how's those eagles?"), but they're nevertheless protective and proud of their wild penthouse charges.

Chris monitors the birds throughout the year since, unlike most North American peregrines that travel to South America for the winter, the New York City population stays home. New York winters aren't severe enough to force the falcons out, and the endless supply of pigeons keeps them well fed. Spring and summer, when the birds breed and raise their young among skyscrapers, helicopters, and humans, are Chris's busiest times of year.

In late spring, Chris bands each nestling with an identification anklet that instructs anyone finding an injured or dead peregrine to contact the U.S. Fish and Wildlife Service (USFWS). During the banding sessions at the nests the peregrine parents, who, understandably, abhor the taking of their young, seriously attempt to erase Chris—which is why he dons a motorcycle helmet and a thick, full-body construction suit to climb to their nest. The attire protects him as well as the birds. During an attack, they could tangle their talons in Chris's loose hair, wristwatch, belt, or anything else. He prefers that the birds simply make a quick, clean hit on him.

The first captive-bred peregrines flew to New York City in 1983, after being raised by Heinz Meng and others, and were released into the wild by the same biologists I had come across in the mountains of Vermont in the mid-1970s. By May 1993, nine pairs of the New York City peregrines had had their most successful breeding season. Thirty-five young were born. But by mid-October, eight young were confirmed dead already and two were missing. In any year "certainly some young will be successful," said Chris, "and others just won't be. Some will starve to death not only here at their breeding grounds but during the time they spend looking for their own new territories. They may run into a tremendous amount of trouble, mostly from man, whether directly or indirectly through construction, power lines, or skyscraper windows they sometimes mistake for sky and try to fly through."

Peregrines prefer open skies in the way whales prefer open oceans, space through which they can move unimpeded, sinuously. But because the birds nest on sheer rock walls, they've adapted, over the decades, to living among the skyscrapers of North American cities. Before Chris's peregrines arrived in the Big Apple, a peregrine pair twice tried to nest atop the St. Regis Hotel in Manhattan in the 1940s, but both times were forced out by human interference. Philadelphia's City Hall in the 1940s and a church steeple in Harrisburg, Pennsylvania, in the 1950s each welcomed a pair of falcons. However, by the late 1950s and early 1960s peregrines were disappearing in the eastern United States due to the widespread effects of DDT and associated pesticides.

By 1972, North America and most European countries had restricted or outlawed DDT and other suspected killer-organochlorines such as aldrin and dieldrin. "But," said Chris, "We're certainly not free of the problem by any means. It's a very persistent substance." And one that is still present in the widely used toxin dicofol, which is an ingredient in the pesticide Kelthane. Kelthane, although available to the general public for home gardens, is used mostly, according to the Environmental Protection Agency, for agricultural purposes. Almost any nonorganic fruit—oranges, grapefruits, lemons, limes, apricots, nectarines, peaches, apples—has been sprayed with dicofol; it kills mites that scar fruit. We're contaminating ourselves and our ecosystems, but our peaches look pretty.

Outside the United States the situation is more deadly for ecosystems since it is legal for U.S. companies to sell DDT to the Third World, where it is often used to eradicate mosquitoes that carry malaria. For instance, Venezuela, which in the past has received large shipments of DDT, is one of the main wintering spots for the more than 200 migrant North American bird species that visit us during spring and summer in our parks, backyards, woodlands, grasslands, and wilderness areas. Some of those species summer in New York City's Central Park. The cycle of poison continues.

After banding the New York Hospital nestlings, we headed south to a nest near Grand Central Station, in midtown, atop the towering Met Life Building that cuts Park Avenue in half. In wilderness areas, peregrines nest on the edges of cliffs inaccessible to humans and lay their eggs in what is called a "scrape"—a simple depression in the rock. In the city, the NYCDEP assists the birds by building, on skyscrapers and bridges, scrapes made of plywood, boxes that open to the sky on one side.

A service elevator took us to the top of the Met Life Building, where we walked out into the sky. At the scrape on the northern side of the building, Chris pulled out three round, three-week-old bodies, like snowballs of downy feathers. They rolled awkwardly on their bottoms, flinging forward their light yellow, reptilian-like feet. While Chris banded the babies, the parent peregrines circled us, calling loudly: *kek kek kek kek!*

If you had been there, nearly sixty stories above Manhattan, you would have noticed several things. For example, the wind whipping around the skyscraper and the apparent ease with which it could flick you to the street. And you would see a landscape beyond Manhattan, a terrain of waters—the Hudson River, the East River, the Atlantic Ocean, the bays—and greener, wider land. On a clear day you would look through the open skies to the Palisades of the Hudson River— sharp gray cliffs where wild peregrines nested decades ago. If your eyes followed the Hudson River south to its confluence with the East River, you would see olive-green bay water surging into the Atlantic. The fetid smell of the city's summer streets, so redolent of trash and human urine, would vanish in the winds. In fact, the city below you would almost disappear. Given the opportunity to look beyond the familiar concrete scenery, you could, with this temporary reprieve from the purely urban, imagine the island of Manhattan three centuries ago, thickly forested and ringed with lime-green marshland. Meanwhile, the Met Life peregrines would keep circling you, assessing you, calling to you: *kek kek kek kek*. Assuming you would welcome it, the mantra of the falcon would rap in your head and slowly you would sense yourself entering, or at least reaching, into something wild, something your body senses, responds to, knows. Some border would have been erased and the world of the peregrine and its life would be ripping in you.

Chris worked quickly but gently on the three nestlings. He secured a black and red USFWS band to one leg of each bird; he misted lice spray under the birds' wings; he checked the insides of the birds' mouths with a small flashlight. And *voilà*. Next.

Before returning the babies, Chris cleaned the nest-box: a piece of wing from a cedar waxwing, several regurgitated pellets of undigested bones and feathers, a blue jay's head, and an unidentifiable piece of some other bird. A few peregrine feathers blew out with the decaying body parts, and although I knew I could not have a feather I considered scooping them up. With another gust of the wind the feathers floated off the roof, and I felt seized then by what could not be seen or touched: the peregrine's voice.

Obviously the birds were commanding us to leave: *warning, warning, warning*. Their instruction was direct, simple: *Scram!* Their command struck over and over, sounding like some ancient music, a music so intense that it plays not around you but into you until finally you surrender to a performance that you don't necessarily watch as much as you eerily feel.

On that windy, urban cliff in Manhattan I imagined the peregrine and the human two million years ago, the beginning of time for both, when the peregrine lived amidst *Homo habilis*—the "handy man" who made tools, walked upright, and who could speak. Over the centuries, the peregrine and *Homo habilis*—and then the later fire-maker, *Homo erectus*, and the modern *Homo sapiens*—co-existed as powerful predators alert to each other's presence in the world. Imagine them if you will, scrutinizing their world, calling into the stillness, wandering the desolate landscapes, choosing their next kill.

While the Met Life peregrines continued circling, playing their music, I wondered: Is it by sheer chance, some impromptu meeting, that we feel we know a wild creature? Is it that simple, sudden? Or does it rise from something deep and abiding, from a mesmeric relationship developed over centuries perhaps, from experiences buried in the body and triggered now by an angle of light on a wing, by an animal's subtle movement, by its calls and colors, by its beauty, through its death?

Perhaps the best we can hope for is a belief that we are born prepared for the world, that it is long-settled in us, and that our job is to be hungry for it, to have predatory cravings for it, to stalk it ecstatically, to discover how we know what we know.

———————

By the following summer, a construction site for a new building in the New York Hospital complex was teeming with activity. Contractors argued with engineers, construction workers drilled holes, hammers pounded, tractors moved masses of the gray urban earth. Ambulances hollered by. Although I had looked for the New York Hospital peregrines in the autumn over the East River, although I'd thought about the Met Life pair as my taxis sped through Christmas down Park Avenue, I had not seen or heard the birds since Chris banded the Met Life nestlings.

I hoped to glimpse the New York Hospital's new brood of peregrine fledglings, who at this time in their young lives would be practicing their flying and, with their parents, would be occupied in hunting lessons. But again they eluded me.

A few days later, walking east on Seventy-second Street, I heard a bird call overhead. Once, and then again, louder: *kek kek kek kek!* The call rushed into my body, silencing the city in my ears. *Peregrine.* I looked up. Two falcons skimmed over the fancy Upper East Side brownstones, over the well-dressed workers, the delivery people, the leashed dogs. The parent peregrine handed off prey to its fledgling—one of the ways a young peregrine learns to hunt. They tangled in the air, separated, swooped in circles, called, and flew behind a glass skyscraper toward the East River.

The air filled again with horns, boom boxes, buses, trucks. Like a gift I'd carried around without knowing it, the voice of the falcon had survived in me. The call of the peregrine is no memento, nothing like a feather that can be held in one's hand or stored in a box. It is an heirloom we hold in our bodies, summoning the ghosts within us: our wild past among peregrines.

LOGGING ON:
A POSTMODERN AWAKENING

David Petersen

Late winter, late night, midlife. My sleep interrupted by a pressing concern, I rise in the chilly dark and stagger naked, by Braille, toward the
bathroom—a short trip—bouncing from wall to door, feeling with a
toe for the smooth porcelain cold of the toilet. It's a relatively recent
concession to midlife and wife, this water-wasting contraption; for
most of our twenty years here in this little cabin on a big mountain in
Colorado, we got on fine with an outhouse. But an *inside* outhouse, I'll
admit, is warmly welcome on a subzero night such as this.

That wee task accomplished, I stumble on, navigating semi-visually
now, eyes gradually accommodating the opaque darkness. Another
short trip, round a corner and up one step, and I'm in what we jok-
ingly call the "great room," in all its 145-square-foot greatness, with a
redwood post in the middle. But the joke—semi-elective semi-
poverty—is on no one but ourselves, and we don't often mind. I built
this little shack with my own hammered hands, and I am as content as
Caroline is long-suffering.

Here in the many-windowed great room, the ambiance is notably
lighter. The moon this late frigid night, hanging heavy in the west, is
plump and bright as an incandescent egg; slung low above a brooding
horizon, it paints a luminist scene stirringly similar to the Thomas
Aquinas Daly watercolor, *Beaver Ponds with Rising Moon,* that watches
over this little room. Aided by that golden moonglow, I open the

woodstove door, stir down the ashes, grab an armload of aspen splits from the woodbox nearby, and shove them in—standard winter routine here at the postmodern Petersen digs, where wood is our only heat. But tonight, rather than shutting down the stove and returning to bed as usual, I swing the stove door open wide, step back and sink into my rocker to watch the world's oldest and still-best late-night movie.

Meanwhile, outside in the brittle Colorado cold—not real near but not too far—some horny creature calls. Moments later—not too far but not real near—its query is answered in kind. I smile, happy to hear them at it again, "twitterpating," as the vegetarian owl in Disney's insipid, insidiously anti-nature *Bambi* dubs it, euphemizing pure animal lust. In fact, those two great hornies out there sweet-talking in the frozen February night have been courting since Christmas, their species being the most eager twitterpaters among all North American birds. By early spring, while snow still falls here high in the Rockies, and less hardy birds still bask in sunnier climes far to the south, these consummate predators of the night will already be tending chicks.

The flickering stove fire, struggling to rekindle itself, is at least visually warming, though I'm sitting too far back to feel its modest heat, and naked as the night I was born, nine months almost to the day after the close of World War II, so very long ago.

I squirm uncomfortably in my bentwood rocker, its oaken ribs deadly cold on my bare buns and back, sending a shiver up my spine and reminding me with a chuckle of a 1950s horror flick called *The Tingler*—the one where a giant millipede-monster grows surreptitiously on its victim's spine until suddenly something snaps and the victim's eyes bug in shock and the Tingler comes ripping out of bloody flesh in momentarily dubbed-in color and everybody in the theater screams and tosses their popcorn. The next moment, the theater lights go out and the chilling voice of Vincent Price pleads sardonically from the darkened screen: "Ladies and gentlemen, the Tingler is loose in the theater, please keep your seats and be calm!" More screams. Then, just as panicked patrons (average age, eight) start stampeding for the exit, the lights come back up, Vince announces that all is now safe, and the movie resumes. Entertainment, like life, was so much simpler back then, so much more fun.

Squinting at the indoor-outdoor thermometer on the pine-plank wall, I read the hard news: minus five out there with the owls, a balmy forty-eight here inside the cabin. It dawns on me that instead of sitting here shivering, I could either go put some clothes on, or move my chair a little closer to the stove. In a compromise—recalling with a bitter-sweet chuckle a favorite book title, *Bald as I Want to Be*—I grab a cap from the hat rack and scoot a little closer to the flames.

I've been mesmerized by wood fires all my life. It's a near-universal human attraction, this Promethean infatuation with flame, tangled deep in the fibers of our species' evolutionary roots. Staring into bright leaping flame connects us viscerally, spiritually, to our ancestral past. Yet it's not the dance of flame that holds me now, nor even the moonlight, golden and bracing as sour-mash whiskey, but something unique and compelling about one of the logs I just put on—the protagonist in this late-night matinee. As I eased it into the stove, by the eerie glow of moon and coals, I recognized this log as a distinct individual among its thousands of near-twins in the firewood pile outside: a stick with a story.

Quaking aspen, like no other tree I know, is a storyteller, a log-book of local life. Inscribed in its soft white bark you'll find rousing tales of deer and elk—recorded as the finger-thick linear scars of autumn antler rubs, as oily smears of sebum deposited via vigorous face-rubbing, and as the twin denticulate notch-scars of winter bark gnawing. Porcupines likewise autograph aspens, with sharp, climbing claws and toothy bark chews. And in the process of shedding their lower limbs as they grow, aspens scarify themselves in provocatively anthropomorphic fashion: Perhaps you've seen them—winking aspen eyes, blackened aspen penises, open aspen vulvas . . .

And speaking of sex, anyone who has spent time walking in a Colorado aspen grove has likely encountered a sample of the soft-porn aspen art carved by homesick shepherds, dating mostly from the late

1920s and early thirties, a greatly depressing time all around. But to me the most impressive aspen art of all—witness the log I'm watching burn now—is the work of climbing bears.

This particular aspen split, taken from midway up a 40-foot trunk, tells—in sigmoid sign language—of a black bear climbing; of thick, muscled arms hugging the slippery pole in a wild and fierce embrace; of scimitar claws gripping, slipping, ripping the chalky bark, cutting five curvaceous slashes, 6 inches long, a quarter-inch deep. In sum, it speaks of passion.

As hungry flames probe the rounded side of the bear-scarred split, searching for a chink in its slick bark armor, the wood begins to speak—snapping, popping, hissing—reciting, I fancy, its own eulogy: a poignant swansong of seasons turning, of the warm taste of sunshine and the cold weight of snow, of annular growth and wooden resolve, of a bear's brief, impassioned embrace and the hurtful scars it left behind—a visual mnemonic for the bittersweet ephemerality that renders all life so precious.

Soon after the old aspen fell, I found its slender white corpse, like a giant stick of chalk, lying in the woods. After severing its skeletal limbs, I sawed the naked trunk into ten 4-foot lengths. Noting the bear scars, I cut carefully around, leaving them intact.

Reflecting now on the beast who left that cursive autograph, I wonder: Where are you tonight, friend bear? Grown old and died naturally? Killed by hunter, highway, or habitat destruction? Or—a happier supposition—snoring snugly in your den, somewhere quite nearby. Bears can live a quarter-century or more in the wild, so even this is possible.

After cutting up the fallen tree, I wrestled the heavy green logs into my old work truck, coasted down the dirt mountain road, motored a ways on asphalt, switchbacked up another mountain, another dirt road, and home. At the top of the rutted two-track drive—in order to keep the chainsaw's snarl, stench, and sawdust a polite distance from cabin and Caroline—I reenacted a ceremony I've enjoyed countless times across my two decades here, a sacrament of sweat of the sort Zen countryman Gary Snyder would call *real work*—a term and concept interpreted by human ecologist Paul Shepard as "not a drudging, slogging subservience to a hated routine, but an encounter with the world in a delicate way central to thought and feeling."

And real work it is: Unload and saw each of the 4-foot logs into three stovewood lengths, cleave each length with an 8-pound awl—depending on its diameter, into half-, third-, or quarter-moon splits—pitch the hundred-plus splits back into the truck, back down the drive to the top of the little clearing that makes a feral yard, toss the splits atop the growing heap of former forest that warms us half of every year, body and soul. . . . Body and soul, since with each bit of wood I feed to the stove—as with each bite of elk I kill and cut and feed to myself—I'm warmed not only by caloric combustion, but by the primal pleasures of self-sufficiency, diffused gratitude, and a direct and deeply intimate, thus profoundly spiritual, connection to life-giving nature. Biophilia spoken here.

As the aspen scars are gradually erased by flame, I think of the tree from which that burning split was cut—its past, present, and future foretold: sprouting, branching, budding; fresh, green, smooth-skinned and limber; growing straight and tall, yet collecting scars even in youth; and heart-rot, like a time bomb lurking, ticking, deep inside. Incrementally aging, stiffening, weakening, leaning, doomed to crash to Earth one day then hauled away and tossed onto the inevitable pyre; up in smoke. And when it's done, when I'm done, my ashes, like those I'll shovel in the morning from the cooling stove, will be returned to the forest and scattered, scribbling long dark lines on clean white snow—bear scars on aspen bark—melting with that snow come spring, seeping into the forest duff to nourish the growth of . . . what?

An aspen sapling?

With a flare of sparks and flame, the remains of several logs collapse in sudden synchrony, recalling my attention to the flickering woodstove fire, which now approaches its denouement. But within moments the sparks die down and my thoughts floats off again, back to yesterday.

————————

As always in winter, when sunrise comes lazy and late, I awoke with the first gray glimmer of dawn. No alarm clock to hurl against the wall in protest of another wasted day of pointless, empty effort. No rush to leap from bed and shower and shave and pull on my daily work uniform: T-shirt, sweatpants, ball cap and moccasins. No force-fed fast-food breakfast. But like most folks these days, I must commute to work . . . about 20 feet, from the cabin to the storage shed-slash-office I call the Outhouse (apropos, some may say, to what's produced within).

But before this morning's commute, making the most of my luxury of wake-up time, I sat and sipped and listened to National Public Radio interview some nutty Harvard professor bent on human cloning. Just what the world needs: more myopic meddling with nature and ourselves, more people—designer people no less—cloned after our own narcissistic self-image. Lower-case poet e.e. cummings put the writing on the wall when he cautioned: "A world of made is not a world of born." Yet more and more of us squander more and more of our imaginations, souls, and fleeting lives on made fantasies, while neglecting, abusing, and destroying the one thing in life that will never fail us: the one true reality of nature.

Anyhow, just as I was moving to ditch this depressing "news" in favor of mellow morning music, the soothing voice of Bob Edwards was drowned out by a cacophony of bird screams outside. Dashing to the west-wall windows I peered out and around, looking to spot the mobbing jays and spilling my coffee in the excitement. From the sound of it, the birds were ganged near the top of a ponderosa pine, 80 feet up, down by the Petersen pet cemetery, blocked from my view by the cabin roof's low overhang and luxurious drapery of icicles. As I searched around, hoping for a glimpse of the hawk I knew had just been there, I noticed something as lovely as it was unlikely: a *butterfly*— small, blue as an October sky, floating lightly along, not using its wings but just easy-riding on some invisible breeze. This, I knew, just could not be—a butterfly at 8,000 feet in the Colorado Rockies on a February morning at two below zero. And then I saw that it wasn't.

What it was, was a breast feather. Then another. And now a whole parade of these lovely blue angels of death came coasting across my view, angling left to right, settling gently atop the night's fresh snow, shadowing the unseen raptor's departure as it winged away with its prey—a warm, fat Steller's jay.

Still hoping for a glimpse of the hawk, I rushed outside, where my leather-soled moccasins slipped on the snow and I fell to my knees. Too late anyhow. The killer—a Cooper's hawk, most likely—had already flown the coop. The deed was done, the drama ended . . . until of course the next time. For life to triumph there must always be a next time.

Winter: so lovely, uncompromising, and clean. If only it didn't go so long.

––––––––––

That was this morning; or, more accurately, yesterday. Tonight, which in fact is tomorrow, I slump low in my rocker, grogginess and gravity pulling me down, down. My thoughts, already weak and flickering, fade like the flames in the near-forgotten stove. But now, just in time to stop my nodding nosedive, comes a slow, sibilant sizzle from a shadowy corner of the room—a soft, susurrous breeze, fetid as the devil's breath—then a low, throaty moan, a dull shuffle, as ancient Angel-dog shifts arthritic bones on her padded bed.

Angel—an Akita-shepherd mix, old and in the way (like me); neglected by her previous family, she (like me) showed her tail to a bad first draw in life, striking out in search of something better, risking all, appearing here one summer afternoon some years ago. For days we ignored her, as best we could, hoping she'd just go home, wherever that might be. But Angel knew she was home, and so she persisted—one ear up, one ear down, brown eyes pleading. Soon enough we relented and let the old girl in. After all, it's not every day you find an Angel on your doorstep.

And then there's Otis, half Lab, half golden retriever, with all the best of both; half Angel's age and nearly as big, black against her blonde, lost in the ozone again, curled on his bed at the foot of our bed. While Angel is blind in one eye and massively arthritic, Otis is half-deaf and waddles like Charlie Chaplin from an old hip injury. And in spite of it all, they both love life.

Otis and Angel—the latest and hardly the last in a lengthening litany of aging, outcast curs who have adopted us, much to our delight. Dogs offer comfort in this increasingly uncomfortable world. If she could, Caroline would have a dozen. Well-loved dogs are loyal, grateful, uncomplaining, infinitely forgiving and, by never second-guessing the meaning or worth of their existence, help keep our own anxieties at bay. Yet these dog-daddy instincts of mine conflict head-on with my neo-animistic worldview, which acknowledges the fact that genetically, dogs are "goofies," pitiful products of mankind's mania to meddle and control, erstwhile wolves crudely reshaped into clownish reflections of our oafish selves. Human ecologist Paul Shepard goes so far as to suggest that dogs and other companion pets are invented and kept by people "who are desperate for the sight of nonhuman creatures because they touch some deep archetypal need."

That need, of course, is for palpable animal intimacy, for wildlife and wild*ness,* for ongoing physical and emotional contact with those suprahuman beings Shepard calls "the Others," in whose numinous eyes we see glimmers of our own neglected wildness, dignity, and freedom. As replacements for the magnificent creatures from which they've been reduced and reinvented, our genetically deracinated pets make piss-poor proxies.

And this I know better than most, since my life is blessed with natural wildness. Yet, in the end, we love our dogs and they love us. And love is good, wherever you can find it.

Suddenly a minor emergency rouses me from my musings. What little remained of the bear-scarred log has just exploded—a pocket of trapped core moisture, I suppose; heartsblood, vaporizing and expanding, hurling glowing shrapnel out the open stove door and across the great-room rug. Old, thin, and tattered as it is, that rug is all that lies between us and a cold wood floor. So I fall to my knees and scamper to the rescue, gingerly gathering the livid embers with bare hands and tossing them back into the stove—grinning to think that I'm inadvertently emulating those exotic fellows who dance barefoot across carpets of glowing coals to prove . . . what?

So ends the late-night movie.

————————

With the rug fire safely extinguished and the indoor temperature having soared to a sultry fifty-four, I shove a few more sticks of wood into the stove, close the door, set the spin-draft for a low, slow burn, pet a snoring Angel and slouch toward bed—where Caroline, my own Sleeping Beauty, greets the icy press of my bony bod with a warm and welcoming sigh. I snuggle closer. So does she; our synergy is perfect.

Nearby, curled like a furry fetus on his own bed, Otis snuffles, shifts, and moans contentedly. Homeostasis returns to the little cabin on the big mountain in Colorado. Not a creature is stirring, not even a hantavirus-harboring deer mouse (thanks to our diligent neighbors: the owls, the foxes, the coyotes). Come daylight, when next I will awake, if it weren't for the fresh burn marks in the great-room rug, I might well dismiss my recollections of this eerie night as merely a weird dream. But that bear-scarred aspen log was as real as life and death. Now it's gone, up in smoke, and no way to recall it.

Logging off . . .

POEMS

Penny Harter

GOING HOME

Going home, your eyes close
as you bounce along the rutted road
visiting a landscape you have made
from fragments—

the face of that cow by the fence,
the neon sign on the all-night diner
set against a black wall of pine,

or a parlor filled with voices
you thought you had lost,
a room through which a stream
from your childhood
is mysteriously flowing,

and you step into the current
on the same flat rocks as always,
only their moss grown thicker
over the years.

TEA CEREMONY

FOR ELEANOR ECOB MORSE,
MY GREAT-GREAT-GRANDMOTHER, 1890

She sits at her worktable,
lifts a blue glass cup
to admire its gilded rim
as she begins to paint
small violets on its sides.

By evening, she will have done
the whole set, blessing each blue sphere
where violets bloom.

She does not feel the weight
of snow that fills each cup she raises
to the window's light, the cold
of blowing flakes against her hands,
or the sudden chill that finds her lips
when she pantomimes a sip.

This morning, the sky beyond her window
deepens to the blue of finished cups
as I hold each one up to catch the sun.

AT NINETY, MY FATHER

At ninety, my father studies the cosmos,
slowly turning pages in his birthday book
to contemplate the glowing photographs
of planets, of galaxies beyond the Milky Way.
He is looking into time.

With his good eye, he reads about
the rings of Saturn, the seas of Mars,
enters giant towers birthing stars.

Here and there, he leaves a fingerprint
    among the spirals
        in the radiant dark.

QUESTIONING THE STORM

If you stand in a black cloak in a stony field,
leaning into the wind, tilted toward thunder
and purple jolts of lightning at the horizon;

if you wear a black cloak with a hood
as the sky darkens and thunder cracks
a fine line across the black egg,
a hairline fracture that splinters into rain,

what difference then
between cloak and cloud,
breath and wind,
skull and sky?

THE HINGE OF PAIN

Each half fits the other,
held by a pin.
How many angels?

The hinge of the jaw
does its good work
until the winding cloth,

and the hinge of the eyelid
blinks away our dust
until the close.

Tonight my bedroom door
creaks on its hinge
as it slowly swings shut,

but a stone from the mountain
holds it open
between you and me.

THE BARN

The barn is empty.

Look, that black hole
is where the animals
used to be,

their warm breath pumping
the pink sacs of their lungs
until the air was wet,

and the ripeness of manure
falling like a harvest
around their sturdy feet.

The barn is so empty
you can see clean through it
and out the other side.

Shadows live in there now,
and echoes, trying to find
their source.

I guess there's nothing
we can do about it.
The barn is empty.

Sleep in there one night
and you will feel the harsh rasp
of dead tongues,

laying their braille
on the planes of your face.

INTO THE DARK

When I was a child, I felt
that shining my flashlight
into the night sky
pulled me with the beam
as I followed it into the dark,

and I believed that light
would shine forever, beyond
what I could see, beyond
my death.

So, too, the thrust of sight
that touches sight, that penetrates
these molecules of flesh
and passes through.

PELVIS WITH MOON, 1943

AFTER THE PAINTING BY GEORGIA O KEEFFE

Fallen from some female,
this pelvis cradled her young
until she lay down to die,
her bones laid bare by desert sun,
and by circling scavengers
whose dark wings folded
over her flesh.

Now her spirit's risen,
a bony cradle holding the moon,
a calcium galaxy
spiraling over blue mountains.

For years it will burn
in the wind's slow flame
above mesas that remember fire
until only white ashes remain—
bone-dust blowing through
the sockets of our eyes.

IN THE DISTANCE

A fire glows in the distance.
The road we travel winds
through the foothills;
now we see flames,
now only a smudge of smoke
above a ridge.

The road climbs, carved
into the mountainside,
taking whatever shape it can
at the edge of the sky;

we see the fire more clearly
from this height, until we turn
to face the deeper mountains.

Out there
wind disperses the smoke.
We are all moving
toward the same horizon.

THE DOOR IN THE SUN

As if there were a door in the sun.
As if somehow that door opened
into a dark heart, its helium frame
blinding those who enter.

As if we would not burn,
would not return to brilliant gas
and dust if we went through,

leaving the blaze behind
like a story we once knew,
its aura still flickering
at the edges of our flesh,
a story we've been feeding
all our lives.

As if we could enter
the still point, the pause
between heartbeats,
the incandescent darkness
where the blood waits
and then goes on.

1808, CENTRAL TEXAS

We, the Pawnee, know this god.
He fell in fire and thunder from the sky
to live near our Red River.

When we touch him, he cures our sickness.
We journey many miles on pilgrimage
to sit in his presence.

Why are you in our sacred place,
and why do you fight over him?
Why do you want to carry him away
down our Red River on your foreign boat?

We will not let you take him from us!
Your blood will run into the furrows
you are making with his holy body
as you drag him across the land.

He will not speak to you
in that place you call New Orleans.

TOTAL ECLIPSE

FOR MY DAUGHTER NANCY AND HER CHILD

At total eclipse, the moon
turns copper, a dusky sphere
on midnight blue. Thin clouds
blow across it, first obscuring
then revealing its journey out
of Earth's shadow.

My daughter is pregnant,
her womb waxing toward spring,
filling with a child who floats
on the ultrasound screen,
flesh transparent, bones shimmering,
the delicate curve of its spine,
a crescent moon that promises
full light.

IMILAC METEOR

Held up to the sky, this sliver glows,
its crystalline layers flickering
as if they were still gaseous,
lit by interior light.

In its patterns, see a bird in flight,
or an amber animal that sleeps
between iron–nickel wings—
random shapes cut out and polished,
given to the air.

Look how they mirror back to us
the density of flesh, that mesh
of molecules that maps our lives
until we fuse with earth or fire
while orbiting the sun.

MAPPING THE METEOR

Harsh lump of rock and iron,
a small meteorite rusts in my palm,
oxidation marking the rise and fall
of craters that scar its surface.

My palm rusts too, the dry rivers
of heart and life lines sketched at birth,
sinking deeper with each breath.

Perhaps four billion years ago,
this meteorite was flung out
by a nascent asteroid, grew cold
as it fell through the void,
then arced in its envelope of light
down through our atmosphere.

Older than the moon,
it found the larger rock of Earth
where I can bear its weight
and make these words
to fling it out again.

THE ALLURE

Dale Herring

My sister, Joan, said the four-letter word to me over the phone. "FLAT," she warned me. We were going on a five-day private river trip, kayaking through the Canyonlands, down the Cataract section of the Colorado River. The trip was ninety-six miles, with only twelve miles of rapids sandwiched between the flatwater stretches. When I tried to cancel the vacation, the airline said, "nonrefundable." I tried to complain to a friend, but he shook his head unsympathetically and said, "You never know what will happen, the Canyonlands is a powerful place."

Within hours of arriving at the Grand Junction Airport, Joan and I found ourselves in a bar, watching a video of Cataract Canyon at extreme high water. Huge rafts with three pontoons and motorboats got munched in monster holes. Our run would be in much lower water, I ruefully thought, as the bar shut down, and we headed to our put-in at Potash. When we arrived, our friend's lantern greeted us. The light had an eerie glare. In my morbid mood, it reminded me of a shrine for the dying oceans that had contributed to the beginning of Canyonlands.

The oceans came and went nearly three million years ago. Each time the sea evaporated, like a corpse baking away on a funeral pyre, it left behind chunky bones in the form of salt, gypsum, and potash. New seas revisited the land, leaving a legacy of sandstone, shale, and limestone, which crushed the salt deposit under its weight. Water collected in the sunken bowl, then drained as the land thrusted upward nearly sixty million years ago. The water's journey to the valley tore at the soft-est, weakest rock, leaving the stronger rocks reaching for God, or for each other, in the desperate balancing acts of buttes, arches, pinnacles, and spires. The Canyonlands and its wild rivers were born. The Colorado took all that geology could feed it, whether rain, rock, or drought. Now it would take us as well, on our river journey through the heart of a desert.

In the morning, our crew told us we were missing two people. Our friend Steve assured us, "They are either drunk and asleep or drunk and in jail." So we packed the rafts, the kayakers geared up, and we ran shuttle, leaving some cars where we'd end our trip. Finally Johnny and Martin showed up.

"Hey, babe," Johnny said in Johnny style. "Do you know why six is afraid?" We shook our heads. "'Cause seven ate nine." I looked squarely at Steve, who cued the trip leader, Dave. "Let's go boating!" they cried.

Our group, sixteen people, slipped into the silky chocolate water of the Colorado. As I paddled, the canyon walls closed in on the river. The current crawled so slowly that the whirligigs moved faster than my kayak. In spring there would have been wildflowers—pale primrose, globemallow, and the fatal locoweed, which is so addictive that live-stock dying from its poison still seek it in their last moments of life. But this was summer and the land was still raw, the jagged tips of rusty-colored buttes and spires jutting into the open, blue sky.

By mile ten, a narrow, 1,700-foot sheer-walled mesa cast a shadow on my boat—Dead Horse Point. Legend has it that a herd of wild horses died of thirst there after being corralled, gated, and forgotten in the 1800s. I imagined the beasts pawing the ground and longing to jump into the river far below.

By lunchtime, my flat-water phobia was replaced by the convic-tion that nature coursed through this desert like a deep, wild force. The beach where we ate was carpeted with warm white sand. Joan and I followed animal tracks on its surface. Five padded toes in the back and four toes in the front told the story of a deer mouse's demise. Sometime last night an owl, soaring with wings stretched two feet wide, had stalked its prey. I wonder if our deer mouse had time to glimpse its yellow eyes piercing through white and brown mottled feathers before the talons seized it. The owl suppered on the rocks just as we had. We found the regurgitated pellets of indigestible brownish-gray fur, and I put a row of teeth about four millimeters long in my life-jacket pocket before getting back on the river. I could feel a parallel world pulsing behind the air, in the rocks, between sun rays in the sky as we propelled our-selves deeper into the canyon.

After twenty miles, our crew camped for the night on a sandbar by a large gooseneck bend. The gooseneck was about four miles long, while gaining only one mile down the canyon. Night settled around us faster than we gassed up the stoves and prepared dinner. Still, Martin broke out some ice from the coolers and opened bar while Steve started a fire. We laughed easily under the summer sky even when Johnny told us about the horse that walked into a bar and asked for a drink. The bartender said, "Sure, but why the long face?"

One by one people drifted away from the fire and into their sleeping bags. When Joan said good night, only Dave and I were left rearranging the wood in the campfire. We spoke unselfconsciously, aided by the dark clear sky and warm night. He was a climber and a skier, and his voice became excited when he talked about deep white powder in backcountry hills. I, too, knew the lure of white water, whether snow or rapids. The same passion for the outdoors ran in both of us.

That night I dreamed that I was a peasant who sneaked into a royal court where a mighty ruler loomed. When I awoke the next morning and saw the sun warming an alcove across the river from our beach, I still felt intimidated by my dream, afraid of nature's own palace sizzling with power ready to burst, like air pregnant with rain in the moments before a storm.

We packed the rafts, cleaned the dishes, smashed the beer cans, and made sure the dry bags were folded snugly with sleeping bags and personal gear. The groover, our travel toilet, got a capful of bleach and a very tight lid. Everyone helped out until we pushed off together into

113

the flat, meandering river. The wind kicked up, pushing my kayak back upstream.

"Do not enter," I imagined a gust whispering as we passed monolithic spires appearing as totems at an entrance gate to the land of ancient peoples. The first known humans to visit the area more than 10,000 years ago were hunter-gatherers. Piñon nuts, cactus fruit, and berries filled their baskets. Flint-bladed spears and darts brought down big horn sheep and deer. It seemed that their rituals and oral traditions were imprinted in an ancient language within the rocks around me.

I continued to paddle with the ominous wind breathing in my face. Don paddled with me as the landscape changed from spires to mesas and buttes. The rock formations' uncanny likeness to lavish temples seemed too perfect to result from random acts of nature. Don told me more about the Old Ones, who were also called Anasazi, or ancient enemies, by the Navajo. He told me how the Anasazi became farmers, then moved into cliff dwellings, probably to protect themselves from raids as natural resources became scarce. Some people even said that the archaeological finds of smashed, cut, and burned bones point to cannibalism or ritual execution.

At this the wind kicked up again. We paddled harder as I scanned the cliffs for dwellings. So many stories seemed etched in its ridges and shades. I saw a mesa shaped like an Anasazi ruler on a throne. I thought perhaps he commanded his people to build it so he could sit closer to the gods. With each year the king sat higher until, too far from the river's wisdom, the king's mind dried up, and he withered just as the horses had at Dead Horse Point. Then his people left the haunted area.

I told Don this. He thought the Anasazi went away because of drought and war, or perhaps as the environment became exhausted a new religion pulled them toward the southeast. I contemplated Don's theory and finally grew tired of fighting the wind. If a new religion could pull people southeast than maybe there was one that could pull me downriver. I headed toward Dave and Austin's raft for a ride.

RAFT. Another four-letter word. On crowded rivers in the East, I had been run down in my kayak by over-eager commercial rafts. But here rowed Dave with a long blond braid so unruly it could have sunk the vessel. He quoted Monty Python, saying "Blessed are the cheese-makers," and his friend Austin answered, "What's so special about the cheesemaker?" While Dave wore his openly, Austin was a little harder to read. Each turn of conversation revealed a new side of him. I liked it. Maybe this raft thing wouldn't be so bad, and I took a turn rowing as bighorn sheep eyed us from the bank.

The miles passed peacefully. Dave rested on the bottom of the boat while Austin and I kept chatting. I enjoyed seeing Dave content. A great blue heron stood like a five-foot buoy as we rowed past. When its daggerlike beak speared the water and came up empty of fish, its three-foot wings unfurled slowly as they contemplated flight. The wings worked laboriously as they pushed through the air. Then, in an act of faith, the prehistoric-looking bird retracted its legs and let the wind take it aloft, like a blue parasail filling with air in the sunset.

That evening, the same wind that had carried the great blue heron recklessly tossed sand into plates of food, sleeping bags, and every crevice of our bodies. My skin felt hot from the sun and breezes, which were changing my color to the rusty glow of the Canyonlands. I could feel water from the river still in my ears and clogging my nose. The landscape was claiming me as its own. No longer small and uninvited, I was becoming a part of something larger. My friends and I sat by the fire after dinner and I gave backrubs to the people who rowed the rafts carrying all the kayakers' gear. Dave sat in front of me for his turn while we listened to Martin connect the constellations into X-rated mythol-ogy. Johnny told us about the bear that walked into a bar and said "I'll have . . . a beer." The bartender replied, "Sure, but why the big paws?"

The bottle of Wild Turkey passed around our circle of friends, and by the time it was finished Dave and I found ourselves alone again. We hadn't separated since the massage. My hands wandered across his bare neck while he told me about little things that made me laugh. The wildness of the landscape poured into the night, and a chill drew us closer together. When the sun finally inched its way over the canyon walls, we stirred the still-warm embers of the fire and began to make

115

coffee and pancakes for our crew. The rhythm of morning chores fell smoothly on the camp. People excitedly planned the day because our fifty miles of flat-water penance was almost over. The current would pick up a little, and we had only twelve miles to cover, so there would be time to surf, hike, and play.

The day's first and best surf wave of the river showed up within an hour. It built to about five feet, and was retentive enough to spin, throw blunts and ends, and cause general chaos. It was a giggle machine with eddy service. Peter and I were the last to leave the spot. The water flattened again for a spell, and I thought of John Wesley Powell, the one-armed Civil War veteran who left on a riveting ninety-nine-day mapping journey of the Colorado River in 1869. Not having the benefit of other river runners' experiences he might have thought of our wave-surfing waves as a dangerous game. He once wrote, "the water of the [river] wave passes on while the form remains. . . . [It] sometimes gathers for a moment, heaps up higher and higher, and then breaks back. If the boat strikes it in the instant after it breaks, she cuts through and the mad breaker dashes its spray over the boat and washes overboard all that do not cling tightly."

Peter and I caught up to our friends who were waiting for us at a shallow beach tucked beneath gray rock undercut walls. Maureen, a salmon-boat captain from Alaska and Peter's wife, had discovered fossils, crinoids, and brachiopods inlaid in the limestone shelves. She pulled out long, fragile tubes from the bank and answered my questions about the crinoids that first appeared on Earth more than 500 million years ago. She also told me about the brachiopods, which have been called lampshells because they look like early Roman oil lamps. We got back in our boats quickly, though, eager to find more whitewater.

The tamarisk grew more aggressively along the banks as we pushed on. At what is mapped as mile ten, we saw a park sign: "WARNING—Dangerous rapids 4 miles downriver! Travel permit required by law."

We heard the white water before seeing it. Sure enough, four miles downstream from where the Green River joined forces with the Colorado, we had rapids. When Powell came upon this same confluence in 1869 he said, "On starting, we come at once to difficult rapids and falls, that in many places are more abrupt than in any of the canyons through which we have passed, and we decide to name this Cataract Canyon." The white water we had been waiting for was here.

After surfing a glassy wave formed on river right we set up camp directly below the flat 120-acre floor called Spanish Bottom, named for the Spanish explorers who penetrated the desert wilderness in the late 1700s. Our hike options included, on river-right, a trek to a deeply fissured mesa known as the DollHouse, and a four-mile climb from the left that went into the Needles District.

We crossed the river and took the old path into the DollHouse. Up out of clay banks, zigzagging 1,000 feet up the face of the canyon wall we climbed. Dave and Steve leapt ahead like billy goats while Peter and Maureen searched for hidden secrets in the nooks and crannies of eroded rock. Iron oxide inked the walkway red, while iron and manganese oxides or clay minerals occasionally created a lustrous smooth varnish on rock surfaces. Butch Cassidy and his crew were said to have roamed these parts, escaping the law by going where few dared follow. We, too, disappeared, just as they may have, over the top of the rim down into a dome-shaped amphitheater—the DollHouse. A rabbit bounded through desert scrub and cactus. I felt like Alice in Wonderland. Massive doll-shaped rocks stood in a circle on the desert floor, properly clad in garments sculpted by the wind. They seemed to have gathered in the juniper garden for tea. Dave sighed. The magic of the DollHouse moved us.

That night while the camp ate roast lamb and potatoes, Dave and I bathed in a private cove on the upstream edge of the beach. The water was freezing and the evening cool. Afterward, we hugged the dry rocks still warm from the sun, and I brushed the knots out of Dave's long blond hair. Stars emerged in the sky and we headed back to camp. Martin, who had swum from his ducky during the day by accident, was forced to drink cheap beer from a neoprene river bootie. Tomorrow we would take on the biggest drops of the Cataract Canyon. I dreamed of white water, and every now and then Dave's nearness felt so strong that it woke me.

"Last call for groover!" Steve shouted in the morning. I had over-slept and now the groover was being packed away. I dashed about tak-ing care of business, slopping on sunscreen, helping with dishes, and finally sliding my boat into the water. From this point on, the river took on a new temperament. It reminded me of a Christmas shopper dashing about frantically for last-minute finds, running down whom-ever, or whatever, got in the way. The first rapid, a couple miles below Spanish Bottom, was called Brown Betty and marked the beginning of four more miles of light white water. Most guidebooks suggested scouting the fourth rapid at low water and the seventh at high water. Scouting is easy along the rock jetties that replace the sandy banks upstream. Then, as if our Christmas shopper had sunk down on a bench for a small rest, the excitable river slowed into a two-mile flat-water pool before sharply leaping left. "Watch this up ahead!" yelled someone from a raft. "There should be some good white water!"

The river mimicked its earlier charge, toppling over canyon debris with its white-capped garment fluttering chaotically. For over a mile we were caught up in its whirlwind of energy. Dave had heard that the fourteenth rapid, Capsize, could present danger. At 7,000 cubic feet per second it was full of splashes and fun. It saved its menace for just below.

The Big Drops rapid has three parts: Upper Big Drop, Satan's Seat, and Satan's Gut. It slipped and fell down the canyon, which was now constricted and littered with bus-sized rocks. We took turns run-ning it—first the kayaks. After scouting beyond the first two horizon lines on river-left, Joan commented, "Making up your mind to run the rapid is harder than actually paddling it." While its crashing water could be intimidating, the lines were straightforward. The kayaks made it through fine. We watched from downstream as the rafts came through. Less maneuverable than kayaks, they can stray off course easily here, and perhaps get a trashing in a pour-over called Little Niagara at the sec-ond drop, and a spanking in Frogg Hole to the right of Satan's Gut.

Dave and Austin led in the little red raft they called the "ruby slip-per," planning far in advance how to let 7,000 CFS and momentum take them where they needed to go. Dave lined up, casually throwing in a few adjustment strokes here and there. "Paddle!" I wanted to yell, but he knew the rubber would make it through. Following Dave came Jamie who took a surf at the third drop in a nasty pour-over. I couldn't imagine one of Powell's awkward vessels making it out of here in one piece. In fact, the men of 1869 often discussed their chances of getting out of the Cataract alive. Powell worried over the very real possibility that "may be we shall come to a fall in these canyons which we cannot pass, and where the water is so swift that we cannot return." At the Big Drop, he wrote, "We are compelled to make three portages in succession, the distance being less than three-fourths of a mile, with a fall of seventy-five feet."

Yet, even as he fretted, he was also awed by the river's majesty. "Wherever we look there is but a wilderness of rocks—deep gorges where the rivers are lost below cliffs and towers and pinnacles, and ten thousand strangely carved formations in every direction, and beyond them mountains blending with the clouds."

After the Big Drops, our group called it a day. It would be our last night resting sleepy heads on the bosom of the wild desert. We sat together under the quilt of a starry sky. Next to me, someone whispered the origin myth of the Colorado River.

"A chief lost the woman who he loved most in life. He mourned bitterly and begged the gods to grant him a way to visit her. The god Tah-vwoats took pity on the crumpled man and created a passageway for him to follow. The path wove through magnificent splendors, otherworldly alcoves, and magical glens. It was so stunning that the gods feared other mortals would be drawn to the path before it was their time to leave life. So they filled the golden road behind the mighty chief with water, and the river became the Colorado."

During our trip we had started down the path made for the chief, but we could never finish the journey—not because the gods had added water, but because man had flooded it with a nature-defying act called Glen Canyon Dam.

In 1963, the U.S. Department of the Interior shut the gates to the 300-foot-thick, 710-foot-high dam—or the "cement plug," as Edward

Abbey called it. A reservoir, Lake Powell, flooded Glen Canyon and its rapids, reaching back to within only a few miles of Cataract Canyon. An entire ecosystem drowned in an unparalleled watery massacre—and a new one was created.

A sad beauty persisted on Lake Powell as we tied up our rafts and motored out through the reservoir the next day—a beauty now haunted not only by the stories of nature but by the consequences of humans' twisted ingenuity. The tamarisk and tall Fremont poplars that marked the wild and free portion of the river upstream no longer softened the transition from water to rock on the banks, but the silt filling the Colorado settled in the still pool, creating beautiful crisp, clear water. As we approached our take-out at Hite Marina, we drank from a bag of wine, saying good-bye to the Canyonland and each other in our own way.

The river now mingled with my feelings for Dave. I felt both the sun and whisker-burn on my face as I dangled my feet in the water. Suddenly Dave was next to me. He had left the ruby slipper and boarded the raft. We looked out over the water at a sandstone arch that crossed the reservoir like a rainbow. I handed him a fossil that I had found and he gave me a stone from the beach where we had bathed. The wild feel of the Canyonlands opened our hearts to each other. I scratched sand from my scalp and breathed dry hot air into my belly, only to be reclaimed by the desert in my exhale, which Dave then shared. A force both wild and powerful had claimed us.

AUTUMN IN LOVE

Gretchen Dawn Yost

Today it rains. Drizzles. There will be snow in the mountains. A harbinger of winter—when this land will be covered white and the most mundane task becomes a chore. I spend the day at home, for the first time in weeks, it seems. The last I can recall it was summer. I devoted most of it to the high country—backcountry patrol, surveying, fighting wildfires. But now I awake and another season is sneaking its foot in the door. Aspen trees with one small clump of south-facing leaves turn yellow overnight, poking out, hanging like a tail or an afterthought. It creeps in slowly like this, then one day I can't help but notice patches in the landscape burning brighter than the sun—yellows, oranges, pinks, and reds.

Autumn is a time of fast-paced business, bears getting fat, ungulates crazed with love and regeneration, migratory folk heading south. In the human community we work, getting winter's wood up, hunting, fishing, berry picking, taking last-minute trips to the backcountry—trying to squeeze a year's activities into one season before the rhythm of winter sets in.

I live in a remote cabin in the foothills outside of Bondurant, Wyoming, a small ranching community caught between the prosperity of Jackson and the simplicity of Pinedale. Hunters, ranchers, outfitters, carpenters, and lovers of the wild, all people this small valley with their log houses and cabins quietly dotting the rolling hills. I've lived in this humble home for only a few years, but long enough to have the winged, planted, and four-legged creatures of this place capture me, weaving me into their lives—and deaths.

———————

With hypnotic constant of rain on my rooftop, and dark-gray clouds engulfing open space, my body can't help but fall into a slower pace. I think of the quilt I will work on this winter during the long dark evenings, pieced of seasons and the colors of this land—the pink and rusty-red hues of the Hoback Range, the lavender of milk-vetch, the pale green of sagebrush in late autumn, the brown and tan coats of elk, the bright yellows of evening grosbeaks in early spring, the greens of spruce and fir, the oranges and reds of leaves fading to fall, the white snow with a breath of blue and gray, the sparkling, deep-blue sky on a forty-below morning. It's a patchwork of memories that live on in scraps from cast-off dresses, old lovers' shirts, pillowcases, and handed-down skirts. I'll use pieces of new fabric as well, promises to the future—of memories not yet made.

Perhaps because I am originally a native of western Oregon, the rain always makes me nostalgic, taking me in circles and bringing me back. It is as though rain is the symbol of the circle of life and of seasons, always on the return—however late or desperately needed. Today I'm taken back twelve months to last autumn.

I remember how I did something that fall. A vegetarian of nine years, I ate steak—elk steak. I was at the house of a man with whom I'd been carrying on a flirtation. He was young, a ranchhand and a hunter. He didn't know I was a vegetarian, and he offered me a steak. I declined in that polite way people refuse something they really want. I wanted to eat of that elk. He insisted and so I accepted.

Cutting into the lean steak and working my teeth into the tough, chewy meat—my jaw moving in circles like an ungulate chewing its cud—I imagined a bull elk grazing in a mountain meadow. I saw his parched, sun-bleached antlers and the drying grasses on which he fed and the sun and the soil and the surrounding pines and the autumn colors of cool heat. And as I ate of that elk and that sun and that grass,

I felt for the first time since I moved here that I was sinking my bare feet into the soil, getting dirt under my toenails, being bitten by ants and cut by small, sharp rocks. I could feel my blood dripping into the land and the land embedding itself inside me. I ate slowly. I did not feel guilty.

Later, he and I made love, and I felt as though I was making love to a young bull elk and to the colors of fall: blood, sex, death, decay, and the coming renewal. In the whirl of it all, I could not tell the difference between eating and making love—between the hunter and the hunted.

Not long afterward—when the earth was white and the sagebrush still stood tall—he disappeared. He was lost to me in the folds and valleys of this place. This man was not a lover, per se. He was more of an encounter, an encounter with a moose, when your paths cross for a few moments, silent words are exchanged, and both parties continue on. Does he remember me? Does the moose remember me? I remember them.

———

Sometimes I realize how city attitudes have followed me here. In that anxious, desperate, hurried way, I grasp at the bird flying south, trying to hold it in my hands as though time were linear and the bird would not come back of its own accord—sometime next spring. I live in a world where nothing, it seems, lasts forever. Entire species enter extinction, wild lands are destroyed, wildlife corridors are severed by mining and logging operations. No wonder I'm always in a hurry to fall in and out of love, to grasp it, hold it—like trying to hold water. But what if love did last forever? Could I flow with the river, instead of trying to hold it still?

Since then, another twelve moons have passed me by. The pine grosbeaks returned to my feeder this winter, the sandhill cranes came back to the wetlands this spring, and now, once again, the aspen leaves are turning the colors of the setting sun. Perhaps living in this place has brought me closer to another logic. The logic of beauty and of seasons. The logic of wildness.

Now I've met another man—Adam. He is the First Man and yet, for me, the last. I found his heart swimming upstream in the Upper

Green River. He is a fisherman and a hunter. He has a bony lump on the back of his head and says it's because he is a Neanderthal. While hunting, he gets aroused—he says it's the chill in the air, being in the woods. But I think he's taken enough elk into his body that he's *become* one. Adam is not entirely human, which—in my humble opinion—is to be *fully* human. Like the deer and elk and moose rubbing their antlers on aspen trunks and on each other, it is that time of year when my wild lover and his prey stumble around the woods, driven by hormones and the desire to love. Hunting season. Mating season. Autumn in love.

Today, as I listen to rain patter on the rooftop, I daydream of the kind of time and space I'll be in this winter, hand-quilting a patchwork of stories—the fabric of place. Every stitch made in mindful meditation, in a slower time. Wintertime. Earth time. My lover is beautiful and he is wild. I think beauty and wildness rest in the kind of space where quilts are stitched by hand, the kind of place where love is born and nurtured. I hope he and I will wallow there this winter—our hot breath meeting cool air, our bodies engulfed in the warmth of a patchwork quilt. And I hope our love is lived not in modern time, but rather in the rhythm of seasons. Earth time—eternally slow. I think I've realized now that love can last forever; that as long as there is wild nature there will be lovers in—and of—wildness.

———

Early evening, and the sun burns through the slowly lifting rain clouds. I sit on the grassy knoll above the cabin, looking toward the horizon, stretched in the pink hues of the Hoback Range. The warmth of the sun kisses the side of my neck with a lover's gentle touch and a loner's timid smile. They say wolves are moving down from Yellowstone into the Upper Green River basin. They say grizzlies are more plentiful and the ravens are getting fatter. There are obstacles, no doubt, and there will be more. Yet now, at this moment, I can't help but think we have everything to look forward to.

SPRING'S OVERTURES

Ann McDermott

EARLY DAYS

A nest is under construction in the scrawny paloverde—the tree that took root among the river rocks I transplanted from their original watercourse and used to line the driveway. The tree is grotesquely shaped because it has been trimmed to keep it from crowding the driveway, and because it has literally crawled out from under a rock. Its deformed contour seems rather a poor choice for housing offspring, at least to my eye, but a cactus wren nested in it last year, and the remains of that residence are still there, tinsel and all. The tinsel was a bit of "pretty" woven into the usual grasses and weeds, scavenged from that year's Christmas tree burning party's honored remains. The wrens insisted on keeping that glittery string, even after I tried to pull it out, fearing it would snag on one of the fledglings. My attempt succeeded only in stretching it to a longer filament that fluttered in the breeze. The wrens announced their decor preference by weaving it back into the mass of sticks and stems. But evidently they have now deemed that nest seriously uninhabitable. Not only is there a new nest underway, but the old one is not even being used for construction materials, even the tinsel. I haven't observed the construction crew at work, but the partially finished nest has the earmarks of belonging to more cactus wrens. That's fine with me; I enjoy having them as neighbors.

Besides the nest-in-progress, I have also seen streamers of male house sparrows in hot pursuit of desirable females, who are fleeing at breakneck speed through bushes and darting around branches. The ladies certainly don't appear willing to breed, but with all those ardent, persistent suitors, they may have little choice.

The Saye's phoebe pair is spending many morning hours around my house again, though they don't seem to be doing more than window-shopping for a dwelling site. They call endlessly to one another. It has been months since they came around the house, but now the nesting urge stirs their senses and they check for possible quarters. So far, they seem to have forgotten about last year's preference for the top of the garage door opener . . . or maybe this is a different pair. I do hope they take up residence someplace very near, but not inside the garage.

I haven't seen the female cardinal all week. Only the male comes around to collect the seed scattered each morning. Bright red with black mask and throat, he pecks for seeds and flies out of sight periodically. Is he perhaps already busy feeding his mate as she sits on a clutch of eggs in some nearby tree?

My dog is again visiting the big galleta. He buries his face in the dry upper stalks, searching for the heart of the bunch from which new green is sprouting, spring tonic for browsing dogs.

An antelope squirrel creeps around the creosote bushes, furtively casing the area for dogs before stuffing a kernel of old dry dog food into its bulging cheeks to bury in a secret cache, hoarding already against the upcoming summer of want. It seems early in the season to be seeing them out and about, but the winter has been so warm that there was no extended hibernation period this season. Still no snakes, though squirrel sightings usually mean the snakes that eat them are not far behind.

Little rain has fallen for the past two months, so spring flowers may be scarce, but the first half of February yielded a half-inch of rain, and that was enough to entice the creosote to open a few cautious yellow blossoms. Another annual, sporting tiny white flowers, always among the first of spring, has decided to go for it. Their blooms are so small I almost need a magnifying glass to see them. I wish I knew what they are, but I have never found them in any of my books. Some of the yellow fiddlenecks are also in bloom, but not with long cascades of blossoms; only a very conservative single blossom graces each stunted plant. The mallow are very small and sparse yet, and the only one in full gorgeous bloom is the one just outside the fence around my garden, where it undoubtedly soaks up the flow provided to the vegetables that many desert creatures steal from me. It is too early for the cacti to get in on the act of flowering. The hedgehog has not begun to form buds, and that is always the first cactus to do so. When the hedgehog blooms, spring has truly arrived, and the annual cycle of rebirth to rebirth, spring to spring, is again complete.

Loggerhead shrikes, distinctive and regal appearing birds, are residents of my desert, but not commonly seen. On several occasions over the years I have spotted one, but I had never before this spring heard one speak. They often sit on a telephone wire or in a treetop, silently surveying their realm. The shrike is often mistaken for a mockingbird, with its largely gray, white, and black attire, but its black mask and chunkier build sets it apart. Shrikes also have a hooked bill and more black in their wings than mockingbirds. They have been nicknamed "butcher birds" for their habit of leaving an insect or small item of prey hanging on the barb of a barbed-wire fence.

Maybe this early spring I have been more observant, or perhaps just more fortunate than usual, but three times I have heard this strong, typically silent bird vocalizing—calling for a mate, no doubt, as this would be the season. While walking one recent afternoon, I followed a masked bandito touring his terrain, calling from the borders in a number of localities, but never was he answered. I hope he has better luck another day in finding a partner, but with a voice like that, any potential lover will have to be pretty nonjudgmental about musical ability, looking beyond that to some other aspect of birdish appeal. I found most of his repertoire strange and outlandish. Still, I suppose that strange chortle and harsh rasp might sound fabulous to a lady shrike.

A pair of red-tailed hawks have begun hanging out together, quite literally. They float on the breeze together, suspended on the air flows, soaring symmetrically. I think they may be considering a particular mesquite tree of grand stature as a nesting site. But the tree is close to a neighbor's house, and there is new construction going on down the road from there. I hope they will not be discouraged and leave.

The signs of spring are upon us. But I still say it's not officially spring until the hedgehog blooms.

PREVIEW OF A RIPARIAN FOREST

It was cold in Wickenburg when we met in the parking lot early that morning to carpool out to the Harquahala Mountains, where we planned to hike up a canyon in the wilderness area just southwest of Aguila, Arizona.

The leader of our group, like myself, had never been to the region before, but others of us had. She was designated as leader mostly because the rest of us were relying on her to teach us botany as we moved up the canyon. Accordingly, we hiked very slowly, stopping to discuss many plants along the way.

One of the first we inspected was the desert trumpet, also known as bladderstem, Indian pipeweed, or *Eriogonum inflatum,* for those lovers of the Latin language. It was not yet in bloom—too early for this plant to be about that—but its unmistakable long green stem shot up from the basal rosette of leaves. Portions of the stem were inflated and hollow, a feature typical of a number of species of Eriogonum. About fifty species of Eriogonum are found in Arizona. Some wasps bore into the stems, if they are hollow, and fill them with captured insect larvae and their own eggs, thus providing meals for their developing young.

We hikers were a casual gathering of friends, all with different goals, schedules, and hiking abilities. A number of folks had lunch and returned to their vehicles in time to make it home to watch Super Bowl XXXII. Several did not have the physical endurance to go very far.

Most of us continued to a spot where huge boulders had tumbled during a recent rain, gouging out a portion of the wash. Just above the avalanche, water from a spring seeped to the surface, providing just enough water to encourage a cottonwood and nine willow saplings to sprout. Tamarisk had also taken root, an invasive plant not native to the area. Several of our group members were volunteers from the Hassayampa

River Preserve and felt duty bound to "tammy-whack," as they did on the preserve, assisting the indigenous willow and cottonwood saplings in their survival, precarious at best. No one could explain how the tiny sprigs of trees had made it through the past summer, with no visible water to sustain them. No one knew where they had come from, as there were no known stands of cottonwoods or willows for miles. But here they were, riparian residents in a marginally riparian environment.

It remains to be seen whether these amazing upstarts survive to become the great trees their genetic encoding plans them to be. Wouldn't it be grand to one day visit the Harquahala Wilderness Riparian Forest? It could happen . . . unless the McMullen Valley becomes the next region to experience a population boom.

TWO FELLED TREES

Fremont cottonwoods—the oldest specimen—have thick, deeply furrowed brown bark and trunks of which can reach four feet in diameter and support a canopy of leaves spreading one hundred feet high. The broad leaves, shiny and triangular, turn a golden hue in the fall before floating to the ground. In the spring, before leaves bud, flowers form. The female trees scatter the cottonlike seeds that give the trees their name. Fremont cottonwoods live in wetlands, along streams and rivers, at altitudes ranging from 1,500 to 6,000 feet above sea level. Beavers favor their bark and wood for food and dam building. The Hopi use the roots for carving Kachinas, the doll-like representations of their gods. It is the kind of cottonwood in residence at the Hassayampa River Preserve, where beside the trail to the pond (imaginatively labeled a "lake") a huge Fremont cottonwood stump tilts toward the pathway. It has been smoothly cut. Its trunk, twenty-three inches in diameter, is severed cleanly, no doubt because it threatened to obstruct the path, making passage difficult or unsafe for visitors. There it sits, a mere shadow of its former self, destined never to achieve the grandeur of the largest Fremonts.

But, on the north side of the stub a sucker sprouts. Throughout the summer, that sucker was the tree's enduring signal that life continued within. Two sprigs headed upward and formed a fine phalanx of leaves.

They were about six inches long when the freezes of winter wilted the robust, green shoots to gray. Undaunted, the trunk has now sprouted a new bunch of suckers below and beside the two dead ones. Not only that, a new patch of green is bursting out of the top side of the leaning truck. One of those is about nine inches long with a stem as thick as a pinky finger. That sucker looks of a mind to begin forming bark, a deliberately serious next step toward reclaiming its destiny of realizing one hundred feet high. I think it may make it.

———

The blue paloverde is a member of the pea family, but you'd only know that if you saw it in full bloom in April or May. The five-petaled yellow blossoms are shaped much like those of the sweet pea. It is Arizona's state tree. Growing at altitudes of 500 to 4,000 feet, it is perfectly adapted to desert life, shedding its leaves during a drought, retaining moisture by reducing surface area. Photosynthesis continues unhindered in the green branches and twigs of the hardy tree, with each twig defended by a quarter-inch thorn at every node. Flowers form flat, brown seedpods that are important food sources for a number of animals, including some humans, who grind the seeds into meal. Seeing a "grandparent" blue paloverde, gnarled trunk up to a foot and a half in diameter and thirty feet high, bursting forth in full spring bloom, is a glorious sight, a feast for eyes and bees.

One afternoon, as I walked a major wash near my home, I happened upon just such a monster paloverde. It had grown in the steep bank of the wash, the trunk crooking out of the bank's side and then straightening toward the sky. Over the years, it became very top-heavy and the crooked trunk eventually cracked right at the kink, toppling the bulk of the tree directly into the sandy bottom of the wash. The bark split at the crook, a gash that apparently circles the tree, but the trunk's interior fibers still hold and still pump life to the limbs. Evidently, this split occurred some time ago. Where the branches have plowed into the gravel bed of the wash, erosion has scooped the sand and stone away from the branches, which nevertheless grip the soil for dear life when blasts of floodwaters attempt to tear the tree away from the trunk base. Those roots still feed life to the green bastion of twigs and branches. It must be quite an obstruction to the water flow, when the water flows. So far, though, the branches have not been totally severed from the roots. Until that day, it continues to live.

Upstream a ten-foot-tall mesquite has washed down and drifted almost to the downed paloverde. When it hits that obstruction, during the next major runoff, the two of them will make quite an effective dam. That may be what takes out the paloverde completely. Or maybe, just for a while, we will have a "lake" forming east of our house, a fitting memorial for such a grand and stubborn old paloverde tree.

PHOEBEVILLE REVISITED?

Two days ago I heard a loud *purrting* sound. I stood in the kitchen, a closed door safely between myself and the noise, and tried to pinpoint the source. I listened closely, then decided it must be a bird making the din, and that it must be inside the garage. Having guessed that much, it was easy for my mind to run over a whole gamut of possibilities.

A bird enraged by a cat? I don't have a cat, but the neighbor's might be visiting, and it may have trapped a bird in the garage. Not likely, though, if my dogs are nearby.

One of my dogs challenging a bird? That battle is usually too action-packed for such a constant *purrting* racket as accompaniment.

A rattlesnake inciting an avian riot? No, too early in the year for a snake to be out and about.

Finally, very carefully, I opened the door to the garage—and spooked a Saye's phoebe from the top of the garage door opener, where it had been warbling at the top of its lungs. Possibly a declaration of intention? An announcement of territorial possession? I could see no sign of a nest under construction and still don't. But this morning, as my son left for school, he said he startled the Saye's phoebe from a perch on top of the garage door opener, and that he too had heard it singing there earlier in the week.

Dear God, does it begin all over again?

UNUSUAL

I saw a sage thrasher for the first time during the Christmas bird count in the Wickenburg area. I had never knowingly seen one before. I may have come across it in the desert in the course of my journeys, but not in the company of someone who could positively identify it for me, and I did not have enough knowledge myself to know it from, well, a hermit thrush, for instance. That's why I like to go out in the field with bird-watchers more expert than myself, those who have spent more time in the joyful hobby of birding.

Then I saw another thrasher with the birding enthusiasts I went counting with a week later in the Arlington Christmas bird count, near Buckeye.

And last Sunday I saw one sitting atop a dead mesquite, the tree a victim of fire or disease. The bird was silent, calmly watching me while I gazed back, first facing me so I could see its spotted breast, then turning its back to me, showing the coloration of its back and wings. Thanks to its obliging nature, there was no mistaking its identity. This winter visitor from northern sage country was indulging me with a long, leisurely look. There, in the desert not far from my home, where I had seen plenty of curve-billed thrashers, I was finally seeing a sage thrasher. Its perch was near a home under construction—an unusual bird near an unusual house being built by a most unusual man.

While talking with that unusual man this past week, he told me he suspected I was an ex-Roman Catholic nun who got thrown out of the convent. He figured I was insane, a crazy, though he did not specify how he had reached this conclusion. I told him I thought he was insane too, so we were even. We may both be right.

In past conversations, he mentioned that he once killed a man and did time in prison for the deed. Incarceration convinced him that he should never again commit murder, which may be the root of his oft-stated preference for coyotes and other wild creatures as neighbors rather than humans, with whom he might be inclined to argue, possibly leading to more violence. I too like having nature and the wilds as my close neighbors, though not to the point of excluding humans quite so thoroughly as he. In any case, I certainly appreciate his regard for the desert and rural life.

I can't relate, however, to his peculiar architectural preferences or his lawlessness. The home he is building is a bright-green, ramshackle plywood affair, three-storied thus far, but with a fourth planned so that, as he told me, he could look down on all his neighbors. I use the word "planned" loosely, because there are no plans in actuality. He is building freestyle, without permits or blueprints. He says he can do this because he rents his land to a rancher who has the rights to graze his property. Therefore, as landowner, he does not need to abide by the usual laws that govern most construction projects. I cannot comment on the logic or legality of his stance. He just continues building.

I also can't relate to his need to collect huge vehicles: buses and trucks of multiple tonnage, barely running, sure to fail the emissions tests he refuses to put them through. He currently lives within the region for mandatory testing in Maricopa County, though he claims the house he is building is not in the region. He wants to use his future address as his abode of record in order to avoid testing. He regularly shows up in Peoria courts, where he is cited for driving unregistered vehicles. Although he drives into town each day to pick up newspaper being recycled and to maintain the recycling bins, he sees no reason to pay for licensing and registering his vehicles. Other folks who live outside the metropolitan area, and commute daily to work, are expected to do so, but he thinks he should be exempt.

He suffers extremely from foot-in-mouth disease. Upon meeting my son for the first time, when he came by my house to use the phone, he announced loudly, "Well, you look like you're used to the good life!" (In my experience, this man is unable to speak at a normal volume.) My son later told me that he started to get offended, then considered that the statement might simply mean that he had all his teeth. An intact set of teeth might well define "the good life" for our desert companion who builds so uniquely to the east of our Homeowners Association property.

The roads in our association are privately owned, and our board is currently embroiled in arguments with nonmembers and realtors of property owners to the east who want to use our roads to access their property. My unusual friend is one of our board's staunchest supporters regarding the sanctity of our roads. He repairs the barbed-wire fences that are cut when landowners to the east move trailers and manufactured homes across our roads to deposit them on their properties. He is on good terms with our board president, because if his immediate neighbors cannot use our roads, it prevents them from developing their land. He mines our roads with nail-studded boards so the nails will puncture the tires of vehicles rolling over them, punishing trespassers and endangering hikers and animals—a point I have brought to his attention, as I am one of the hikers.

I asked the fellow how he got to his property each day. He told me he used our roads, but that was okay because he had permission from our board president, who is grateful for his services as self-appointed security patrol.

A favorite pastime of his is hassling neighborhood kids who ride their ATVs on our roads, motorcycle and ATV riders being among his other pet peeves.

Clearly, he sees no need to obey laws not to his liking. Conversely, he believes others should obey the laws that he supports. I can relate. Isn't the posted speed limit optional? He detects no irony in any of this, so far as I can tell. For all our differences, this is where we are aligned. We both want to obey the laws that make sense to us and disobey the rest, a position pretty much shared by the rest of the human race. And we both grieve to see development squelching our rural ways and the lives and livelihoods of those wild neighbors we have both come to value. Perhaps even more significantly, we each believe that the other is crazy. With so much in common, I am compelled to beg leniency for us both, for we assess land values not by the amounts recorded in the state treasurer's office, or by the percentage of the transaction going to the real estate agent handling the sale. We assess land value in wild animals and sage-thrasher sightings. I guess that makes us both crazy.

IN BETWEEN

For the first time this year, I sat outside and drank my morning coffee, no coat or jacket, no discomfort from the cold. I wore jeans, socks, shoes, and a long-sleeved shirt—not exactly summer attire, but still, no coat! It must be spring.

Yesterday morning's walk featured a shrike vocalizing from the innards of a hackberry bush. So busily was it serenading that I came quite close, within about 15 feet, before it sensed my presence and fled. As I continued past the hackberry, coming around to the west face of the thickly-leafed plant, I saw another shrike leave cover and fly to the south, where the first had reperched, waiting. So he has found a mate, or she has found a mate, or they have found each other. Whichever. It matters not, except to future generations of shrikes. Another successful pairing, another indication of spring.

My neighbor and I have ventured into winemaking, determined to produce at least one batch of elderberry wine. We needed to start our project while temperatures were still conducive to yeast activity, for the must (the technical name for wine-in-the-making) must not drop below sixty-eight degrees nor rise above seventy-five degrees, lest the yeast become inactive, lest the must not become wine. This rules out winemaking in the summertime, as we both keep our house thermostats set at eighty degrees to avoid the high electric bills associated with air conditioning. This past week's warmth, close to eighty degrees for daytime highs, has brought the temperature of the must close to seventy-five degrees. From another neighbor, my partner and I borrowed a tub that we filled with water, and in which we parked the carboy, the five-gallon glass jar that holds the must. The must is now an acceptable seventy-two degrees, but doesn't the task of cooling it mean it's spring?

Then again, the sage thrasher I saw last weekend is mostly a winter visitor to our area, and the white-crowned sparrows are still amongst us, not yet having followed migratory urges to wing to their Arctic summer homes. Nor have the white-winged doves returned from their Mexican wintering grounds. These are all signs that spring is lagging. As final proof, the hedgehog cactus still has yet to show buds. This is my arbitrary indicator of the season. When the hedgehog blooms, it is spring.

'Tis the season of in between.

ON THE CONTRARY

Penelope Grenoble O'Malley

I forgot the sheep might be dead. From a distance, I saw she was down and far from the others. I walked into the pen and opened the far gate to let the rest of the ewes into the pasture, all the while evaluating the possibilities for a dead sheep. Dead on a soft spring morning, full of sun in a cloudless sky, a soft, rainless spring day.

She was a Barbados sheep, brown and tan, small-boned. Not much meat on her, not much fleece to my eye, flighty like a deer, picky about what she ate compared to Katahdins and Rambouillets. Like the rest of the "Barbies," she came from Jan's farm, borrowed to help our small flock eat down the growth from the El Niño winter, and to keep the barley and rye and oats from maturing into foxtails that trouble the collies' eyes and feet.

The Barbies have been driving me crazy for weeks. When my male dog drives them forward, they don't stop when he lies down. They fly past, frantic. When the sheep move wildly like this, a dog loses its sense of timing. Ideally he leaves from your side, travels in a wide arc to the rear of the sheep, and "lifts" the stock forward in a controlled burst. If all goes well, you are neatly lined up: dog–sheep–handler. The Barbies don't seem to have learned their part in this ballet. They don't stop when the dog eases the pressure. They don't settle but instead vault off at a tangent, leaving the dog yards behind feeling duped by your commands. On the next try, things get worse. The dog is suddenly deaf. He can't hear your voice or whistle and he ignores your best growl.

He knows without doubt that he cannot abide the disorder you have created.

———

The weather made training difficult this year, the winter of our long-forecasted El Niño, when warm water flowed north from the equator—"The Little One," as South American fishermen call it, because the warm water always appears at Christmas. In southern California the predictions were that we would either fry or drown. Preparations began in mid-June, just as my husband and I moved into our new house in the canyon, when the prospects for a record-breaking wet winter seemed laughable. The mustard and white sage blanketing our acre was fried toneless by the dry heat's temperatures that rose regularly past ninety. Still, county crews ventured out to clear vegetation from nearby creeks and streambeds, ignoring the environmentalists who worried that such enthusiasm with bulldozer and backhoe would damage sensitive creeks and wetlands. Road crews built berms where they thought water-saturated soils might slide, and cleared debris from erosion-control channels that hadn't seen a rake or shovel in years. Homeowners in rural areas like ours were urged to do their part, to check runoff drains and clean out gutters. Signs advertising sandbags appeared in the canyon.

"Gutters," said the county building inspector, pointing to the un-protected right angle between the roof and the walls of our new house. "Without gutters, the water will roll right off that roof and pool next to the foundation."

"Yes," I agreed, "gutters would be ideal."

"Without gutters, if the winter's bad, you'll have a moat, right there." He pointed again, this time at the strip of unplanted soil next to the house.

The real estate agent stepped in where the inspector had left off. "The driveway won't cause you problems?" She pointed out the car window to the three inches of water in the arroyo that cut across the front of the property. A drake mallard skimmed larvae off the surface of the thin flow. "The creek could flood."

My husband and I watched the duck and smiled. "Not us. We're looking forward to it."

———————

The first storm hit on a Saturday the first week of February, just as I set a 12-pound turkey on the kitchen counter. I told the checker at the market I'd come to buy bread. "I thought it might make me feel better." She smiled, then went back to ringing up my bag of broccoli, a pound of potatoes, two cans of cranberry jelly. "Some food is comfort food. God knows we need it with all this El Niño business," she said.

"Turkey always makes me feel better."

"Cold?"

"No, stomach. Nothing seems to sit right."

The truth was I'd been feeling poorly for months. I was afraid that this new house, this acre of land we had bought for all the right reasons, might be too much for us, this canyon we'd spent a year hunting for among the small pockets of rural land still left north and west of Los Angeles. I no longer felt so smug about escaping sidewalks and city lights. I was no longer soothed by our view of clouds and moonlight through the kitchen skylight or the scent of sage and mountain lilac that floated in from the wild land at the back of the house. I was no longer sure I had what it takes to keep a garden going, to chop our own wood for the fireplace, to compost waste. And the final proper thing, to manage our own herd of sheep, for dung to use as fertilizer and for wool to send east for my sister to spin.

The cashier, too, predicted rain. "I hear we're in for the big one." But we'd been talking about El Niño for so long, who could take anything seriously?

———————

The dogs wandered into the kitchen and sniffed the groceries, then gave me the no-sheep-again-today look. "Tomorrow," I tell them, as if tomorrow I will feel any more like being humiliated by the skittish

Barbies. "Tomorrow I will put you in the truck and drive you to the sheep field like a canyon mama taking her kids to school."

I have never been to Scotland, but I imagine Border collies fanning out over the hills in search of sheep, the shepherd watching his short-legged dogs shrink into black-and-white dots against vast swells of gray-green. The Border collie was bred for this, to run fast and long and bring back sheep scattered in unfenced terrain. Our dogs have less dramatic work to do. The co-op field where the dogs now train is fenced, a six-acre remnant of the pasture that once covered this entire area. Our land is leased from month to month, our sheep all but tame. For some of us the aim is competition, the goal a silver belt buckle. For me it's a matter of ethics. It's good and reasonable for me to give my dogs the opportunity to do what they were bred to do.

"Tomorrow," I say again to the dogs as the first drops of rain begin a drumbeat on the skylight above the kitchen sink. The drops become a steady flow, then a downpour. My husband goes out to check and comes back for his raincoat and boots. A half-hour has gone by when I realize he's still outside, shuffling garbage cans and plastic buckets, the dogs' galvanized washtub, anything he can find to thwart the moat that's forming as predicted. I help empty water buckets, and I bail where the water pools six inches deep. Twenty minutes later, the water is back and I am soaked through my raincoat to my underwear. My clothes are so heavy I can barely walk. My husband finds another raincoat and develops a rotation. He puts his wet coat in the dryer, and bails for the ten minutes it takes the coat he's wearing to soak through and the other coat to dry somewhat. Then he trades. I feel guilty watching him move through the kitchen to the dryer, his thin hair plastered against his skull, his eyes glazed. A legion of drummers beats at snare drums above us. *Tap-tap-tap, b-a-r-o-o-m. Tap-tap-tap, b-a-r-o-o-m.*

For three hours the drummers march. I have always liked rain, the way it makes me feel snug inside a house, the way it reminds me things go on without me. I have always liked the way rain takes me out of myself, the way its tapping makes me dream. I have always liked the scent of land after a rain, the way grass shines. But this was no tinkling, picturesque rain, no benevolent farmer's rain. This was a rain that came in on the heels of ten thousand booted soldiers, a rain that sailed in on a ship of malevolence and took pleasure catching us off guard. Finally my husband and I are at the kitchen table staring at each other over white meat and gravy, residents of a besieged city that is finally quiet after the big guns have stopped.

"I thought it would never stop," I say to my husband. Exhausted, he eyes his plate of food.

"Good turkey."

———

After I let the sheep out, tie the gate open, and watch to see they were grazing, I turn to the dead ewe. She is sprawled in the sun, her neck arched up and away from her body, her belly distended. I notice no signs of vermin. This is the second dead sheep I've attended, and I expected flies and ants and the horrible threat of maggots—like the maggots that swarmed in a cold slime over the dead rat under the bathroom floorboards and oozed up through the drain in the tub, the maggots in the garbage cans behind the drive-in restaurant where I worked in high school.

Two years ago in a different place, I encountered another dead ewe, this one with an unborn lamb. I helped load the body into two layers of plastic garbage bags, then lift the bags into a rusty, pockmarked dumpster. I felt my arms bow beneath the ewe's weight, smelled the sweet, acid stench of early decay. It was deep in summer then. Pale blue light crimped the edges of the sky but blackness lay at our feet. I couldn't see the dead ewe as we loaded her in the garbage bags and lifted her swollen body over our heads, but I remember her legs were stiff and tore the thin plastic. I feared the bags would explode and drench us with bile and undigested hay. More than anything I remember our furtiveness with the bloated body, as if we were trying to hide a natural function. But in a place with no room for burial, what do you do with a sheep carcass, with a body that will burst and spawn maggots, with a once-living animal that is now no more than garbage?

Such memories are out of place on this warm May morning, this quiet Sunday after our vengeful El Niño winter, with women in light dresses and men in short-sleeved shirts.

———————

We had many days like that first storm in February, when the arroyo in front of the house ran thick with mud the color of milk chocolate. During a lull one Sunday morning, we rushed across the stream to the fire station and loaded the truck with oily burlap bags filled with wet sand. The day before my husband had brought home a dozen sandbags, filled too full in his determination. From the kitchen window, I watched him strain to lift and drag the bags in place. Day after day, we watched the milk chocolate in the arroyo darken to bitter-sweet with branches and tree roots and boulders. Day after day, we heard the county snow plow mangle its way upcanyon, pushing mud and rocks off the road. Upstream, a man who couldn't get his car through the swollen creek tried to walk across. A neighbor fished him out before the boulders got him.

The big one hit just as February turned into March. The storm started in the morning with a warning tap-tap against the kitchen sky-light: "Notice me, notice me." The sandbags were in place; so were the new plastic garbage cans and the makeshift drain my husband built to funnel water off the roof. Raindrops, still sparse and light, bounced off my umbrella, so thin I thought for a moment the storm might not be as bad as predicted. But the conquerors weren't finished with us. The advance troops had been kind, but the regular army was on its way. The heavy water started at noon, so thick there was no way to distinguish individual drops, so dense it drowned the drumming. A battalion of giants emptied cauldrons of water from above, so many and so fast the water merged into a single flow. Water swamped our makeshift drains, pouring off the roof into the saturated soil. Water rose outside the front door, took a right turn, and headed toward the arroyo. The stream by the side of the house overran its outfall pipe, and water backed up into the kitchen. I bailed for thirty minutes, forty-five minutes, an hour, knowing I couldn't make a difference, but fearful of not trying. The water was above the foundation, three feet deep in the arroyo out front, above the first two rails of the horse fence at the ranch across the road, and I was wet completely through my foul-weather gear.

The sky dumped eighteen inches of rain in one month, more rain than this region of southern California usually gets in a year, the highest monthly total in the forty-nine years the weather service has kept track.

Sheep don't care if it rains, but it can be hard on dogs, especially dogs like my male, who has long legs and a heavy chest. As the rain continued, the sheep pens grew thick with mud and dung. The dogs wanted to run but couldn't, wanted to execute their precise right-angle takeoffs. They visited the sheep only to assuage their own addiction, to pretend they had an opportunity to do their job. The sheep sensed they had the upper hand and moved nonchalantly or stood in place and waited for the dogs to race around them. The dogs came home exhausted.

———————

I walk closer to the Barbie lying in the hot May sun, wondering what to do with a dead sheep on this fine Sunday morning. I could drag her to the top of the field and let the varmints have at her. I think I can stomach the idea, but other members of the co-op might not think it so benign. Perhaps I could call the county animal control office and claim it was an emergency. But what emergency is there in a dead sheep? What if someone in a house above the field called later to complain—would that, too, be an emergency?

I fight the urge to let the ewe be, to wait for Monday when the animal shelter will be open. I try to rationalize there's nothing I can do. Sheep die, dogs die. What would a rancher do? Dig a hole and throw her in? Would a rancher spend money on a vet and a needle? Would he own his own needle? Knife her across the throat perhaps?

I am irritated that I have to think about such things on such a fine spring morning. We should have a protocol for this. The woman who heads our co-op is out of town. Who else can I call? William, who handles the finances? But William takes his specialization seriously and makes few other decisions. The vet: should I call the vet? She'll know what to do with a dead sheep.

My ranting turns out to be pointless. As I walk toward the body of the dead ewe, I pull up short. Lying in the hot Sunday sun, her stomach bloated, her head curved high and back against her body, she is still breathing. I groan when I see her chest heave up and down, a trace of an effort. "She's still alive," I say to myself. "Oh, she is still alive." But obviously dying. The realization plunges me into new torrents of speculation. That the ewe is down means there is little hope. Sheep would rather stand, even in distress. She was standing last night when Phoebe called to tell me she had found the sheep sick. She had checked with a vet, and the two of them had forced soapy water down her, the prescribed treatment for bloat. The ewe had belched up gas, confirming the diagnosis.

"Sheep die," I say to Phoebe, as if I am suddenly wise. "I'm not going out there tonight."

But standing in the spring sunlight, I am confronted with a different picture, an animal in obvious distress, suffering perhaps. "Careful," I think. "Don't get carried away." But how do I leave a dying animal? How do I justify doing nothing? I stand and stare at the ewe. I resist the urge to poke and confirm the diagnosis. I look around, as if there is anyone to consult. Slowly, softly, the wind washes away the effort of my thinking. I walk to the gate, close the latch behind me. I leave the ewe where she lies.

"She's still alive," I say to my husband. He nods and turns the key in the ignition.

"Wait," I say, reaching toward the steering wheel. "At least I can give her some shade." The ewe struggles as we pull her by her feet into the shelter. She kicks, but just barely. I collect sheets of black plastic and build a third wall to block the sun as it comes around. I unlock the old fruit stand and copy the vet's number from the card thumbtacked on the wall. At home, without telling my husband, I call.

"Someone could force more soap down her," the vet tells me quietly.

"She's lying down."

"That's bad."

"Yes," I say. "She's dying."

"I could come by. Put her down, make it easier for her." We are quiet at opposite ends of the telephone line.

"It's Jan's sheep," I say finally.

"Jan doesn't spend money doctoring sick sheep."

I tell the vet I'll see what I can do. I call Jan and leave a message, then I call Susan, who's on duty with me this weekend. Susan tells me the sheep is ours.

"Then the co-op should pay?"

Susan says she'll call William. I walk into the kitchen for a cup of coffee and tell my husband I think we should pay to put the sheep down. "What for?" he asks. "Let nature take its course."

"Yes," I agree, adding sugar to my cup. "Let nature take its course." But the ewe is ruining my day. Across the road, someone is running one of our neighbor's trotters through her workout. Every morning at ten o'clock the trainer comes, hitches the horse to a sulky, grabs a whip and climbs aboard. Does the horse look forward to this? I wonder. Having achieved her twenty minutes around the track, does she feel satisfied, and does this satisfaction stay with her as she stands in her stall hour after hour doing nothing? The phone rings.

"Put her down. Tell the vet the co-op will pay." William's voice is shaky. It has taken four people three hours to make this decision, three hours while the ewe lies dying. I call the vet, then stand at the window and think again about the horse across the street. I think of the woodpecker that slammed into my truck one day as I drove home from the mountains. I pulled over and picked the stunned bird off the highway. The fly it was after was still caught in its beak. I laid the woodpecker under a tree to die. But the bird opened its eyes and tried to move, forcing me to rethink my actions. I picked up the woodpecker, wrapped it in a towel, and laid it next to me on the front seat. The vet I took it to thought the bird had broken a bone in its wing. "I'll keep it overnight." I called the next day but no one could tell me how the bird was faring. Finally, after three days, I called again. The vet told me the woodpecker was still in its cage at the hospital. "I was just going to put it out back and see if it could fly."

"The wing isn't broken, then?" A long pause, silence.

"I'm sorry," she said. "I've got the wrong woodpecker. The one you brought in died."

"Died?" I tried to keep the disappointment out of my voice.

"Head injuries," said the vet.

"How do you know?"

"The way it held its head when it moved around in the cage."

Dead, a handsome black-and-white woodpecker with a full crown of red and all the sky to own. Dead, in a cage in an animal hospital, by my hand.

A friend tells me I'm too dramatic. "You did the best you could."

Did I? To die in a cage in the glare of artificial light and the smell of disinfectant? Nothing the woodpecker could have expected. Nothing it knew how to handle.

————

Today is Monday. The animal shelter will be open. I will drive to the field. I can't lift the dead ewe into the truck alone so I will set a piece of plywood against the tailgate. I will put the ewe on the plastic I used to shelter her yesterday and pull her through the pens to my truck. I will push and pull the bloated body onto the truck bed and close the tailgate. It will be hot. I will sweat.

There is a line in the shelter office. A woman sits with a black collie-shepherd cross she had adopted two days before but is "relinquishing" because her children aren't sure they like the exuberant puppy. The woman behind the counter isn't pleased.

"I'd take the dog," I tell her, "If I didn't already have two of my own."

My turn comes. I tell the woman I have a dead sheep. She picks at the keys on the computer keyboard, damning the outdated machine.

"Cause of death?"

"Bloat."

"Bloat?"

"Yes. It's a condition, not a symptom."

"A condition of what?"

"The vet said sheep get if from feeding on grain or if something gets twisted inside." The moment the words are out of my mouth, I want them back.

"No surgery?"

"Hundreds of dollars of surgery for a twenty-dollar sheep?"

The woman nods. I sign the forms, pay five dollars, relinquish the sheep.

Why bloat, when the ewe fed on pasture? All winter I have been starved for sun and light and green, for the earth springing to life, for soil drying beneath the collies' feet. There are fifteen members in the co-op. If they all felt as I did when the rain stopped, we might have overworked the sheep, the skittish Barbies that don't know enough to cooperate and are less likely to stand a dog down. Perhaps the dead ewe had had enough. Perhaps giddy with sun and warmth and light, we allowed our dogs more leeway than we should have.

"Drive to the back of the yard," the woman at the counter tells me. I open the gate, drive the truck through to the back of the property, and park close to the loading dock. A young woman with an official patch on her sleeve and waist-length hair wanders over.

I shout at her from the truck window. "I've got a dead sheep!"

"Sheep," she says. "I'll have to get another barrel." The young woman ambles away, comes back with an oil drum painted white.

I lower the tailgate, grab the Barbie by her stiff legs, pull her out. The young woman helps. We stuff the sheep into the dented barrel and wheel it across the parking lot. The young woman opens the door to the deep freeze, then holds the door open so I can walk in first. We each grab one side of the barrel and together we roll the dead ewe into the freezer, into a vacant spot next to the stiff carcass of a buff-colored beagle.

———

I thought I wanted to tell you about the time my husband and I spent in the country, my attempt to escape Los Angeles where I had

147

lived since I moved west. The word "country" derives from the Middle English *contre,* from Old French *contrée,* from the Latin *contrata,* meaning opposite, contrary, against, "that which is beyond." Beyond the city. Fair enough. Beyond, as I said, the lights and noise, the congestion and confusion. To me cities have always meant disorder. Cities are unpredictable. I have always felt off-kilter in a city, that I can't handle what's being thrown at me. I thought I wanted to escape to the quiet and even pace of country life, the opposite of what the city represents. I didn't realize the city had seeped into my bones and into my blood, that the city I had lived in for thirty years had become a permanent part of me. Although I railed against what was uncomfortable about city living, I was steeped in its rhythms and in its constancy, in the street lights that—even as they block the stars at night—enable me to see what I'm doing and where I'm going (and what other people might be up to), in the stoplights and stop signs that keep traffic moving so people in cars and people on sidewalks are safely separated, in the orderly way the streets are laid out (get on Wilshire in downtown Los Angeles and drive straight to the Pacific Ocean, the same with Pico Boulevard and Olympic), in the streets and sidewalks paved to uniform standards, in city-built drains that carry off storm water; in the policemen trained to keep order and the paramedics and firefighters who are on call twenty-four hours a day, in mail delivered directly to my door, in regular garbage pickup. I was unaware how much my experience with the city's regularity and its continuity had influenced my standards for how I would live once I had decamped.

What I aspired to in the country might be "right" in the sense of responsibility and environmental correctness, planting a garden, composting waste—but my expectations about how these activities would be accomplished were distinctly urban. I would tackle the gardening and the composting and the tree-pruning systematically. I would work methodically to get the job done, then move on to whatever else needed doing. I expected things in the country to be regular, tied to the seasons or whatever other forces dominate rural life, and things being regular, they would be predictable, and being predictable, the amount of time required to spend on them could be methodically and accurately allocated. The trees would require a steady amount of trimming at the same time each year (what did I know of droughts, early frosts, unpredictable cold snaps?) I could count on having enough water (but not too much) for the garden. The soil, once properly prepared, would remain so. Complicating the situation, I expected to accomplish all these pastoral tasks at the same time I continued my urban preoccupations, inviting guests for elaborately prepared meals, going off to concerts or my husband's favorite jazz club an hour away in the city, keeping an eye on local politics, keeping up with the *New Yorker* and the *New York Review of Books,* reading up on the latest fashions, foods, and music. No wonder there is so little *contra* living going on close to cities, even with what little land is still left. The temptations are too great. No wonder so many people who leave the city to escape noise and crime and to see the stars at night move into subdivisions that mimic what they've left behind. Their cause is as hopeless as my own. The city follows them just as it followed me; worse, they bring what they expect from a city with them, in their demands for urban services—state-of-the-art schools, law enforcement, fire protection, convenient places to eat and shop and be entertained.

The day I found the ailing ewe in the co-op sheep field, we were on our way to meet friends for dinner in Beverly Hills. I knew better than to traipse through the sheep pens in a silk dress and thin sandals, but looking back, I see this was my small revolt against the forces that had kept me under their thumb all winter, my own private celebration that things were returning to normal. The vengeful El Niño winter had passed and I would get back on schedule: practice with the dogs for an hour three or four times a week, running through our regular routine, then take fifteen minutes to feed and water the stock on the days in between.

Sitting on a sofa in a friend's living room in Utah, I picked up a book of photographs from the coffee table. I was attracted by the title, which promised portraits of "real" working women on farms and ranches in the West. I didn't need the blurb on the back cover or even the text that accompanied the photographs to get the point: It ain't easy, honey. I saw women up to their knees in snow and mud, the snow dirty with manure, the women's boots and jeans spotted with mud and cow shit. Tired women warming their hands over a dirty iron stove or sitting in front of a fireplace or a TV. Overweight women, scrawny women, women with muscles, women with dirty gray streaks in their short or long hair, women with mangled hands but bright eyes, two women laughing over a cup of coffee at a battered kitchen table. The captions told me of mothers and daughters, just in from rounding up strays or fixing fence or whatever it is you do when you run thousands of cows on who knows how many acres. What do these women know about regular garbage pickup or county-maintained storm drains or city cops or paramedics that respond pronto? What time do these women have to sort out what's left from dinner—this to the burn pile, that to be composted—or to plant an herb garden? What do they know of our manic urban urge to control the forces we think threaten our well-being (no more than three dogs per household, no cattle or sheep—or roosters—in neighborhoods zoned residential), our insistence that there be a solution to every unforeseen circumstance, as small as, say, a woodpecker slamming into the side of an automobile, as large as . . . what? An El Niño winter? They figure they're lucky if they can keep up with what they encounter day to day, trucking feed to cattle stranded in a blizzard, getting enough water for livestock in a summer without rain, not just one sheep dead but hundreds.

I didn't know I was thinking about the city when I began to write about that heavy-handed El Niño winter. I thought I wanted to tell you what happened when I left, how I'd escaped the movement and agitation that bugged me, the crowded streets and unclean air and how different my life had become—and what I learned from the time I spent living *au contraire*. But I have lived among the city's mean streets so long that in many ways it may be impossible to really leave. Like it or not, it is in the city where the forces by which we live coalesce, natural and man-made, where trends evolve. It is from the city that my life, whether it unfolds there or on the land, is controlled and regulated.

Perhaps this is why so many people born and raised in rural areas dream of escaping to the city—dream with as much lust and idealism as do urban dwellers who long for the land, for a lifestyle that is as unattainable as it is idealized.

I heard once of two couples who settled together on 4,000 acres in northern California, northeast of Sacramento. The man and woman who owned the property had been successful with a chain of hardware stores. Like me, they had a dream, but compared to me, they went at it big-time. The other couple were country folks, well enough prepared to renovate an old farmhouse and set out pasture for sheep and cattle, to lay out stables and exercise areas for horses. The arrangement lasted less than a year. The businessman, who liked to inspect his property from behind the wheel of his new Chevy Suburban, expected the country folks to establish a plan and a timetable for what they would accomplish. He wanted to know when and in what order the barn would be refurbished and the house renovated and the stables built and the pastures laid out. The country people took it slow, as they would on their own property, watching the way water drained across the acreage, where the good grass was, what the wind and air currents were like, confident that what they had to do would fall into place in due time. When the experiment fell through, they went home to their own five-acre ranch in California's Central Valley, where they figured they were old enough that, by the time the city caught up with them, they'd be in the ground.

When I speak of rural, I think of life as it is lived on a farm or a ranch. But lacking the experience of the women in that book of photographs, I have discovered I can only think of country life in a way that distinguishes it from how I have lived in the city. I am stuck in the contrast. I want the opposite of how I have lived so far, and I vaguely define this opposite as clean, open, free. I am all too familiar with what I want to escape from but not nearly familiar enough with what I think I'm running to; perhaps my dreams of running away are just that, daydreams.

The United States census defines an area as urban if at least 2,500 people are settled there. It hardly seems enough. To "settle," the dictionary tells me, is to become fixed, resolved (as in resolving my conflicts with the city?) or established (set down in one place), to become quiet and orderly, to take up an ordered or stable life. Not in the country. Not in the way I went about it. Not by a darn shot.

STRIPERS WERE MY ELK

David Stalling

It was a cool September evening and I was seventeen, on my way to pick up a date for a high school dance, when I caught a glimpse of the rising moon. Bright and fat as a peach, it stirred in me inexplicable urges. I rushed back home, grabbed the keys to Dad's boat, and headed for offshore islands in search of striped bass. In my delirium I had forgotten my date. But it was, after all, a striper moon.

The incident inspired my oldest brother to create a collage of images clipped from magazines. On a beach in the foreground stood a beautiful woman glancing longingly out to sea. Far in the distance was a figure fishing from a boat, a small Boston Whaler like my father's. The caption read, "Oh well . . . I guess he'd rather chase bass."

Adaptable, migratory, alluring, striped bass are more like elk than any other fish I know. Like elk, female bass are called cows. In countless hours of pursuit, their enigmatic lurkings have haunted and taunted and baffled me. Stripers, like elk, have the power to take you over.

"That is the magic that rides the striper's shoulders as it swims through the ageless pattern of its autumnal migration, south along the shore and deep into the souls of the men who live on it," wrote John N. Cole in his 1978 book *Striper*. This book was a revelation for me. Although I was a senior in high school, *Striper* was the first book that I truly read and enjoyed. Cole tells of his passion for stripers and fishing and how both shaped his life, his values, and his thoughts. I could relate.

I had already spent a childhood, and then some, chasing stripers along the shores and islands of my Connecticut coastal home. One of my earliest memories is of a dusk-to-dawn foray in a boat. Still too young to fish seriously, I napped to the rocking of waves, and woke to the screech of monofilament rapidly departing a reel, my dad hooking and fighting a big bass, working the fish close enough to the boat to gaff. When he hoisted the fish over the gunwale, I was enchanted by the lean, pearly white giant scribed with vivid black stripes, its grand, sharp-edged dorsal fin and sweet, pungent odor. Later, I came to savor the white flesh which is, as 1600s-era New England fisherman William Wood noted, "One of the best fishes in the country . . . a delicate, fine, fat, faste fish."

Known to reach 125 pounds, these anadromous fish commonly weigh 40 pounds or more and live twenty to thirty years, torpedoing up and down the New England coast, their powerful tails and armor-like scales chiseled by the harsh, rocky surf where sea and land meet.

But even as Cole's book captured the magic of striped bass and the joys of fishing for them, it also clarified what I was already feeling about the stripers' future—and my own. "Ten years from now, at its current rate of decline, the striped bass will no longer roam the inshore waters of the Atlantic from Cape Charles to the St. John," he wrote. "The northeastern migratory striped bass, that creature with its genesis in the great glaciers, will have vanished as a viable species."

———

From the start, my father taught me conservation basics: to keep only what I would eat, to fish fairly and honestly with respect for the quarry. Later, he showed me the varied ways of pipers and horseshoe crabs, jellyfish and sea robins, scallops and mussels, and all that makes up the world of the striper. Eventually, he also spoke of the importance of clean water and healthy estuaries for stripers and all ocean creatures.

From spring through fall, from shore and by boat, mostly at night and on rainy or overcast days, I madly pursued these fish as they migrated between their spawning grounds, in Chesapeake Bay and Hudson River estuaries, and their summering grounds, as far north as Maine. Along the way, I sometimes caught bluefish and weakfish, dug clams, trapped lobsters, netted blue crabs and jigged for flounder. But always stripers swam through my thoughts.

I cast hefty plugs from the surf. I drifted chunks of mackerel, eel, and sandworm from the boat. I anchored off the islands, hooked three-pound baitfish called bunkers through their backs and let them send distress signals out among the barnacled-covered boulders where I hoped a huge striper lay waiting. I constantly hounded my father with questions: *Do you think the cows are coming through? Where's the best place to fish tonight? Can you go? Can you leave work early? Can I skip school?*

Like elk, stripers can tempt you to extremes. There was the night the surf slammed our small boat into a bon reef, swamping us in the dark, frigid Atlantic where we struggled, near to hypothermia, for our lives. A rogue wave filled my waders, stole my breath and pulled me under. Failed engines left me drifting helpless in dark, foggy, rough seas. But there were countless crisp, starry nights flanked by brilliant crimson sunsets and sunrises. There was the amiable smell and bitter taste of saltwater; the feel of salt spray, sun, and wind; the clamorous, rapacious cries of seagulls, terns, and cormorants.

Between bouts of fishing, I slept on the fiberglass deck of the boat or on island beaches rife with sand fleas. Resting during one spontaneous four-day striper binge, I was awakened by the Coast Guard. They were combing the reefs and islands after my distraught mother reported me lost at sea. Thereafter I was confined to shore for a while but still managed to fish the surf. In an area otherwise congested with humanity, the beach, bass, sea, and islands were my wilderness. Later, I recognized my pleasure in Thomas McGuane's collection of essays, *An Outside Chance,* in which he tells of fishing for stripers in Sakonnet, Rhode Island, within casting distance of mansions: "And, to a great extent, this is the character of bass fishing from the beach," he writes. "In very civilized times it is reassuring to know that wild fish will run so close that a man on foot and within earshot of lawn mowers can touch their wildness with a fishing rod."

I remember one night in particular, with my father, anchored alongside a narrow reef, stretching nearly a mile from a sumac-covered island to a boat-wrecking pile of barnacled rock exposed only at low tide. It's an unusual reef because the tide flows over it in the same direction whether coming in or going out. The trick is to stay close to where reef meets island as the tidal current flows through the eel grass, carrying food to hungry, waiting bass. Suddenly my bunker began to splash along the surface, and in the moonlight I could see the fins and wake of a long, lean striper slice toward my bait. Then there was a brief chaos of sound and flying water as though a flat rock had fallen from the moon. Then silence, and a dead rod, my bunker now floating motionless.

When I began to reel in, my father hissed, "Wait!" Soon we saw a swirl, followed by a huge dorsal fin, then a tail, moving with leisurely purpose toward my bunker. Like some great cat batting a mouse, the big bass had stunned my bunker with his powerful tail. Now he snatched it up and ran, the line, lots of it, spooling freely in the general direction of Long Island. I counted anxiously to ten, flipped the bail switch, leaned back with all my weight, and drove a 4/0-size hook into the bass's jaw. In the twenty minutes before the fish came to gaff, I was as alive as it is possible to be.

———

Sometimes, particularly on cold, overcast autumn days, I would spot a mad swarm of seagulls and terns diving the surf, picking at bait fish frantically sandwiched between sky and boiling bass. There might be time to drift close and cast a Goo-Goo-Eyes lure among the fray. I would swim the big plug across the surface, tracking the swirls as a fish closed in. Then the horde of bass and baitfish would vanish as quickly as they had appeared, leaving me to wonder where they had gone and why. There was so much mystery about them, so much to learn.

Happy that I shared his passion, my father taught me the most promising reefs and jetties to fish at certain seasons and tides, his knowledge based on a lifetime of fishing this shoreline and keeping meticulous notes, always searching for patterns and cycles. He might have caught a great silvery beast under the full moon off the southeast corner of a particular rocky island in late October, when the tide was two hours out. Or he might have seen a school of cow stripers throwing shadows like a squadron of dirigibles on a certain grassy sandbar the first week of June as the tide began to turn and rise. So we studied tide charts and calendars and fish those places when the conditions seemed ideal. The stripers weren't always there, but we found them often enough to keep us hungry to learn more. The pursuit of stripers, like hunting elk, requires knowledge, time, patience, and persistence.

My father loved to show me the best places to look for stripers, but he also took me to the places where he *used* to look for them—the salt marshes that are now Saugutuck Estates, the estuaries turned golf-course resorts, the brackish waters, where freshwater meets salt, that are now industrial dumping grounds. I was baffled by those who would fish for and eat stripers, yet think nothing of filling in a salt marsh to build a new home—just as I'm now puzzled by those who hunt and eat elk, yet glibly build houses in the heart of elk habitat. Later, through books and college, I learned of ecology and biology, and Leopoldian notions of a conservation ethic. But such studies were affirmations of what striped bass, and my father, had already taught me.

Like elk, stripers once numbered in the millions. In 1614, a Captain John Smith, sailing off the coast of New England, reported, "I myselfe at the turning of the tyde have seene such multitudes passe out of a pounde that it seemed to me that one mighte go over their backs drishod." The fish spawned in every major tributary from Virginia to Maine, and were so numerous the colonists used them for fertilizer. In 1629, colonists passed the first conservation law of the New World, forbidding the use of stripers for fertilizer.

In 1879, trainloads of striped bass began making overland journeys from New Jersey to San Francisco part of a zealous effort to establish a West Coast fishery. It worked. Stripers now range from California
to British Columbia. When the Army Corps of Engineers built the
Santee and Pinopolis dams in the 1940s, they unwittingly trapped
spawning stripers that had run up South Carolina's Santee and Cooper
Rivers from the Atlantic. Surprisingly, these fish survived and thrived,
living year-round in freshwater. Fishery biologists have since stocked
this strain in reservoirs across the country, including labyrinthine Lake
Powell at the border of Utah and Arizona. They've also mixed the eggs
and sperm of stripers and white bass, creating a hybrid that is stocked
in lakes and raised commercially for food. Good, I once thought. Why
not spread the majestic striper wealth!

But now I wonder how this quintessential East Coast native is
affecting aquatic species endemic to North America's Pacific coastline.
Should a fish that historically has spent ninety-nine percent of its life
in saltwater displace the native fish, amphibians, and other wildlife that
evolved, adapted, and live in rivers and lakes? Do stripers belong in a
man-made lake that was once a maze of beautiful desert canyons? Should
we devise our own species from two wild fish to suit our whims? Is this
desire to improve upon nature like moving elk to Alaska or red deer to
North America? Are hatchery-reared fresh water stripers any wilder
than domesticated elk behind game-farm fences?

———

By 1979, when I was a senior in high school, the future of
stripers looked dim. My dad and I caught our share of older, bigger
fish, but the number of young bass had plummeted, and we no longer
ate their sweet meat. PCBs had contaminated their flesh. These toxic
chemicals had worked their way from industrial plants along the
Hudson and Chesapeake estuaries into the wild food chain all up and
down the East Coast. That year, Congress enacted the Emergency
Striped Bass Act, directing the U.S. Fish and Wildlife Service to inves-
tigate the causes of decline and recommend restoration measures. The

resulting efforts have mostly focused on fishing restrictions and raising stripers in hatcheries.

At meetings of the local striped-bass club, in which my father served as president, I observed heated debate about the causes and cures for the striper decline. It was popular, if not easy, to blame commercial fishermen. I despised those who would haul stripers from the surf with nets. But later, when I read Peter Matthiessen's book *Men's Lives,* a tribute to Long Island's haul seiners, I had second thoughts. Matthiessen relates eminent striped-bass biologist Dr. Edward Raney's view on whether commercial fishermen are the real bogeymen: "If the sportsmen would put equal energy into the correction of known contributing causes to scarcity of stripers, the future of the species would be far brighter."

Stripers populations periodically cycle up and down, but each "high" in the cycle is a bit lower. With our proclivity for damming rivers, filling wetlands, and dumping chemicals, we've destroyed the spawning and rearing habitats needed to restore their numbers to Captain Smith's days. With stripers, as with elk, few people seem willing to address the bedrock issues of habitat, pollution, human greed, population, and consumption. But, like elk, stripers are astonishingly tenacious, surviving in spite of our continued desecration of their home.

Although they have recently made yet another remarkable comeback, nobody seems to fully understand why. Fishing regulations and hatchery-reared stocking may have contributed, and certainly efforts to reduce contamination in the Hudson River have helped. But the Chesapeake—where nine-tenths of the East Coast's migratory stripers spawn and spend the first three years of their lives—is still laden with acid rain, aluminum, sewage, chlorine, and industrial and agricultural chemicals that poison water, deplete oxygen, and decimate aquatic nutrients and vegetation vital to striper eggs, larvae, and fry.

Cleaning up the Chesapeake, like protecting elk winter range and migratory corridors, is the key to the species' survival and viability. Even if the Chesapeake is cleansed, though, it seems sad and unwise for so much of the striper's fate to precariously hang on the health of one estuary.

I've known striped-bass fishermen who love to catch the fish but care little about protecting the waters in which the great bass dwell. A fellow elk hunter recently confided that he's more concerned about bowhunting opportunity than elk. I can only wonder why the magic of the species—and the oceans or mountains—eludes such people.

———————

In 1985 a forestry job brought me to Montana and elk. I fell in love all over again. I began summer mornings with devout studies of Olaus J. Murie's *Elk of North America* and the Wildlife Management Institute's *Elk of North America: Ecology and Management.* I spent every day I could pursuing and watching elk, year-round, on foot, snowshoes, and skis through steep alder and ninebark jungles.

Elk have lured me through many long, lonely nights of extremes in cold, snowy mountains. I've hunted hard, killed elk, and savored their flesh. And in the countless hours and miles of unpredictable adventure chasing these magnificent creatures, I've come to deeply cherish elk and the land they animate.

As with stripers, my devotion to elk and elk hunting kindled concern for their well-being and their habitat. Like the East Coast stripers migrating through the shadows of the most heavily industrialized and populated stretch of the United States, elk continue to adapt to and survive human expansion and development. But how much can they stand, and how long can they continue to adjust and subsist? And what will they become in the process? Stripers cruising a desert lake are like elk that become dependent on human feedgrounds. They seem different, something *less*, not the enigmatic, wild animals that can evoke our passion and our stewardship.

Elk have become my stripers, and stripers were my elk, and through an obsessive quest for these mysterious beasts I've come to admire all that they are and all that sustains them. From the barnacles, plankton, and sharks of striper country to the lichen, sedges, and grizzlies of elk country, I relish and respect what makes these creatures whole—and how they, and their habitat, have helped make me whole.

In *Striper,* John Cole wrote, "If we allow fish and fishermen to vanish, we deny our heirs this critical opportunity to find themselves in the nets they pull from the sea." The same can be said of elk and elk hunters.

When I walk with my father along the rocky Connecticut shore where he has spent seven decades fishing for stripers, he often shows me where, as a boy, he and his pals would skinny-dip, steal corn, hunt ducks, dig clams and oysters, catch blue crabs, and fish. In his youth the Connecticut coast still held wild expanses of hardwoods, miles of rugged, empty oceanfront, small farms, and fishing villages. But cornfields are now country clubs, and duck marshes have become gated communities.

My father tells of a moonlit night in his youth when he watched, for hours, the green backs and spiny dorsal fins of thousands of bass (some the size of punching bags) as they pushed their way through shallow surf over a sandbar, headed for southern breeding grounds. I have never seen such a gathering of stripers, but his stories still feed my dreams.

When my father visits Montana, he sees the same forces whittling away at the country. When he reminisces, I hear a wistfulness born out of his vanished youth, but beneath this lies a deeper sorrow for all the wild country that has vanished with it.

Stripers and elk have furnished me immeasurable adventure, joy, and nourishment. I do what I can to aid efforts that sustain the wildness on which they, and I, depend. When I am old, I hope to look with content, not sorrow, at oceans and mountains still clean and wild— a world where stripers and elk still captivate and inspire their pursuers.

THE RUNAWAY MOTHERS CLUB

Jeri McAndress

The runaway moms are on the roll again. We're not all mothers but we all mother. We're chicks who dig canyons, babes who disappear at the drop of a death wish. We started our wild women's getaway coalition to enable us to leave the premises in the space of a sphinx moth, because we're femmes who can't do dishes every day. Or laundry either. Otherwise, we're normal. We take care of our loved ones. It's just that we need retreat from being needed, and we lust after outdoor motifs. So our pattern is pack up, grab the topo maps and any available psychotropics, and go for it. Remote canyons and spots that have clear blue pools are our goal. Off the beaten path, sprung from the grid, out in the hemisphere of anything-could-happen-next. Thads da plan.

Our escape: Lois and I drive in Lois's car and Rose drives in hers because she can't stay as long as we can. We leave Ophir at an altitude of 10,000 feet where it is snowing like crazy. We leave Lois's two kids and husband to journey west. On an icy highway past Sheep Mountain and Lizard Head Pass we wind down a narrow corridor of rock. What would Odysseus be called if he had been female, I wonder: Odessa? There is a little bit of Odysseus in every one of us.

Nearing the town of Dolores, we take the McPhee Reservoir cutoff. Dolores is a laid-back little town next to one of Mesa Verde's large side-canyons. This canyon brims with ruin sites and pictographs, but McPhee renders all that inaccessible now. You can pop into the visitor's center and see pictures of what it all looked like before the dam was erected. Rose says we look like "The Blues Brothers Go Camping." We is, whiz-wise, a trio of muses whose duty is to answer the desert's call, which this time around is: Blanding, Monticello, across the Colorado River to Hankesville and Capitol Reef, later on, Escalante Canyon— yo we be there.

———

This is the wettest spring we've had for years. My mind keeps thinking about Hans Blitz, a Colorado state patrolman who gave me two speeding tickets in the same month. He caught me on that straight-as-steel stretch of Highway 17 between Moffat and Alamosa. Most people drive this fifty-mile span between seventy and ninty miles-an-hour 'cause it's empty, so vacant that it looks like Utah's Salt Flats. Hans Blitz stopped me on the edge of Hooper, where he said, "I clocked you at seventy-three miles an hour."

"I'm just trying to get to my eight A.M. class, at Adams State College so I can become a teacher and get off welfare."

No response whatsoever. Two weeks later in the same place, at the same time, he pulls me over again and goes through the same nightmare routine. "Hey, give me a break!" I protest. "Pick on somebody else. What is this déjà vu ticketing? I'm going to court to fight this one. I can't believe it."

Nothing I said made any difference to Hans Blitz. He just kept writing like I was windshield smear. He tore off the ticket, handed it to me, and walked back to his car. He had radar and quotas to consider. Two years later, at forty-nine years old, Hans Blitz was crushed by a tree that fell on his car on the west side of Wolf Creek Pass in southern Colorado. Circumstances beyond his patrol, I guess. Mother Nature gave him a ticket to heaven, and he doesn't have to appear in court to contest anything ever again. All decisions erased. His thirty-eight-year-old wife was killed along with him. They had no kids, according to the Monte Vista newspaper. Crack, whack, smack, and it's over. History happens. Two people wiped off the face of the earth in the mad snow, rain, and winds of spring of 1995. Ours is not to answer why. Ours is just to watch each other die, either from disease, old age, or ruthless catastrophe. Catch the show and go. That's our ticket on this stagecoach.

———————

Since I'm still here, completely unmolested by nature for the moment, I decide to look out the window. Blue trueness is stretched out with immaculate cloud puffs. It is so cold the aspen leaves haven't even opened yet. The ground on Highway 145 is saturated with snowmelt. The grass is pounded flat against the slopes. These slopes have hathair real bad. Rico scenery: huge avalanche vestiges; cracked tree limbs; raging Dolores River bursting its banks, gouged with slow-moving snow chunks. The highway's pavement is a wreck, full of potholes from winter's freeze. Rico, an old mining town completely the antithesis of Telluride, says "time warp." Rico has no skiing or tourist industry. It's plain and chilly. My Navajo friend Glenda had to live in one of those Rico mining shacks when she was a kid because her father worked the Rico Mine. It must have been freezing for them here at 8,827 feet in this narrow dark canyon. Not like the beanfields and red-rock country of Glenda's origin. The first signs of spring are starting to show—the ochre-colored willows and new grass. The aspen stands are still naked, but wrapped up in mists and sung to by a swollen river. Rivulets squiggle through the grass. Ponds polka-dot the place and instant estuaries materialize. On the outskirts of Dolores, because we're just a little farther south now, the aspens sport their first leaves, tiny starts of itsy-bitsy leaves.

It's the last day of May. Snow on the Henry's, and snow on Capitol Reef's highest flanks. But we're warm at last. It's delightful here in Caneville Wash, where we pull up at 7 P.M., following some cowboys up a draw. Last night we parked on this multicolored slab of sandstone and strolled at dusk through a paint pot of hills in mauve, milk chocolate, pink-and-white stripes. We're in mounds of ash and volcanic rock and uplifts of different heights, some squared-off butte style with sharp edges and fallen chunks resting on their inclines. Others are curved mud piles in raspberry and white gypsum. It's a magical place at sunset.

Big, heavy clouds illuminated by late-day sunrays. The wildflowers are unbelievably plentiful here—angiosperms that have been hiding for decades sprout in fiesta bouquets. We are awestruck by this otherwise ordinary stretch of cow country. One guy comes by and says hello. "Gee, I never see anyone walking on this road."

Rose answers, "Don't know why not. It looks like somebody turned the sprinkler on for days. There's so many flowers around here."

The next morning, the cowboys herd their Hamburger Helpers right past our camp. After months of imprisonment in jeans, we euphorically slide on shorts and sandals.

We head to the visitor's center, sighting cottonwoods swaying along the Fremont River. Soon we're on Highway 24, just west of Caneville, traveling toward Capitol Reef National Park. Three camper-trailers pass us as we drive through multicolored cinder piles carpeted with tiny yellow flowers. More enormous recreation vehicles go by. What do these guys do at night while we're in our tents, have generator-noise contests? This is the geologic environment we are in today: Bentonite hills, Morrison and Mancos formations, Kayenta sandstone, limestone and Cutler formations.

At a park ranger's suggestion, we jeep over to this perfectly empty spot in the water-pocket fold. On the way, atop this hairy hill, we find some large, flashy chunks of silica protruding from the sand. Lois tells us that before taking her new jeep down this stretch she needs a shot of brandy. "Mother-fucker! Watch out baby 'cause here we come." We give lots of encouragement to our designated driver on her descent.

———

We're on the Notom Quad now. What a great campsite Tantalus Flats is, with its old fire ring and cowboy kitchen consisting of a few boards nailed to a tree overlooking a virgin meadow. Here we reside in an outstanding section of water-pocket fold, and we don't have to give our license number, cash, or credit card to get in.

Thursday (who cares what date): we wake up from our private car-camping dream spot and hang out gawking at the stupendous monoliths in every direction. A Navajo sandstone escarpment 700 feet above our heads has a tiny arch at the top big enough for a bird to fly through. We leisurely dine on coffee, pancakes, and eggs. I'm telling you that yesterday the wildflower tapestries we walked through in Sheets Gulch were like nothing I've ever seen. Everything imaginable was up. Some sort of purple begonia with red-purple leaves set onto heaps of pastel-colored clay silicate hugged the ground, marching over slope after slope, carpeting the lavender mint mud just right. Every kind of penstemon was up too. Georgia O'Keefe would have gone wild.

We jeep across this meadow on a sketchy road. We have to ford this wash with mud pits and maybe quicksand in it. But there's a sweet spring here, so we fill our bottles and prance around the car, splashing through puddles, surveying the situation. We decide we can make it and go for it. Ten minutes later, our brave move has provided us with luxurious sunbathing on slick rock lounges and skinny-dipping in aptly named Pleasant Creek. No one else is here. Oh, how I love the simple life.

———

I don't know how many trips we've done so far. We've been to the Grand Canyon twice, but Lois and Rose never want to "hike it" again. Rose is so primed for the river rat's life which, compared to our Sisyphian backpacking stints, seems a breeze. So let's put our names on that infamously long list of someday-it-will-be-our-turn and see what happens.

PADDLING SOLO IN THE FIORDS OF THE FAR WEST SHORE

Jon R. Nickles

Waves crash on the rocks below me. Whitecaps roil the sea and spindrift sails high in the air. Thick white clouds stream down the knife ridges that buttress Mount Gilbert's craggy summit like water over a dam. Four-foot seas generated by williwaw winds leave no doubt that I'm shore-bound here in Prince William Sound's Harriman Fiord. My reading material includes Jan DeBlieu's book *Wind*. But how can I read about wind while engulfed by the heavy exhalations of these mountains and glaciers and the exuberant dance of wind on water? It's August 22, and I'm midway through a 250-mile kayak trip in the northwestern part of the Sound. I welcome this unplanned day of leisure.

Twenty miles south, Blackstone Bay is also rocked by wind and waves. A thirty-eight-year-old man from Maryland, paddling a rented kayak, is due back in Whittier before dark. He tries to stay on schedule but never arrives. The entrance to Blackstone Bay is only fifteen miles from the community of Whittier, the jumping-off place for water recreation in western Prince William Sound. Surrounded by mountains and glaciers, it's a popular destination. At noon the next day Alaska State Troopers recover Michael McGovern's body floating in a cove next to his badly damaged kayak.

How many times have I heard the admonition, "Never travel in the backcountry alone"? Friends, family, and wilderness travel literature all dispense this generally sound advice. But sometimes my soul cries for solitude, and so I go alone. On a sunny August afternoon I paddle from Whittier's small boat harbor into whitecaps on Passage Canal. Food and gear are stowed beneath blue canvas decks, and a daypack full of camera equipment occupies the front seat of my two-person Klepper kayak. For the next three weeks weather, tides, and sea conditions in Alaska's Prince William Sound will dictate my rhythms.

Setting out, I'm dogged by trepidation, which I consider a healthy feeling. There's an element of uncertainty and concern about those things that are within my control and those that are not. Once I am committed and underway, other feelings and perceptions drift in. A profound sense of freedom and self-sufficiency washes over me. Everything I need to live comfortably for several weeks is stowed in my kayak, except fresh water, and the land will provide that in abundance. I'm accountable only to myself, but carry an obligation to travel safely, not only for my sake but for the sake of family and friends.

Propelled by a southwestern wind, normal here in fair weather, I cross a mile and a half miles of open water to a cliff where 5,000 black-legged kittiwakes nest. Near the sheer rock face the confused sea undulates beneath me; waterfalls plunge from unseen heights; and hundreds of kittiwakes wheel about in cacophonic flight, alabaster white with coal-black wingtips against the stark sky. Water, wind, and birds synergize into one dynamic life force.

Beyond the cliff I beach in the calmer water of a small cove. After carrying food bags and gear above the high-tide line, I clear a fresh heap of berry-filled bear scat from the most promising tent site. Pink salmon thrash in a nearby stream, and ripe blueberries hang plump and plentiful. I silently promise to be a good neighbor and hope the apparently well-filled bears will do likewise. With my small tent set up and gear organized, I begin dinner preparations. These are not elaborate— I boil water. I call my meals elegantly simple; tonight's dinner is uncannily like those I will eat for the next twenty days. Noodles, summer sausage, cheese, and crackers are the main course; cookies are dessert.

Before I savor my first bite, a sow black bear with two small cubs appears at a pool in the stream a hundred yards away. Salmon torpedo through the shallows and the bears pounce. Jaws clamped tightly on a squirming fish, mom retreats into the woods, trailed by her distracted young. Before dinner is over another bear saunters out of the trees, nonchalantly snags a fish and disappears the way it came.

Evening brings a gentle breeze that caresses my face, fresh and cool. I put on a pile jacket against the chill and take an after-dinner stroll, carrying my food bags away from camp. Skeletal trees stand like ghostly sentinels in the shadows, mute testimony of the subsidence caused by North America's greatest recorded earthquake more than thirty-five years ago. The land here dropped five feet. The epicenter, beneath Unakwik Inlet, was not far from where I'm camped.

Later, resting against a driftwood log, I revel in the darkening night sky, spattered with stars. Each twinkling pinprick in the firmament reached critical mass millions or even billions of years ago and ignited into a nuclear furnace that burns as bright or brighter than our sun. The stars' dim light, just now reaching Earth, has traveled the vast expanse of interstellar space for eons. Bathed in ancient starlight, man and bears share a narrow strand of rocky beach on this blue-green planet in the void, each made of stardust, each a part of an incomprehensible, expanding universe. I finally turn in and sleep soundly.

I'm not a food hanger so it's reassuring the next morning to find my food bags where I left them, by driftwood logs in tall beach rye grass, beyond high tide's reach if not the bears'. After hundreds of nights camping in bear country I have yet to share my food. Careful food selection and packaging, a clean camp, and luck all contribute. Or maybe elegant simplicity just doesn't compete with ripe berries and fresh salmon. Hanging food in bear country is accepted practice, but I've camped many times in treeless tundra and gotten out of the habit. And people who hang their food bags often do so improperly—"bear piñatas" a friend calls them. Hung food should be suspended between two trees and beyond a bear's reach from both the ground and the trees.

———————

Point Pigot marks the entrance to fifteen-mile-long Passage Canal. From my campsite I watch boats heading into and out of Whittier—the state ferry M.V. *Bartlett, Klondike Express* and other tour boats, pleasure craft, and fishing boats. Climbing the hill above the beach, I'm embraced by temperate rain forest. Sitka spruce and hemlock shade saturated ground from which the improbable huge leaves of skunk cabbage emerge. Rain is the lifeblood of this northernmost temperate rain forest. Whittier receives 160 inches more precipitation per year than Anchorage, which is only fifty miles away as the raven flies.

Low clouds and patchy fog greet me in the morning. Over oatmeal and coffee I ponder the 7-mile crossing of Port Wells. The water is calm but I keep a wary eye on the cloud-truncated mountains of Esther Island. I have a compass but no desire to be engulfed in fog. After awhile I decide the weather and water conditions are good enough.

Hans Klepper, a German tailor, publicly introduced his ingeniously crafted kayaks in 1907; the basic design has changed little since. Now constructed of wood, canvas and hypalon, these collapsible boats have many virtues, but speed is not one of them. It's comforting to finally paddle close to the southern shore of Esther Island after two and a half hours of open water.

Frenetic salmon leap everywhere when I paddle into Quillion Bay; at any moment at least ten airborne pinks are in my line of sight. Midway into the bay the high tide delivers me to a camping spot atop a huge granite rock. Pink salmon by the hundreds stream past the rock below my tent. Finally I yield to temptation, rig a fishing rod with a red Mepps spinner, and cast half-heartedly. The fish have no interest in heavy metal and soon I lean my rod against a spruce tree and just watch, considering their fate. After two years at sea they'll soon entangle in a fisherman's net, or they'll spawn and die, their rotting bodies providing nutrients for the next generation.

After I eat my dinner, laden clouds release their burden and hard rain urges me inside.

———————

The sea is calm as I backtrack from Eaglek Bay toward eleven-mile-long Esther Passage. I glide on the smooth water in a dreamlike state, and only the rhythmic splash of my two-bladed wooden paddle punctuates the silence as I dip left then right, left, right. Stopping to rest, I'm soon lost in reverie, suspended on the glassy surface between dark abyss and azure vault. Much of the glacier-scoured sound is hundreds of feet deep with the deepest areas exceeding half a mile. Wondrously diverse creatures swim below me while others creep their way along the ocean bottom or burrow into it. How easily we take these largely unseen miracles of creation for granted. We harvest what we want from the sea's web of life and discard or ignore the rest as if it doesn't matter. I dream of an unfathomable universe of sea stars below and the infinite star-filled heavens above. One star among billions energizes this beautifully complex planet and sustains life in all its myriad forms. If only the wounds we've inflicted on this sacred Earth could heal as readily as those of the sea star when it regenerates a damaged arm. How can we fail to revere all creation? How can we do any less than our very best to be good stewards of our precious inheritance?

Midway through Esther Passage, I pitch my tent as high as possible on gravel right at the edge of tall beach rye grass, which I know will be heavy with dew in the morning. The tide book shows tonight's high will reach 12.4 feet at 3:00 A.M. I've been jarred awake before by the sound of high tide lapping at my door. A contingency plan is warranted, so I put only a few essentials in the tent, stash most of my gear in the kayak and set my alarm for 2:00 A.M. I awake to a still, clear night surrounded by ghostly mountain silhouettes. A nearly full moon casts faint shadows and illuminates a trail of gold across the glassy water . . . and the glassy water is perilously close to my tent and rising. In bare feet I drag the tent into the grass. When morning sun rouses me I emerge well rested—better to wake up in wet beach grass than in a puddle of seawater.

———————

Valley glaciers come into view one by one as I paddle into College Fiord, whose arms were all named for eastern colleges by the Harriman Expedition, sailing these waters in 1899. Harvard and Yale Glaciers calve into the head of the fiord. John Burroughs, a naturalist on the expedition, wrote, "Indeed, we were in another great ice chest—glaciers to right of us, glaciers to left of us, glaciers in front of us, volleyed and thundered; the mountains were ribbed with them, and the head of the bay was walled with them." At Fiord Point I'm within sight and sound of Bryn Mawr and Yale Glaciers. Riflelike shots and the deep voice of moving ice reverberate through the night, reminding me of a Midwestern thunderstorm.

It was forty-eight degrees and drizzling when I turned in last night. Now slanting sunlight dapples mountains and glaciers, and patchy clouds shroud the peaks in mystery. There are no other boats in the Yale or Harvard arms. My feet push the rudder pedals hard left, then right as I turn one way then another to dodge ice calved by the glaciers. The dense ice crackles and pops as it expands, releasing long-trapped air.

Late in the afternoon the *Klondike Express* roars in, banging ice aside with its catamaran hull. I watch until it disappears against the massive face of Harriman Glacier and then search for it with binoculars. Where it calves into the fiord, the glacier is about twenty stories high and nearly two miles wide. It is the second-largest tidewater glacier in Prince William Sound, covering an area of 200 square miles.

As large as they are, present-day glaciers are mostly retreating remnants. At the maximum extent of glaciation more than 12,000 years ago, ice covered most of the Sound to a depth of a few thousand feet. These mountains and deepwater fiords bear testimony to thousands of years of gently falling snow, compaction of snowflakes into ice, and the inexorable grinding, scouring, plucking, and polishing of glaciers.

From my camp near Wellesley Glacier, I watch a flock of twelve black oystercatchers whistle in fast and low, circle and land on intertidal rocks. Distinguished by outlandish red bills, these crow-sized birds remind me of clowns as they converse noisily among themselves and probe the rocks for invertebrates.

Later the Holland America cruise ship *Statendam* glides quietly by. Tour ships transit Port Wells once or twice a day, sailing up College Fiord and a short distance into Harvard Arm. Their looming presence seems grotesquely out of place here; they compromise the spirit of wildness. Although separated by only a few miles of water, their insulated passengers and I are a world apart. These multistoried floating cities carry nearly 3,000 people, more than live in most Alaskan villages. Occasionally their loudspeaker announcements slice through the silence. I imagine well-fed diners glancing up from the dessert table for a glimpse of the glacier. More than an hour after their passage, a plume of blue smoke hangs low over the water.

———

Camped near the entrance to Harriman Fiord, I scan the water with binoculars and spot more than fifty sea otters. I hear the cracking of shellfish and the whining of pups. These large, endearing members of the weasel family were decimated by over-hunting, first by Russian hunters, then by Americans after the purchase of Alaska. Driven nearly to extinction, sea otters made a dramatic recovery following protective legislation in the early 1900s. From a population estimated low at 2,000 animals, sea otters rebounded to over 150,000 in Alaska alone. Their population in the sound was still increasing when the Exxon *Valdez* spilled its black cargo in 1989. About 500 carcasses were recovered here in the aftermath of the oil spill. Sea-otter fur is the densest, most luxurious of any mammal. Unlike all other marine mammals it is the fur, not blubber, that provides insulation. Fouled by oil, sea otters succumb to hypothermia. The northwestern corner of the sound was not directly impacted by oil, and otters seem to be doing well here. They have yet to recover in oiled areas.

The Harriman expedition is credited with discovering twelve-mile-long Harriman fiord, though I suspect the indigenous Chugach Eskimos, who had occupied the area for several thousand years, knew something of it. In 1899 Barry Glacier nearly blocked the entrance to the fiord. Harriman encouraged Captain Doran to take the steamship *George W. Elder* through a narrow water passage close to the glacier's face into uncharted and unsounded waters. John Muir, one of the naturalists on board and an expert on glaciers, was ecstatic. Describing Harriman Fiord he exulted, "It is full of glaciers of every description, waterfalls, gardens and grand old forests—nature's best and choicest alpine treasures purely wild—a place after my own heart."

Following his physician's advice that he take a long vacation, railroad magnate Edward Henry Harriman originally planned a summer cruise for family and friends. But with extra room on the ship, he invited many of the most renowned scientists and naturalists of the day—paleontologists, geologists, geographers, foresters, biologists and others. In two months the expedition covered 9,000 miles; thirteen volumes constitute the trip's official scientific reports.

Just inside Harriman Fiord I meet a solo paddler from Spokane. We compare notes for an hour, drifting with the outgoing tide and dodging an occasional chunk of ice. He is well equipped with safety gear and I vow to at least carry a VHF marine radio the next time I go sea kayaking. A borrowed cell phone is packed in my gear but I soon learned the sound was beyond its range.

Parting company, I paddle to a protected bay where trails through the vegetation indicate many others have camped. From open muskeg I can see three of the five tidewater glaciers in the fiord. Surprise Inlet and its glacier are directly across from me and hanging glaciers cling to mountains on each side of the inlet. Looking north, Serpentine Glacier snakes down from the heights of 9,638-foot Mount Gilbert. Harriman Glacier fills the head of the bay. At twilight four kayakers beach and carry firewood to their camp, which is a few hundred yards beyond mine and out of sight. In the midst of this wild country I feel a twinge of guilt for camping so near them.

An Anchorage kayaker died in nearby Blackstone Bay in 1993 when a large chunk of glacier ice fell on him and broke his kayak in two. His girlfriend narrowly escaped injury. In 1989, an Anchorage attorney and his visiting brother drowned there when caught by wind and waves. Two women in the party capsized but made it to shore. They had apparently already missed travel deadlines. One survivor is quoted as saying, "We just didn't want to be out there anymore."

Engaging in outdoor activities beyond our normal routines carries inherent risks. Important considerations include limitations of equipment and the ability to use it properly; weather, wind, and water conditions; and animals. The idea of risk has much to do with perceptions, familiarity with and knowledge of a particular area and activity, and what we choose to take for granted. There is truth in the saying, "Familiarity breeds contempt," but "complacency" might be more accurate. I'm more alert, aware, cautious, and sensitive to my environment when I go alone. While I'm comfortable spending days or weeks at a time in the wilderness, I know I've lost much of an ancestral intimacy with nature and her elements, and every day is a learning experience. I make mistakes, but with reasonable precautions, I have no doubt I'm safer hiking or kayaking in the backcountry, even when alone, than driving the streets of Anchorage.

In late afternoon the wind-tossed sea is calmer but the ride to Harriman Glacier is bumpier than expected. I realize I'm paddling too close to shore when a submerged rock slices the hypalon rubber of my kayak hull. Field repairs are easily made with duct tape and I carry enough of this Alaskan repair-all to make another Klepper if I have to. Alone in the upper six miles of the Fiord I enjoy an icy before-dinner bath in full view of the glacier. Refreshed, I dry and dress just before mountains swallow the setting sun.

Glassy water mirrors mountains and glaciers in the morning calm. Gazing into the crystalline reflections, I feel like I'm floating in a scene within a scene. Later, with camp set up two miles from Surprise Glacier, the thunder of calving ice turns my head. I watch waves radiate along the shoreline and time how long it takes until they lap the beach where I'm camped. Almost three minutes. Taking my camera gear I paddle toward the glacier. The recommended safe distance from a tidewater glacier's face is at least half a mile. Seeking quiet water, I pull the kayak close to a rock wall. I'm alert to the possibility of large calvings, but suddenly waves hit from the side, banging the kayak against the rock. With the paddle I push off hard and stroke for open water. Only then do I realize the waves are the wake from the tour boat *Tanaina,* which is making a slow pass nearby.

———

Another williwaw pins me to the beach, but with a warm sun the day is perfect for washing and drying laundry. I carry my clothes to Baker Glacier stream, weight them with rocks and toss them in for a fifteen-minute wash cycle. After wringing them dry I adorn one of the many standing snags with shirts, socks, pants, and underwear. My other laundry method is to toss weighted clothes into the lapping shoreline waves where a twenty-minute wash cycle is sufficient. I've decided I prefer tide for doing my laundry; this method is best employed on the outgoing tide to avoid wet feet when retrieving the clean clothes.

I spend my last night in Harriman Fiord across from Cascade, Barry, and Coxe Glaciers, the triumvirate that guard the entrance to Harriman Fiord. A mixed flock of several hundred scoters moves back and forth a few hundred yards off shore. White foreheads and napes indicate most of these large sea ducks are surf scoters. Sometimes they string out in a long line and then regroup. Their feeding appears synchronized when most of them dive at the same time.

The incoming tide sweeps around the point and up Harriman Fiord. I estimate its flow at four miles per hour, close to my top paddling speed. I carry my gear close to the fast-rising water then load quickly, keeping a watchful eye on the kayak. Paddling out, I fight to keep the flow from pushing me back into the fiord. Even Harriman's steamship *George W. Elder* had difficulty here. Having broken one of its propellers on an underwater rock, it was heading for repairs at Orca, a now-abandoned cannery near present-day Cordova. John Burroughs reported it was caught by the tide, and being slow to respond to the helm was carried perilously close to the glacier's face.

———————

The thrum of rain on the tent fly reminds me of the saying, "Bad weather always looks worse through a window." In my case, rain always sounds harder when I'm inside the tent. During a late morning break in the weather I pack quickly and launch. Wind-driven rain soon returns, and I don rain gear for only the second time while paddling. Fog obscures the far side of Passage Canal. By mid-afternoon I'm back at my "bear creek" campsite. I could paddle the remaining distance into Whittier, but I'm reluctant to end the trip.

I venture out of the tent when the evening sky brightens. A dark animal waddles through the sedges near the creek. At first I mistake the porcupine for a black bear cub. During my dinner, three bears (or perhaps one bear three times) come to the creek to scoop up salmon and fade back into the forest. The lights of Whittier shine across the water, stars appear one by one in the clearing sky and a freshening fair weather breeze arises from the West.

I rise early and pack, not anxious to end my trip but expecting the wind to increase later in the morning. Outside the sheltering cove I'm hit with a headwind, three-foot seas, and more exhilaration than I want. Beyond the kittiwake colony, with its noisy tenants and growing chicks, I turn toward Whittier. After clearing the breakwater and entering the harbor's calm water I rest my paddle across the gunwales and slump in my seat. I give silent thanks for three weeks of good weather, safe passage, and the sensory feast spread before me each day.

Fragments of a poem about the "fiords of the far west shore" play through my mind. Penned in Prince William Sound by Charles Keeler, a member of the Harriman Expedition, the poem is my benediction. It closes with these words:

> *What joy is this to float upon thy tide,*
> *So blue so beautiful to gently glide*
> *'Mid islets forested, past shores that stand,*
> *Dark portals opening to enchantment's land,*
> *Where all is but a dream, soon to be*
> *Lost in the purple mist of memory.*

WHERE THERE'S HOPE

Jill Hindle

FOR OWEN ASHER GUSTON AND ETHAN KHOI

What makes a place special is the way it buries itself inside the heart,
not whether it's flat or rugged, rich or austere, wet or arid, gentle or harsh,
warm or cold, wild or tame. Every place, like every person, is elevated by
the love and respect shown toward it, and by the way in which its bounty
is received.

—*Richard Nelson,* The Island Within

There is nothing more disarming than discovering beauty in a place
where you least expect it. I stepped outside today into a street full of
people and sunlight and noises rushing through the brisk, February air.
I took my usual right onto Sixth Street and headed toward the East
River. Within the space of twenty paces my senses were struck with a
rich waft of incense, the savory smell of meat cooking on a grill, and
the puissance of an old man's pipe. Smoke tumbled elegantly into the
street over the tarnished eaves of a snug row of brick facades. A beautiful little girl with hair the color of summer squash hopped and
clutched her father's hand, explaining in an exquisite, elfin voice the
feeling of going down a slide backward.

I run to the East River on weekends because I like to get outside
when I can. During the week, most of my daylight hours are spent at
a desk in a building on the other side of town. So on Saturdays and
most Sundays, if my weak knees and the weather permit, I go east as
far as I can, then south along the edge of the water. There is a path

along the river that'll take you all the way to the Brooklyn Bridge. When I run along this path, I stay as close as possible to the railing, because seeing the water pleases me, and feeling the wind whip up off its surface makes me breathe deep and strengthen my stride. Today I concentrated on keeping my gaze up off the ground. My back straight, my chin up, my quadriceps conscious of their ability to cushion my battered joints, I drew my eyes across the landscape that makes up Brooklyn. Just south of the Domino sugar factory, the view is bisected by the wide stretch of the Williamsburg Bridge. As I get closer, the bridge looms—I sense the weight of its great steel girders and beams—and as I pass beneath, vibrations from the cars and trucks passing overhead send down a shower of old rainwater from somewhere. A fisherman leaning against the railing beyond the shadow of the bridge watches me shake the water off my hat as I run past, and he smiles.

I am telling you about these things because in this landscape of my life in New York City, all of this matters a great deal. This is a different kind of community for me; I am not well-adapted. I grew up in a place where it wasn't dangerous to lay in the street for hours on hot summer days, the cool, rutted pavement at my back, watching the oaks arch their great, feathered limbs overhead like old ladies in emerald gowns bending to gather their skirts about them. There are no such luxuries in this city; there is no room for them. Yet the most important thing I have come to realize since I moved here (exactly one year ago today, in fact) is that, however alien or extraneous I feel, I *am* a part of it. I have to be, if I want to live well, or feel committed in any way to my own notions of democracy or happiness. Indomitable: that is what this city is. But the human spirit is indomitable, too.

———

The figs are falling from the trees, they are fine and sweet: and
as they fall their red skins split. I am a north wind to ripe figs.
Thus, like figs, do these teachings fall to you, my friends:

now drink their juice and eat their sweet flesh! It is autumn
all around and clear sky and afternoon—

—Friedrich Nietzsche

Not long after I arrived at my apartment on the Lower East Side last February, I started compiling a list of moments, events, facts, truths and myriad other tidbits that, in one way or another, had given me reason to smile, had slowed me down in the rush of a day, or had generated some productive thought. Hope is the one quality that all of these things have in common. When I realized this, I also realized that landscape—the physical fact of my immediate surroundings—had been playing a huge role in the sustenance of my spirit and general well-being for years. This sudden need to witness and record every fortifying, enlivening, even remotely piquant shred of my daily reality in the city was a direct response to the lack of the basic beauty (or what I had come to think of as "beauty") in that landscape. But it wasn't only aesthetic satisfaction I longed for; I wanted community, charity, identity, solicitude. Like an ulcer, a cyst, a little pocket in my gut hungered—no, ached—for sights, smells, sounds, even tastes that reinforced a steadfast, perhaps stubborn, certainty that all the crimes of our species might somehow be overthrown by some inherent impulse to do, and be, good. It had merely been misplaced; it was harder to see in this linear land of Get and Spend. So I set out to find it.

I remember the day I sat down to begin the list. I was feeling frustrated and alone, but very fired-up all the same. I had just come in from off the street—it was a warm day; I wore no coat—and I was in one of those moods where I found it difficult to make light conversation with my house mates because there was so much else roiling around in my head. I clamored into my windowless room (I have since moved out of that one, thank God), collapsed onto my creaky wicker desk chair, and nudged my lap-top out of sleep-mode. A blank screen appeared, the same blank screen I had stared at for a good hour-and-a-half the night previous. I started fidgeting immediately, cleaning the dirt out from under my fingernails, spinning my pen around my knuckles. I was breathing heavily from my sprint up the stairs. What had driven me to run? What was it about the day (the unseasonable temperature, or the angle of the sun?) that pushed me past the store where I had meant to buy groceries and hurried me up the stairs to this chair and this desk and this irritating cursor, blinking at me like some mechanized version of Chinese water torture?

In fear of losing my momentum, I went to the bathroom to wash my hands, then into the kitchen to get a glass of water. When I returned, my eyes landed on a recent issue of *Orion* magazine lying in a pile of other "things to read" on the floor. The cover pictured a cresting wave, and in the curve of gray water, printed in a pale white-blue, were the words *Where There's Hope.* I sat down immediately and pounded into my keypad the first thought that came into my head: *There is hope in the kidney that my mother gave to my father.* I wrote other things too, but that sentence echoed inside my head for days.

After the extreme physical distress of end-stage renal failure, a bucket of mood-altering medications, and five weeks of dialysis, my father found out that my mother's blood type and cell tissue matched his own and that his body, spent as it was, had a minute chance of functioning normally again with the help of her healthy kidney. The nephrologists called it "miraculous" in spite of their earlier, emphatic claims that it was "highly unlikely." My mother, exasperated with the doctors' professional skepticism, at last could celebrate her determination to endure all the testing and re-testing (sometimes three and four times over) for accurate results. When the implant was finally confirmed, she marched into the New England Medical Center and all but screamed *I told you so!*, much to the amusement of her husband, who had never felt so grateful, or so proud.

Polycystic Kidney Disease: it's one of the most common, least understood, insufficiently funded diseases around. I've got it. My brothers have it. Their children might have it, too, but we won't know that until they're old enough for the symptoms to be testable. My uncle, now in his mid-sixties, is the first male member of my father's family who has lived past age fifty-four. If it weren't for the drastic advancements in research and drug technology over the past twenty years, he would have died decades ago. My father would have died in 1990, when I was still in high school, my eldest brother, a few years later, and I wouldn't have made it past New Year's day, 1995. I was a sophomore in college at the time. Every day I forget how fortunate I am, but every day I'm also reminded. All it takes is two weeks packed in ice with a temperature of a hundred and four to drive home the fact that we're expendable, some of us actually helpless, without the aid of intravenous drugs, antibiotics, cyst aspirations, attentive nurses and parents, friends, lovers.

Since that warm day in February when I ran up the narrow stairs to my East Side apartment to try and pin down words for something I had felt in the street, I have significantly expanded the Hope List. An optimistic sampling from the last twelve months of my life would include the following: forgiveness; wildness; dreams you remember; pain you forget; the old Ukrainian man who carries around a plastic bag and cleans up all the trash—cigarette butts included—between St. Mark's and Fourteenth Street every morning; an adult's willingness to keep learning new things; the day the construction workers clapped and howled when I decided, after weeks of ignoring them, to say hello; my grandfather's ability to make strangers laugh; the bakery down the street where you can still get a bagel and a coffee for a dollar; the woman who crams hundreds of flowers into a tiny three by four-foot plot of two-inch-deep soil outside her apartment on Sixth Street; the way light, at certain times of day, can make you see something differently; paintings; music, especially when it happens on a street corner or on a subway platform or in an elevator, and it makes people smile, changing the whole mood of the place; a mother bird I watched tending to one of her young that had fallen from its nest in a signpost at the corner of West Eighteenth and Sixth Avenue; the other people on their way to work who stopped to watch her with me; instinct; adrenaline; the feeling you get in the pit of your heart when you're about to see someone you love; the men who gather on the sidewalk by the chain-link fence of their apartment complex to play dominoes every summer night between 6:30 and 7:30, their radio blasting out crackling Spanish

185

dance music louder than the traffic on the East Side Highway; when you're reminded of how good something feels; raw talent; good books published by small presses; perseverance; the post card from Terry Tempest Williams that I keep wedged into the frame of a mirror in my room; the man I saw sitting in the doorway between a bondage shop and a tattooing parlor staring at a naked baby in his lap; the free movie screenings held every Monday night of the summer in Bryant Park at Fourty-Second and Fifth; the homeless man on Thirteenth, jingling his coin cup, stomping his feet, and singing about the Knicks making it into the finals; community gardens; the kids that play in community gardens; how the man who runs the laundromat downstairs scrubs all the stainless steel in the joint at least weekly because he believes in a job well done; the fact that education, health care, and conservation are (if only loosely) at least addressed in presidential debates; sunsets from the Brooklyn Bridge; everything about the Brooklyn Bridge; the impetus we have to share; the exhibitionist who rode through the East Village one day on his oversized homemade tricycle wearing pink sequins, a top hat, singing vaudeville, and dragging behind him on a Fisher Price wagon, an oversized harp spray painted gold; watching someone smile quietly to themselves in the street; imagination; ideas; Nina Simone singing "Memphis in June"; the Truth and Reconciliation Commission in South Africa; the feeling in my legs after a long, hard run; Walt Whitman; George Eliot; Rachel Carson; Rick Bass; the change of seasons; the tone in my brother's voice when he speaks to his newborn son.

I will stop there. The list goes on, as it should, and I am thankful for it. Here in the city life sustains itself in ways I never thought possible. There is a will about everything; a will to conquer and glorify, eclipsed by a ruder will to endure despite the odds that is astonishing and often sad. But it is this will, this unassailable desire for the continuation of (if not the propagation of) oneself that has made me stop and think hard, time and again, about who we are and why we do what we do. As removed as we may become from our origins or our emotions, we are and always will be, as T. S. Eliot puts it in one of his Choruses from 'The Rock,' "controlled by the rhythm of blood and the day and the night and the seasons."

The specialists keep telling me that by the time I'm my father's age, I won't have to worry about kidney failure. They will have developed some preventative drug which inhibits the spread of cyst tissue. They will have isolated the gene that stimulates cyst growth. They'll have a pill, an injection, a shock treatment. Whatever "they" project, I can't count on it. I won't. I don't doubt the effectiveness of modern medicine (I even suspect there's a cure), but I do question the amount of time it will take to establish the public and financial support necessary to solve this puzzle. My father is the president of the New England Chapter of the Polycystic Kidney Research Foundation. He coordinates bike-a-thons and walk-a-thons and holiday book wraps and bake sales to generate awareness and support locally. My mother works with him, more than side-by-side—her left side in his right, hooked up to a leg artery. She attends his meetings, his speeches, his fund-raisers and serves, I think, as a gentle though potent reminder of what he calls his "new lease on life."

"I can always take it back," she says playfully, as we sit around the dinner table, recalling the months when my father couldn't mow the lawn, or stack the wood, or make it up the stairs without stopping to grasp the railing and breathe, closing his eyes to gather his strength. Now he laughs and swallows the dregs of his wine. And unwilling to broach the deep sentiment pooled there, shaded by all his relief under the jokes and jibes, he gets up from the table. We hear the faucet go on in the kitchen, the rough clatter of silverware, and my mother smiles a smile so full of grace and patience and intemperate love that I stare at her for a moment, astonished, before smiling back. There is hope in this, too.

Humanity's relation to the rest of life is unimaginably complex,
and includes the deepest of all mysteries on this planet.
Those who embrace it own the gift of a bottomless well of hope.

—E. O. Wilson

I have come to understand the role of mystery in the perseverance of hope. On February 5 of the year 2000, my first nephew (my brother's first child and my parents' first grandchild) was born. Though I am young and my experience is limited by this, I feel confident making the assumption that there is nothing so enigmatic, so resplendent, so perfectly sanguine, as watching a life begin. I refer to the words I wrote in my journal because, although they are rough and indulgent—too clipped in some places and bloated in others—they are the product of pure awe. I have never been so spellbound.

February 5, 5 A.M.: *I keep adjusting my brain to the idea, and there's always more adjusting to be done . . . here we are, holding him and talking to him and developing our relationships already with this new person, and incorporating him into our movements and our decisions and our eating habits and our every thought. To watch my brother cradling his son in the crook of his arm, to watch his head bending over a tiny face; there is something in the angle of his neck that exhibits a quality in my brother's character that I have never seen before. His whole physicality has changed, his role in the family, his position within the framework of his own life. Everything has changed. This husband and wife, these two artists—now parents—have created their own core around which they will circulate for the rest of their lives. Their priorities will shift in the same way the angle of our horizon shifts relative to the background stars. The fact of this child is as fixed as the stars; our orbits adjust accordingly. We have been realigned.*

February 6, in transit: *New York-bound again, after yet another all-too-brief weekend home with family, which has, in the past forty-four hours, grown by one. And this one . . . I can hardly believe the hard evidence—a boy. Even though I have held him and rested my lips against his skin; even though I have heard him cry and seen his naked, stretching limbs, so unfamiliar with this sudden range of motion; even as I have marveled at the size of his toes, the clutch of his miniature fist, the tiny pulse of his nostrils as he breathes; even as I have studied the intricate curve of his ears and the dark movement of his eyes mysteriously scanning our mammoth faces; even still, I am in total disbelief. I leave the room where he lies and he becomes a dream—the most ethereal and beautiful kind—and I am drawn back in to look at him again. The small curve of*

his skull fits into my palm, and I am wordless. I think I can actually feel the
expansion of love in my chest, and picture it as a blossom opening at high speed.
I notice everyone's movements toward and away from him, taking turns, move-
ments like spokes radiating out from the hub of a wheel. I notice we can't talk;
we hardly think of anything else. I notice that something very necessary is hap-
pening: an event so deeply biological that, even though many of us have wit-
nessed it before, or at least have been entirely conscious of its eventuality, we are
nonetheless struck dumb with reverence for the fact of this fresh life. We are
amazed that all of his parts are intact, that a little heart, the size of a nut, moves
inside his ribcage, which is smaller than the breadth of a palm spread wide. We
search for the parts of his face that are Catherine's, the parts that are Michael's,
and this thrills us to no end. Our minds reel with foreign thoughts of chromo-
somes combining and crossing each other out, of two separate gene pools sharing
and exchanging billions of complex units of energy to create this unique, singu-
lar being. And even though we are what he is, it is his delicacy and inviolable
secrecy that engrosses us and makes us wonder. . . .

For brains and bodies that are tied up in the complexities of their
own present reality, the birth of a child is astonishing and therapeutic.
Perspective floods our consciousness like a surge of gasoline into the
fuel pumps of an old car. We sputter and lurch, searching for the right
words, suddenly conscious of our own size and clumsiness. We recognize that we are all the products of this same, most natural, reproduc-
tive act. We are at the root of this universal enigma, which is so
common and so inevitable and so obvious, yet so obscure. It is our own
mystic puzzle we are so enchanted by.

Paradox: this is what keeps me living in the city, for within the
paradox of science and spirit lies the source of so much hope and
renewal. Sometimes, in a landscape that is superficially decrepit, even
shreds of hope and renewal are difficult to find. When my cousin died
"unexpectedly" in a motel room, all traces of hope and renewal were
instantly drowned in an overwhelming tide of devastation, confusion,
total loss, even anger. Like the obvious poverty spoiling the streets of so
many cities, Eric's death felt insurmountable; in spite of our tiresome
efforts to come to terms with it, no measure of reason or understanding

189

could make it easier. And I will never forget the image of my brothers alongside Eric's brothers in their dark suits, heads down, ties dancing in the wind, teeth gritting against the weight, as they hoisted the great wooden box into the back of a car.

Three months have passed. Eric is still dead. The family has dispersed and settled back into our own separate realities. We feel his absence like a powerful ache that dulls with time but never releases its hold. Some days it is heavier than others. We resume our lives and gradually find ways to work and sleep and smile comfortably again. Hope and renewal, like battered angels, finally descend and relieve our exhausted hearts and brains. The next time I walk through Alphabet City, I find what I thought was an unused playground crowded with local kids. The sun blasts a patch of technicolor graffiti on the wall and I stop walking to blink at it. I don't know if it's fresh, or if I've just never noticed it before. Kids are all over the place, skating, swinging, calling to each other. One girl draws big circles on the pavement with a wedge of blue chalk. I think of Eric giving drawing lessons to prisoners on death row, and of the job he was traveling to when he died: to teach art to children at an elementary school in Byers, Colorado.

I plan to leave here soon. For all that it has revealed to me—for the ways in which it has challenged my notions of community, ambition, harmony, and hope—I am not made for this place. I wonder if anyone is. For the sake of my own lifestyle, I have decided that too much must be compromised to survive in the most immediate and rudimentary sense, let alone to feel productive or fulfilled over time. This, after all, is what a body must do: understand itself well enough to know when it is unhappy, and then have the courage to change. Because life is happening. It has a beginning and an end. We all fall somewhere between these two definite points. And it is the puzzle of the progression from point A to point B that defies any sort of measurement or tabulation.

Despite all the systems that structure our lives (the government, the economy, the stock market, and now the Internet) we are inexorable, inexplicable creatures of impulse—complete suckers for beauty, passion, and the end-all: love. We witness birth and then death over and over. We wonder endlessly at the mysteries of both, and then we remember where we are, and that time passes. We shake our heads and blink our eyes at this solid, indisputable fact of life that whispers and sometimes screams, "You are here now. Do something!"

Once in his life a man ought to concentrate his mind upon the remembered earth. He ought to give himself up to a particular landscape in his experience; to look at it from as many angles as he can, to wonder upon it, to dwell upon it.

He ought to imagine that he touches it with his hands at every season and listens to the sounds that are made upon it.

He ought to imagine the creatures there and all the faintest motions of the wind. He ought to recollect the glare of the moon and the colors of the dawn and dusk.

— *N. Scott Momaday*

I have a memory of the old Ukrainian man (number five on the Hope List) cleaning up the street on a cold, blustery day last winter. Instead of the usual plastic bag, he was carrying a long-handled dust pan and a brush. His eyes were focused on something as we passed on the crosswalk. I glanced back just in time to see him trotting after a piece of paper tumbling along the pavement in the wind. That was the last time I saw him. Spring came and bloomed and I left the city before summer set in. But in those last weeks and days, I looked for the old man, hoping to have one final opportunity to talk to him.

I had spoken with him only once before—one early morning on my way to work. I was at the corner of Second Avenue and Thirteenth Street when I saw him about half a block ahead of me, grinding the toe of his boot against something apparently imbedded in the sidewalk. I caught up with him to ask what he was collecting in his bag. Startled, he tried to explain that he didn't understand English, so I pointed at the ground, then at a scrap of newsprint floating by and crinkled up my nose in distaste. The confusion in his eyes cleared. Leaning toward me, as if in confidence, he opened his bag. Pointing with a coarse, gloved hand at hundreds of cigarette butts and indiscriminate scraps of old food wrappers, styrofoam, bottle caps and dirty rags, he said, "Sheetty New Youk." Then he smiled and waved his hand back and forth, indicating Second Avenue. It looked like he was swatting at an invisible fly. "I pick it oup, see, I pick it oup."

Before I could reply, he was hobbling onward, so I walked with him until we reached Fourteenth Street. At the corner, he turned and fixed his eyes upon the crossing signal on the other side of Second. I asked if I could buy him a cup of coffee but he shook his head vigorously and, bowing slightly, stepped off the curb. Half-way across the street he bent to pick up what looked like a straw wrapper. The other people crossing the street moved past him, not looking to see what, or whom, they had stepped around.

The marvel of this man was not that he managed to clear a few sidewalks in Manhattan of all their visible trash each day, but rather that he would be compelled to do so. I don't know how long he had lived there or what sort of allegiances he may have made to that place, but he had evidently decided that improving his surroundings (however ominous) to the best of his ability (however meager) was well worth it. Mornings when I watched him, I couldn't help but wonder what motivated him to clean and re-clean those dingy stretches of cement slab. They never stayed that way; but he came out every day just the same, working his way north and then south again, plastic bag in one hand, pointed stick or broom or dust pan in the other. Take the roots of this impulse, I would think to myself, and multiply. Take the compassion, commitment and indelible hope of an old immigrant in New York City and sow it in the minds of other, younger, abler bodies.

To some people, the story of the Ukrainian man is not a story of fidelity, but a more complex and sobering story of isolation, recklessness, and abandonment. In a country congested with so many educated minds, the image of an old man toiling away at an endless wash of city trash is a clear and shameful measure of our grossest failures. I see their angle, all too clearly. But I don't lose sight of mine.

One of my good friends, Alden, has committed his present youth and ability to a wonderful school in Vershire, Vermont that is built on the basic foundations of awareness and investigation and compassion for the land. During a recent phone conversation, he recited a laundry list of horrific statistics printed on the back cover of the latest issue of *Orion*. I groaned and swore as he read them aloud: "More than 500,000 trees are required to make the newspapers Americans read *in one Sunday alone* . . . our country's daily use of computer paper could stretch around the world forty times . . . we waste 27% of all the food we produce" (and in the spirit of the holiday season, *Orion* thought it pertinent to note that "if the pilgrims had used aluminum cans at the first Thanksgiving, the cans would still be around"). This is not to say that Alden, or the good people who publish these statistics, are insufferable cynics. No, these folks would be the first to send all cynics to the slop house to give them a healthy shovel-ful of their own medicine. But I don't doubt that they would be the very last to buy into the happy metaphors, the neatly packaged explanations, let alone the uninformed ideals of so many "environmentalists" in our country. Nonetheless (I say, with my fingers crossed and my sword raised) a good story, whether it be about an old street cleaner in New York City or a young truth seeker in Vermont, has the power that no statistic could ever muster.

Alden took me on a long walk a few weeks ago. We got lost. It was wonderful. But I should probably start by telling you about Alden's personal investment in this land, a variegated stretch of remote Vermont backcountry. Alden is one of those people who can look at a pile of scat and tell you, not only what kind of animal left it there, but also when, and whether or not the animal was in a hurry. I like walking with him. I always learn something. But I'm also made much more aware of the extent to which my senses have waned over time in comparison to the way his have sharpened. He knows all the trees within walking distance of his back porch; he has favorite swamps, favorite game trails, favorite logs. He knows where the lone beaver has made his scent post, and why the otter scatters her dung in a ring. He looks at a beech tree and predicts a blight coming on. He stops in mid-stride for what appears to be nothing at all, and then slowly I hear it—straining the way I used to strain to hear Santa's bells in the yard—the soft, squawking volley of a flock of high geese. "They're way up there tonight," he'll whisper, unmoving, "nearly a half-mile above the clouds . . . " Stock still he stands. They've come and gone. My toes are aching with cold and he still listens, head cocked, eyes down, back taut. Then a rustle of leaves and he's paces down the path.

One day, a few weeks ago, Alden brought me to his favorite place, a forty-five minute walk from the nearest dirt road. A game trail runs along the edge of a marsh beneath balsam fir, some hemlock, a few old beech. The shore is littered with ragged, pointed branches and gnawed stumps—all the tell-tale signs of beaver activity. But Alden points out that the teeth marks are weathered and the wood rotten. The beavers abandoned this site long ago, leaving their ponds to swell into marshland.

The trees lining the trail are loaded with bear sign: grey bark scarred with pulpy crescent moons. It's impossible not to think of the size and strength of the claws, and it's just as difficult to imagine several hundred plus pounds of fur, bones and flesh hauling itself gracefully up the trunks in search of beech nuts and berries. We get up close and squint at the gashes looking for hairs. We find gobs, coarse and black, a few paler and almost downy. They shift under our breath. Practically every tree along the trail is marked, like some inert gauntlet merely suggesting the blows an angry bear could inflict on the unfortunate passer-by. The bitten trees, the balsams, are my favorite. Organic totems of raw drama, unbroken instinct, monster strength. I have been told bears rub, scratch and bite trees simply to mark territory, but I imagine an impetus more remote—something felt—rumbling deep in the chest of the bear. This rumbling is wildness, and when I look at the great gashes, the great chunks of tree torn off and splintered on the ground, I think, "Yes. Good. This still happens."

Past the marking trees, the land slopes downward into a slight, soft cradle strewn with mixed deciduous leaves: maple, beech, white birch and yellow birch, cherry, ash. Resting in the cradle parallel to the quiet edge of the marsh, an old log sinks into decay. We sit on the ground for awhile in silence, our backs against the softened meat of the dead wood. Then Alden tells me about the moose that stood less than ten feet from the spot a few days before, and about the two grouse that he shot on the other side of the ridge after eight hours of walking. Falling silent again, we see that the sky over the water is growing dim. Alden stands and says, "Not much daylight left." So we hoof it back along the game trails to the road. By the time we get there I am sweating, and the rutted old logging track is a dun-colored swath set off from the thick dark wood on either side. We fumble along.

Though my guide has been on the road before, this section is not familiar to him. We are looking for the path to a clearing at the top of Patterson Mountain. From there we can get our bearings and set a direct course back home. We walk for fifteen minutes in the wrong direction and wind up in a different clearing, staring at the outlines of a decrepit ranger station. Alden is angry and apologetic about his miscalculation, but I surprise myself with a laugh and say, "Let's just walk west." The last luster of the sun still hangs in the clouds above the darkened Adirondacks on the other side of the state. We retrace our steps cautiously, laughing at our decision not to bring head lamps and blinking blindly at the lightless, snapping trees. Only the birches burn slender shapes against the darkly wooded weave of nighttime.

With good sense and better luck, we find the path leading to the lost clearing and, though it is completely dark and getting colder, we sit and watch for the earliest stars. When we can no longer see each other's faces, we start the trek down the mountain. The leaves are loud under our feet as we feel for rocks and roots and the edges of the trail. This is the part that Alden knows well. He's been up and down this trail more in one year than most people would walk it in a decade. "This is where we saw the deer browse earlier," he says, as we maneuver our way around a sharp bend and down the face of a slanted rock embedded in the ground. "The creek is just up here. Watch your feet." And moments later I hear its soft gurgle interrupted by the crunch of his boot in fresh ice. I don't know my backyard as well as he knows this mountain.

Born and raised in Tennessee, now a resident of a very small, very rural village in eastern Vermont, my friend feels he belongs to two parts of the world. He has immense affection for both places, and he feels torn, as though between two lovers: one old and loaded with memories, the other new and entirely distinct, both physically and emotionally, from the first. One nurtured him in his boyhood and the other has helped him mature into his present, twenty-nine-year-old, land-loving self. Sometimes when we sit and talk about devoting the rest of our lives to one place, he becomes silent, as though waiting for an undercurrent, far deeper than reason, to swing his compass in either direction. As for me, I have one lover, one mother, one place that defines me. Though I have traveled across the country and around the world, there is nothing more wondrous, more simple or sound, than coming home again to New England.

Does the Ukrainian man, shuffling over the cracks in the sidewalk of the Lower East Side in his rumpled woolen trousers and boots, his white hair clamped down under a greasy grey cap—does he have this kind of home? Does he understand where he is? Does he remember where he came from? Does it matter after all? In an *Orion* article from the "Where There's Hope" issue, Brian Doyle writes, "Why hope, how hope, in a culture inured to death, in a world fouling it's nest, a politics driven by greed? Because there are giants; because there are children; because life leaps." I will add to this: because we do belong someplace. Home is much more than a pleasant idea. Or rather, we need it to be.

The conscience of a blackened street
Impatient to assume the world.

I am moved by fancies that are curled
Around these images and cling:

The notion of some infinitely gentle
Infinitely suffering thing.

—*T. S. Eliot,* Preludes

I am young, and yet I sense the youth in me shifting, altering its shape to fit my older organs, older eyes, my older notions of happiness. It has been almost a year since I started writing this way about hope. I was an editor then; now I am a teacher. Then I lived in New York City. Now I live in Saxtons River, Vermont. Then I longed for fresh air and space and growing things. Now I can walk out into forests for hours at a time and not see another person. As much as this setting feels more suited to the rhythms of my psyche, I do miss those streets stringing awkwardly through neighborhood after overcrowded neighborhood. I miss the markets that would spring up on Saturdays, all loaded with fruit and breads and cheeses and steaming cauldrons of cider or soup. I actually miss the pulse of the morning crowd, surging like blood through the clogged arteries of the city. I miss that frenetic energy always humming, churning, writhing on the other side of the door at the base of my apartment building's narrow stairwell. It's a zealous city, an agitated city, a city with a fever. Some days I had to think for a moment before stepping outside. It became a real decision: to become a part of the mass, or isolate myself from it. The choice was a conscious one, often dictated by the alternating desire for stillness or movement, silence or noise.

Here, in this quietly contained community, clustered against a river running between the old, low hills of southeastern Vermont, the pace and purpose of life is completely different. Everyone knows about the homemade molé served at The Golden Egg on Friday and Saturday nights, the calamari and bruschetta on Wednesdays. People actually go the speed limit through town. Nobody seems to feel especially inconvenienced when we get a heavy snow. The milk and honey and cheese that I eat is produced and packaged down the road. There are no working ATMs within five miles of here, and the General Store closes at seven on weekdays. I left New York in search of something else, and I

have found it. I left a job where I was confined to a four-by-four cubi-
cle of temperature-controlled office space to spend my days in a class-
room, in the dorm, the dining hall, on the soccer field and the ski trails
with 250 unwieldy, infuriating, wonderful adolescents. I changed the
setting of my life, and now the setting is changing me, just as it always
does. But the change is environmental; it works from the outside going
in, like ice thawing. The elements are the same, but they alter according to the tenor of their surroundings.

The city was ominous and impressive at first, something completely "other." Until I moved there, I had kept that reality in a remote
corner of my consciousness, boxed up and labeled DOW: Dirty
Overpopulated Wasteland. Then one day in February I found myself in
the middle of it. I almost got hit by a cab. I threw away six dollars on
a paper cup of novelty soup, plastic lid not included. But the biggest
obstacles I ran into were my own preconceived notions of the place,
my own violent biases that were so eager to nail it, pin it to the wall
like some grotesque beetle specimen, reduce it to its LCD, even dis-
regard its importance in the larger sociological scheme of things. It
wasn't until I started really looking at the place, really living in it, the
way Alden really lives in his present home, that I began to appreciate
its own peculiar, incomparable beauty. I am different now. I have melted
down and learned to take on other shapes. I am not so "impatient to
assume the world," and I realize, naively, that coffee vendors and street
performers can be as "infinitely gentle" or "(i)nfinitely suffering" as
children and corn crops and wildflowers.

It avails not, time nor place—distance avails not,
I am with you, you men and women of a generation, or
    ever so many generations hence,
Just as you feel when you look on the river and sky, so I
    felt,
Just as any of you is one of a living crowd, I was one of a
    crowd,

Just as you are refresh'd by the gladness of the river and
the bright flow, I was refresh'd,
Just as you stand and lean on the rail, yet hurry with the
swift current, I stood yet was hurried,
Just as you look on the numberless masts of ships and the
thick-stemm'd pipes of steamboats, I look'd.
—Walt Whitman, "Crossing Brooklyn Ferry," Leaves of Grass

Yesterday was Thanksgiving. Like every other Thanksgiving I've known, I spent it with my family. Gus, my nephew, born last February when I still lived in New York, is now flipping light switches and tearing around on all fours. Michael, his father, talks about the challenge of teaching classes at an art school on top of his regular job working in a Boston art gallery to help foot the diaper bill and, eventually, pay for preschool. Catherine, Gus's mom, tells me in her placid, playful way that when she's away from him, teaching or painting or on a quick errand at the store, there is a significant portion of her brain and a larger portion of her heart that can think of nothing but getting home to be with him again. Later I watch my parents take a break from mashing potatoes and thickening gravy to quietly toast their thirty-fifth year of life together. My eldest brother Desh plays us a recording of his first orchestral composition, which should be finished the day before the due date of his first child. Phuong, his wife, sits on the floor Indian-style, her hands clasped around a taught, mounded abdomen. She watches Desh listening to his own music and smiles.

I feel like I am more of an observer than I am a participant in the day. I find myself thinking instead of talking. I wash dishes to give my hands something to do and my mind the time to settle into a comfortable train of thought. After two pots and a ladle's worth of dwelling on work that needs to be done and relationships that need attention, I end up thinking about tradition. I think of what might have happened in this room between other people on other Thanksgivings. Then I decide that, despite tradition, no holiday, no gathering, no graduation or memorial or christening or union happens twice. But tradition threads through all these many-colored memories like a string holding beads. No matter how removed we become from our origins—from that basic question of why we are here, on this continent, and not someplace else—no matter how altered the landscape or how lucrative the economy, no matter who is elected (fairly or unfairly) into office, we will always gather to share food and drink on the third Thursday of November. It's been happening for centuries and will continue to happen in millions of households for more centuries. There must be something in the chemistry of the *Homo sapien* brain that recognizes the importance of celebration, reverence, ritual, communion, promise.

As I toss the net of my memory back over the past two-and-a-half decades, I think of those who were present and those who were not, which years were spent at our house, which were at Nana's. And of the years that were spent at our house, which tablecloths were used and how many leaves were needed in the big, lion-footed mahogany table to make room for everyone. My father did the table setting, always. And I helped him sometimes, waited patiently by the crystal cabinet as he counted out the family on his fingers, his head tilted, eyes squinted and forced upwards as though trying to look at his own eyebrows, his voice listing the names in animated swoops. It wasn't so much a chore as it was a game—no, it was a puzzle, a word problem: so many guests are coming to dinner and we have so many square inches of surface area to accommodate them. This year, he actually planed, cut and sanded extensions for my brother's table out of scrap wood, carrying them into his kitchen as though equipped with the solution to end all problems.

The food memories are the strongest. They've lodged themselves into the corners of my consciousness like burnt casserole. I can recall the years pie crusts were too tough and the squash experiments failed ("Hey, Julia Childs uses marshmallows, why can't we?"), the mulled cider years and the raisin sauce years, the year we had artichokes and my great aunt's car caught on fire, and the year of baked apples and deviled eggs when my brother recorded the cocktail hour conversation then played it back to us after dessert, chuckling wildly to himself. The year my mother and I made nine different kinds of pie, all spread out on the sideboard in the dining room like a doll's wilderness of sugared valleys, cinnamoned peaks and cream-soaked tarns—that year the dog died. I remember the year of radishes, of broccoli instead of peas, when my grandmother was hooked up to an oxygen tank. And the year after that, when her apartment had become a guest wing, we forgot the Hollandaise and her blue chair stood emptily in the corner of the living room, the ghost ring of her martini glass still embossed on the table to the left of it.

This year was the last year my mother's parents spent Thanksgiving in their own home. Next year, they'll be in "assisted living," and we'll have to drive to Massachusetts to pick them up and bring them to our house. Nana will still make the rolls, but she probably won't have room in the kitchenette oven to make her celebrated apple pies, or her cherry and mince with the basket-weave crusts. "I'll miss the smells," she told me when I visited her last. I nodded distractedly and said *Mmmm*. "Don't you *love* the smells?" she demanded, shoving my arm with the tips of her fingers. But before I could agree she was asking about the "nice boy" I brought home last summer.

About a month ago Nana fell and broke her shoulder in two places, and the two men she lives with, her husband and her son, realized they didn't know how to operate the stove. They thought they might have to go without a hot meal until she healed, and they would have if it weren't for the local church and my mother, who has been driving an hour and thirty minutes from New Hampshire every other day to keep the refrigerator stocked and my grandmother bathed. Papa can't help. He suffers from dementia, but suffering isn't the right word for it. He's not in any sort of pain. It's as though his brain has simply decided that it's tired and it doesn't want to work anymore.

"He's like a child," my mother said on the phone this morning. "He holds my hand now when we go to town to do the shopping. We finish one thing and he turns to me and says, 'What're we going to do next?' So I take him to buy a chocolate doughnut and he's happy as a clam. 'These are my very favorite, you know,' he says. Just like a child."

We talk about how life moves in full circles. She tells me another story about my great-grandfather, Grampa Bunker, who looked at his wife just moments before he died and said, "Oops! I tripped over my dress, throwing my stone!" An old daguerreotype in one of Nana's dusty stacks of albums shows him as a boy, his hair wound in curls hanging down to his shoulders. He's posing in front of a velveteen backdrop, wearing a light organza dress with an empire waist and a bow trailing down to the floor. He was about four years old at the time.

When I go home for Christmas, I will help my mother and my aunts box up all the china, the silver and the plate in preparation for my grandparents' move out of the big house on Nelson Street. Nana is worried; she doesn't know what to do with it all. She is also sad, because so much of her life is bound up in these things. I keep telling her that we'll all come together to help decide what will go where. I told her it'll be like a huge picnic. "We'll rally all the cousins and every-one will bring some food and we'll get the old drum set down for Papa. Room by room, we'll just get it done." This doing, this helping, is the only thing that comforts my grandmother these days. It was hard for her to come to terms with out-living a grandchild. "Eric always said he would do an etching of this house," she told me recently. "Or pen and ink. He did a lot of pen and ink. But he never got around to it I guess. You wonder, don't you . . ." When she said this she looked down at her pale arm, motionless in its sling. I'd never seen her look so tired.

She is eighty-seven, and though she is an incredibly fit eighty-seven, she needs us more than she ever has. She's so accustomed to giv-ing that receiving is difficult for her. She is not convinced that the move will go smoothly. I tell her that such a big task is really just a bunch of small tasks in a pile. She laughs and says, "You all loved this place, too, didn't you?" And we did. We spent entire summers there in the pool, in the barn, riding Big-wheels down the driveway, Janna and I scheming attacks on the boy cousins from our headquarters in the bathroom. We crammed more people into the dining room on more occasions than I could ever count. And the stove, an old Custom Imperial Frigidaire, has been cooking without a glitch since 1965. All the strands of our memory loop back and through the rooms, along the walls, up and down the twisted stairwells, out the multi-paned windows and back in through the bright-knobbed doors. Through all our living and dying, the house has stood and held us, like a tradition, like a physical manifestation of the secret familial love that keeps us fighting together through everything.

———

Children's voices in the orchard
Between the blossom- and the fruit-time:
Golden head, crimson head,
Between the green tip and the root.
Black wing, brown wing, hover over;
Twenty years and the spring is over;
Today grieves, tomorrow grieves,
Cover me over, light-in-leaves;
Golden head, black wing,
Cling, swing,
Spring, sing,
Swing up into the apple-tree.

—T. S. Eliot, from Landscapes

Desh and Phuong's child was born today: a boy, six pounds, thirteen ounces, twenty-one inches long. She was screaming *"I can't do this anymore!"* when the doctors realized the umbilical cord was wrapped around the baby's neck. They severed it, and it was over. He slid from her, and before she had a chance to see him, they rushed him to the other side of the room where a nurse put him under a heat lamp and gave him oxygen. From where he stood gripping Phuong's hand, my brother could see the infant's body shivering. He said it was dark purple. I imagine the color of a bruise, of dusty grapes, turnip roots or unpeeled beets. And there was silence—no words of encouragement or comfort from the nurses as they quickly moved over and around the child, prodding him, stretching his limbs, handling him like something inanimate, unidentified, not like a son. Desh let go of his wife's hand to cross the room to ask, just to see, but then stopped halfway, stunned and blinking in that stringent hospital fluorescence, feeling, for the first time, a responsibility for two.

After a while, Desh said the baby's skin started "pinking up." When they heard the first cry, they started breathing again, practically convulsing with joy and relief. And when they finally placed the boy in Phuong's arms, his chapped, tiny lips found her breast within seconds. Exhausted from worry and from watching his wife in so much pain, my brother sat down in a chair and slept. But by the time I reached him on the phone, he was wide awake and totally estatic. "He's really cute, Jill," he said, and I could tell he was smiling. "He's really adorable . . . I'm looking at him right now. He's got Phuong's nose and my mouth and eyes. They're deep blue, dark blue, and he's looking all around the room. When Phuong moves somewhere, his eyes follow her. And he's constantly trying to suck on his fingers. They put mittens on his hands to keep him from scratching himself and he puts those in his mouth, too . . ." I hear the baby sneeze and then Desh's voice go soft: "It's okay, it's okay, it's okay little guy."

People need this kind of reinforcement—this devotion to landscapes and houses and children. Because we need to care, and we need to identify what's meaningful, what moves us. We need to be totally mystified, and learn to appreciate the extraordinary, fugitive fact of our lives. At all costs, we need to hold onto the memory of a young man who (according to his three brothers who wrote the obituary) "was a lover of nature and people . . . a great artist, deep thinker, and gifted musician." We need Thanksgivings and births. We need the common things, the shared things, things to love entirely, unabashedly. Because this is where hope grows.

If they will listen, sing them a song.

— *Confucius*

HEART LAKE

John A. Murray

i.

The great tragedy of life is not that men die, but that they cease to love.
—Somerset Maugham

We begin in the hour before sunrise, a few stars still to the west. The lodgepole forest is dark, but the sky to the east is bright. The morning air is cool, as it always is in Yellowstone, even in the month of June.

Soon we do not hear the passing cars on the road.

It is morning and the uplands are full of expectancy and invitation. Woodland birds twitter. Treetops stir. Aspen leaves rustle. Small rodents move in the grass. Insects murmur. Woodpeckers thump. Pine squirrels chatter. A raven caws.

Spider-threads, thinner than a baby's gossamer hair, crisscross the trail. Everywhere there is the wet forest scent of fresh wildflowers opening to the day and fallen leaves turning to earth in quiet places. Sometimes in the air there is the faint suggestion of a large animal, of fur and musk and movements that are seldom heard or seen. Other times there is the incenselike fragrance of sagebrush, the tangy sweet essence of the Yellowstone backcountry.

At some point in the first mile we cross an invisible boundary and are no longer part of the world from which we came, but are silently absorbed into the older and richer community of Yellowstone.

It is quiet on the trail, and soon the ringing in our ears from the drive is gone.

After half an hour we stop so that my son can tie his bootlaces. He says that his hands are cold, and so I reach into my pack and give him the pair of gloves I always carry. This is his first overnight trip into the wilderness.

He is ten years old.

My son, Naoki. How to describe him? His mother was Japanese and so his features are a mixture of those Asian and European. Sometimes I see him as he was when he was a baby. Other times I see him as the man he will become. This summer he has been crossing the bridge from boyhood to youth. The passage can be described as a gradual loss of innocence. On this trip to Heart Lake I am trying to teach him something more of my world, of our world, of that broad outer landscape that so brightens the horizons of life. I see myself as a kind of Sherpa guide on his larger journey, pointing out landmarks, noting history, indicating routes, warning of hazards, suggesting side-trips, examining possible objectives.

The rest will be up to him, whose name in Japanese means "like a tree, straight and upright, never does the wrong thing."

As we walk I draw his attention to things: the cloven tracks of elk and deer and moose, the deep cut impressions of horseshoes, the tiny cuneiform scribblings of field mice, the three-toed imprints of birds, and, once, the familiar four-toed marks of a coyote. It being summer, the wildflowers are everywhere—wild roses dropping soft pink petals as smooth and glossy as silverspoons, the yellow balsamroot with arrowhead-shaped leaves, coral-red fireweed, lake-blue day lilies, honey-orange paintbrush, and shooting stars with delicate blossoms of blue and black and yellow.

The sun rises slowly by degrees, and where the light strikes the trail scattered flecks of mica in the dust sparkle. In the woods sunbeams fall here and there, brightening the flower patches and angular rocks and fallen trees. In places the trail is no wider than my son's shoulders, and the grasses nearly cover it. In other spots it becomes broad enough to accommodate two horses. We take our time along the path, stopping often to rest and talk. We do not hurry. We have all day to reach Heart

Lake. I am trying to teach my son that the trip is as important as the destination, and that every step across a landscape is full of wonders.

The trail is gentle and climbs hills and follows streams and crosses meadows. The altitude is comfortable for Naoki's first long hike with a pack—around 8,000 feet. This is the southeast corner of Yellowstone, the least visited area in the park. The "Thorofare Country," as it is known, is the wild heart of the central Rockies. Fittingly, our destination, at the head of the Snake River, is a place called Heart Lake.

We stop for a break midway, about five miles, and have a snack. There are no clouds. The sky is as blue and luminous as the enameled blue of a wolf pup's eyes. The day has become warm, and the gloves go back into the pack. We eat crackers and Colby cheese and drink water. We sit in the shade of a solitary standing tree. Our hearts feel good, beating rhythmically from the walk. An iridescent green hummingbird buzzes near, attracted by the red of Naoki's bandana, and then, like Prospero's Ariel, disappears into the remains of what was once an extensive forest.

All around us are burned lodgepole pines. Most of the dead trees are still standing. Bereft of branches, the upright needlelike trees resemble porcupine quills. The trees range in color from bone white to charcoal black, from ghostly blue to pewter gray. Some still have their spire tops. Others are broken over a third or halfway up. A few are collapsed together in groups. One lone pilgrim has fallen into what remains of a charitable neighbor. A gust of wind will soon bring them both down. In places the indefatigable lodgepole seedlings have begun to recolonize the slopes. Most of these cheerful pioneers stand about eight or nine feet—roughly one foot for each year since the fire. In the understory, wild raspberries and fireweed, dwarf willow and bluebells have taken over. The hillsides are green with new plant growth. Over the last decade what had been a sterile patch of overgrown timber has become a fertile open country elk paradise.

Naoki wants to know what happened to the forest. I explain that for a hundred years fires were religiously fought in the park. Dead plants and dropped branches and storm-felled trees piled up, often chest-high, on the forest floor. Then, in the summer of 1988, there was a drought. Conditions became ripe for a conflagration. Lightning strikes ignited a fire on Two Ocean Plateau. Within days the blaze had moved north into Yellowstone, searching as if by intuitive sense for areas of accumulated dead wood. By the time the snows fell in October, more than a third of the park had burned. Despite the efforts of more than ten thousand firefighters and the expenditure of more than one hundred million dollars, the forces of nature prevailed. The fire swept like strong medicine through moribund stands, clearing out dying and decayed trees, opening canopies and bringing in sunlight to nourish the green plants that sustain the animal kingdom.

The real lesson, I emphasize to Naoki, is that in nature destruction is powerfully wed to creation. The Yellowstone fires show that what appears to be destructive and negative can actually be creative and beneficial.

"Like when President Lincoln waged war to stop slavery?"

I pause, surprised. Like his great-grandfather and his grandfather, Naoki loves American history.

"And now the world is a better place?"

I smile.

What I most enjoy about Naoki—and this is often the case for children of nine or ten—are his Heraclitean statements of truth, his simple, unadorned statements that come out of nowhere and cut right to the heart of the matter.

We mount up and move out. Gradually the pungent odor of sulphur fills the air. "It smells like fireworks going off," Naoki observes, hopefully. Like all little boys and girls, he has a fondness for fireworks. Shortly we are standing on the northern edge of Heart Lake Geyser Basin, a treeless burning region about the size of a college campus. The sprawling wasteland is filled with boiling mud pots, beautiful geothermal springs, barren baked earth, and trickling streams of steaming hot water. To the west is Factory Hill, especially hard-hit by the big fire. To the south is Heart Lake, gleaming in the sun, almost too bright to look at.

Naoki is speechless. He has never seen a geothermal basin. I had not told him about the place, so as to give him an unexpected surprise. With the irregular jets and puffs of mist, billowing white columns and dissipating vapor clouds, the area resembles the month-old bivouac of a large army, with the smoke of a hundred campfires and bonfires rising into the air.

"Dad, what is this!" he exclaims, jumping up and down.

Again we take off the packs and have a closer look. Down the hill is a bubbling mud pot. I caution him not to get too close. A few feet from the edge he stops. The mud is churning and burning and turning over and over, as if in a pot over a gas range turned on full. The sounds—random belches and rumbles, burps and gurgles—are comical.

"Where does the heat come from?"

"Subterranean toy factory," I joke.

"Seriously, Dad."

I describe the geological miracle that is Yellowstone—how heat is generated by the friction of rocks shifting beneath the earth, and how that heat then leaks to the surface to become geysers and hot springs, sulfur pools and fumaroles.

He is as excited as I have rarely seen him, and, with the boldness of Captain William Clark, insists we continue deeper into the basin.

Shortly the trail drops down a steep hill. At the base of the hill is a stream, Witch Creek, so hot that it's steaming. Gingerly, he touches a finger to the water. There follows a smile I'm sure I'll recall in the final moments of life, reflecting on the high points of the passage.

Further on we reach a series of geothermal pools. The colors are so intense I set up the tripod and take a few photographs. Most of the pools are a deep azure blue in the center with a jade-green rim. A few are colored by algae beds—ochre yellow, brown sienna, pastel pink. Photography involves waiting for the wind to blow the steam clouds away, which occurs about once a minute. Through that lens, or window, you then try to capture the brilliant color, the seething water, the ephemeral mists rising like the spirits of the departed.

A few minutes later we are back on trail, continuing south to Heart Lake, now less than half a mile away. We pass the ranger cabin, no one home, and then veer down a grassy footpath to the right to the lake and to our campsite in the trees. I set up the tent in the clearing—the old North Face that has sheltered me faithfully, without one leak, from the caribou grounds of northern Alaska to the cactus country of southern Arizona. Naoki immediately disappears into the depths of the tent, refusing to come out, playing an electronic game on his sleeping bag and insisting that he needs a proper nap. "I'm a city boy, Dad," he protests. I surrender to the absurdity of the situation and read a worn paperback copy of Turgenev's *Sketches from a Hunter's Album,* a book I first read thirty years ago, when I was fifteen.

Eventually he tires of the bat cave and emerges blinking into the sunlight.

We walk down to the lake—that perpetual fish smell coming across blue and white-capped water—and gather driftwood for the kindling pile.

Afterward I take him to a special place. In the woods behind camp there is a knoll with an immense spruce that burned in the great fire. The tree still stands, most of the branches intact, in a place where it probably lived for three or four hundred years. At the base of a tree I had, the previous fall, carved a heart with the following inscription: "Patricia Hall Murray, 1928–1998." I explain to Naoki that I had distributed some of grandmother's ashes here, and a lock of her hair.

"Why did you bring her here?"

"Because when I was a little boy she always read to me from a book about a grizzly bear in Yellowstone."

"Who wrote the book?

"A nature writer named Ernest Thompson Seton."

"Do you think she gets lonely up here?"

"Nah. Not with all these wonderful animals and friendly people visiting."

"What do you think death is like, Dad?"

"I think it's like a snowflake falling on the water. I think we go back into the stream."

"Does grandmother being dead make you sad?"

"Oh I don't know, she had a pretty good life. Nobody lives forever, you know. Not even these trees, not even these woods. Not even these mountains. That's what places like Yellowstone teach you—to accept the changes of life. If you stop and think about it, Yellowstone is like a great university. That raven over there, he's a dean. That tree behind him, he is a distinguished professor. He can teach you a lot of things if you only stop and listen. And that lake down the hill is like a giant lecture hall. There is so much to learn in this country. I've been coming here for twenty-seven years, and I'm just beginning to learn the lessons."

"Hey, what's that?"

Naoki spots something moving off in the woods. It is a fisherman from one of the other campsites, with a creel and a rod, headed down to the lake. Naoki insists we follow, and so we walk down to the lake and watch him cast against the wind and across the waves in the middle of the day, having no luck whatsoever.

An hour later Naoki proclaims it is dinnertime and so, with a little assistance, he builds a good cooking fire. Dinner is a gallon aluminum pot full of lake water and boiled carrots and potatoes, onions and celery, green beans and peas, with a little freeze-dried tenderloin mixed in, and served with French bread. We call it Heart Lake Stew.

After dinner is story time.

I tell him about my great-great-grandfather, Charles Evers, who first came to Yellowstone in the summer of 1883, and how he took the train to Miles City, Montana, and then caught a stage coach to Gardiner, and how it was difficult for him to get around because he carried a Confederate miniball in his leg from Chickamauga. And I tell him of my father, who came with his parents to Yellowstone in the summer of 1929, and how Dad still remembers the black bear sticking his head in the car window and how bad the breath of the bear was. I tell him of how I first came to Yellowstone in the summer of 1972, at the age of eighteen, with my girlfriend Paula and my father and little brother. And how I returned two summers later to work as a horse wrangler at a ranch, and how Doc and I packed some dudes into the headwaters of the Lamar River, and could only watch, laughing, as a herd of buffalo stampeded through camp, flattening all but the cook tent.

"You guys laughed?"

"Sure, sometimes things are so bad all you can do is laugh."

The conversation turns to bears. The rangers had us watch a mandatory orientation video on bears before setting out on the hike. Naoki is concerned about bears, but I tell him not to worry, that Daddy studied grizzlies for six years in Alaska and knows what to do and what not to do. I do not tell him about the Swiss woman who was killed by a grizzly at Heart Lake about fifteen years ago, while sleeping in her tent; or about my Alaska friend Michio Hoshino, who was killed by a brown bear while sleeping in his tent in Kamchatka three summers ago.

I show him how to put the food up at a considerable distance from camp and to have absolutely nothing resembling food in the tent.

The stars thicken, the fire dwindles, the night darkens, my son yawns.

"What will we do tomorrow, Dad?"

I point to the mountain behind us, a 10,308-foot massif named Mount Sheridan for an old Civil War general who was not unfamiliar with these parts.

"Climb that thing behind us, if you're ready."

"I was born ready."

"That's my man."

Sometime in the middle of the night a great wind comes up and blows the fly partially off the tent. When I go outside to secure the covering, I see the stars being rapidly blotted out by a black cloud coming in from the west. There are flashes of lightning in the hollows of the cloud, the bolts illuminating amphitheaters and antechambers of darkness. The thunder rumbles across the land. Ten minutes later the rain hits us—torrents and sheets and unbelievable waterfall-like deluges.

Naoki is a Buddhist, like his mother, and begins to recite a Buddhist chant. I tell him not to worry and make a few jokes. Even when the lightning hits nearby we find ourselves laughing.

I listen to the rain for a long time after he goes to sleep, and the storm is rolling out across Yellowstone Lake toward Montana and the wind is making gentle sounds in the trees.

ii.

Thy love to me is wonderful.

—Samuel 2:26

Breakfast the next morning consists of granola with coconut chips and dried pineapple bits, served up in bowls of evaporated milk, with some powdered orange juice to wash it down. Naoki is accustomed to a heavier meal at home—omelet, bacon, hash browns—and I explain to him that you don't want too full of a stomach if you are going to climb a mountain.

He nods politely, unconvinced of the logic.

The trail begins just south of the campsite, veering north into the old burn on the south-facing side of Mount Sheridan.

Dewdrops sparkle in the grass, the woods ring with birdsong. The day is filled with happiness and hope.

Not a quarter of a mile up the trail we spot a cow moose and calf moving from right to left through the timber. I find a fallen tree and we sit there, watching. Naoki takes out his disposable camera and composes a shot. I want to teach him to know the value of long intimate moments with the landscape, to be patient, and to become acquainted with deep time, because that is where all the best ideas come from.

Gradually the cow moose drifts off. The calf, browsing intently on some dwarf willows, suddenly realizes it is alone and nervously looks for its mother, bawling every step of the way. From the woods the cow huffs a response. The young one trots off to join its parent and we continue up the trail.

Higher and higher we climb, following switchbacks, moving in and out of old burns and green timber, ascending closer to the sky.

Everywhere there are the trails and paths of elk and moose and deer. At one point, in a grassy clearing, we come upon the contoured beds of five elk—three cows and two calves.

Always we are moving toward the light, toward the summit.

We round a bend in the trail, overlooking an avalanche slide, and Naoki shouts, "Dad, look!"

He points into the slide and I see nothing.

"What?"

"There—by that rock shaped like a triangle. Something is moving. What is it?"

I squint and find a rock that resembles a pyramid, cast around, and then see it—a black bear.

We sit down and observe through our one pair of binoculars.

"What is he doing?"

"It is a she, son. You can tell by the shape of the head. She appears to be digging for ants."

Naoki is incredulous that something as large as a bear would eat insects, and so I have to explain the facts of life to him—that Yellowstone, a high and fairly dry plateau, is a hard place for a bear to make a living, and is not nearly as rich a habitat as Alaska, with the salmon, or Canada, with the huckleberries.

We watch the bear for nearly an hour as she scrambles up and down the snowslide, looking for something to eat. I explain that a person can learn what is edible in the wilderness—leaves, roots, berries—simply by watching bears. What they can eat we can eat. Finally, her lovely ebony fur rippling in the sunlight, the bear ambles downslope, toward the timber, looking probably for a cool spot to nap away the hot hours.

Near the summit a strange thing happens. A golden eagle and a magpie, both startled by our presence, rise up together not twelve feet from us. We hear the whoosh of the wind through the eagle's wing feathers as it strains for altitude. We see the blue of the sky between its torn tail feathers. Both fly off in different directions. What were they doing? Why were they together? We search around for a carcass of some sort, but find nothing. It will remain one of life's mysteries.

After several false summits, we finally reach the real top of the mountain and sit down to survey our kingdom. The view is panoramic, and expands to the horizons. Far to the east are the Absaroka Mountains, jagged purple peaks that carry snow on them through summer's longest day. Nearer is the vast cobalt expanse of Yellowstone Lake. Nearer still is Heart Lake, which is, we can now see, shaped very much like a heart. To the south is Two Ocean Plateau, thoroughly burned over, the place where the fire started. Colter Peak, named for the first American visitor to these parts in 1807, is visible beyond the meadows of the Yellowstone River. Far to the south and west are the jagged Tetons, the mountains from which we just came. Due west are Lewis Lake and Shoshone Lake, sparkling like two twin sisters.

"Hopefully one day you can bring your son here," I say.

Naoki nods, gazing off pensively. His expression reminds me of the little boy in Winslow Homer's painting *Nooning,* a canvas I first saw when I was his age at the Metropolitan Museum of Art in New York. I am glad that I can give him this, the timeless treasure that is Yellowstone, at such a young age.

On the hike down we sing songs—beginning with contemporary songs and working our way back through the decades to show tunes such as *Oklahoma!* We end with folk songs like *Shenandoah.* I tell him that we used to sing songs on long marches in the Marines, songs like *She Wore a Yellow Ribbon* and *When the Saints Go Marching In.* A good song can carry you along for many a weary mile.

Back in camp we raid the food box and then set out for Witch Creek to rest our feet in its warm waters. Naoki relates his theory that animals can talk to each other, and that certain children can talk to them as well. It occurs to me on the walk back to camp that he just might be right.

iii.

A society is a group of reasonable beings in common agreement
as to the objects of their love.

—Saint Augustine, *City of God*

In the morning I open the tent flaps and discover that the cold has unexpectedly paid a visit. During the long hours before dawn the world has been silently but thoroughly covered with a thick frost. The green mosses near the tent are stiff and coated with tiny crystals of ice. Every blade of grass, every weathered stone, every wilted flower, every tree is covered with white. My breath makes a cloud in the tent. Our boots, left outside under the fly, are stiff. The air feels like November in the city.

An hour later we are on the trail, heading briskly back to the road, the sun already warm on our faces, the songbirds calling out, leaving it all behind for another day.

Although it is, by human standards, mute, Yellowstone has often spoken to me in the quiet way of all landscapes that have not been adumbrated by the works of man. It has reminded me of how short life is, and how long death is. It has demonstrated to me what is noble and enduring in wild nature and what is valuable and unperishable in the human spirit. It has illustrated the necessity of establishing lofty but achievable goals. It has taught me humility and good humor. It has shown me that I must be strong and that to remain strong I must stay rooted to the earth. When I have fallen short of virtue, I have found purity again in its springs. When I have known solitude, I have found companionship in its hills and valleys. Grief and loss have been healed among its fire-charred trees. Implicit in every aspect of Yellowstone, and my attachment to it, has been everything that is evoked by the word freedom. Above all, the park has underscored to me the importance of love—not just love of family and friends, but love of culture and country, ideals and ideas, truth and beauty, forgiveness and compassion.

The importance of love comes to you most when you are alone.

In the end, Yellowstone, like so many of our finest parks, is too large to be folded into a map, captured in a photograph, or compressed into an essay. It is a trumpeter swan paddling quietly in the backwaters of Yellowstone Lake and a pack of wolves trotting out from the aspens in Hayden Valley. It is the roar of the wind in a bristlecone pine on Mount Washburn and the thunder of the Lower Falls in the gorge of the canyon. It is the travertine terraces along the Firehole River and the quiet splendor of the Morning Glory Pool. It is a wide-eyed little girl from Tokyo seeing Old Faithful for the first time, and an elderly couple from Indiana seeing it for the last time. It is a place to carry deep inside and hold close whenever you feel yourself in turmoil, and instantly be at peace.

In the Middle Ages the faithful, at least once in life, made the pilgrimage to Canterbury, where they beheld the most beautiful cathedral in the land. In our time, we have Yellowstone.

Somewhere in the final mile of the trail, as we pause for a water break, I tell my son that everything he knows will one day pass away like the leaves of the trees around us or the clouds in the sky, and that one day even I will be gone, but that Yellowstone will always remain, like the truest and oldest friend in the world.

NOTES ON CONTRIBUTORS

Lisa Couturier has published numerous articles and essays about wildlife and urban nature in a variety of journals and books, most recently in *The Mountain Reader* and *Heart of a Nation*. She holds a master's degree from New York University and is a contributing editor to *Potomac Review*. Couturier writes from her home in Brookmont, Maryland, where she lives with her husband and children along the Potomac River.

Penny Harter's recent books include five collections published since 1994: *Shadow Play, Stages and Views, Grandmother's Milk, Turtle Blessing,* and *Lizard Light*. She has published fifteen books of poetry. Her work appears in numerous anthologies and journals, and she has won fellowships and awards from the New Jersey State Council on the Arts, the Geraldine R. Dodge Foundation, and the Poetry Society of America. She teaches in the English Department at the Santa Fe Preparatory School.

Dale Herring is a graduate of the University of Colorado, Boulder. She has worked for a number of years as assistant editorial director of National Geographic Books. An avid whitewater kayaker, she has kayaked around North America and the world, most recently in Patagonia. Her writing has appeared in *American Whitewater* and other publications.

Jill Hindle is a graduate of Middlebury College in English. After working as an editorial assistant at The Lyons Press in New York City for several years, she began teaching English at The Vermont Academy in the fall of 2000. Jill Hindle is a graduate student in the Breadloaf MFA Program, and is the co-author of *Voices of the Land: An Introduction to the Waterworks.*

Vicki Lindner is an associate professor of English literature at the University of Wyoming, Laramie, where she also directs the visiting writers program. Her work has appeared widely in literary journals, including *Ploughshares, Northern Lights, The South Dakota Review, The Sonora Review,* and *The American Literary Review.* Her fiction has won an NEA grant and two New York State fellowships.

Jeri McAndress lives with her husband at the base of the Sangre de Cristo Mountains near Crestone, Colorado. Her writings have appeared in *Northern Lights* and *The High Country News.* Formerly a ballet dancer for George Balanchine in New York, she has in recent years taught dance at Adams State College and elsewhere in the Southwest. She is currently at work on a book that chronicles a dancer's journey from traditional urban settings to unconventional wilderness locations.

Ann McDermott has lived for over twenty years in the Sonoran Desert west of Phoenix, Arizona. Her writings, which have been published widely in journals, explore the relationships between the human experience and the southern desert landscape. She is the author of an unpublished memoir, *Songs from the Desert,* and a work-in-progress that explores the desert as metaphor.

Jon R. Nickles is a retired biologist for the U.S. Fish and Wildlife Service. He holds master's degrees in both botany and zoology. His writings have appeared in *Alaska* magazine, *Sierra*, and the *Anchorage Daily News* (*We Alaskans*). He has lived in Alaska since 1977 and currently resides in Anchorage, when not kayaking his double Klepper far from civilization.

Penelope Grenoble O'Malley is the recipient of three Los Angeles Press Club Awards for journalism and holds the rank of Fellow in the Society for Technical Communication for her work interpreting science and natural history for the lay public. She has written extensively for newspapers and magazines on urban planning, land use and environmental conservation. She is the former director of communications for the Santa Catalina Island Conservancy. She lives with her husband near Los Angeles.

David Petersen is one of the West's most distinguished natural history authors, and has written such acclaimed books as *Ghost Grizzlies* and *From the Nearby Faraway*. Petersen also served as editor for the journals of Edward Abbey (*Confessions of a Barbarian*) and later for Abbey's poems (*Earth Apples*). He lives with his wife in a cabin home deep in the wild San Juan Mountains of southwestern Colorado.

Suzanne Ross is an English professor at Saint Cloud State University in Minnesota, where she teaches undergraduate and graduate courses in both literature and creative writing. Her work has appeared widely in popular magazines and literary journals over the last decade.

Dave Stalling is conservation editor for *Bugle*, the monthly publication of the Rocky Mountain Elk Foundation. He lives in Missoula, Montana with his wife and young son. An avid outdoorsman and devoted environmentalist, Stalling has written numerous articles and essays in both popular magazines and book collections such as *A Hunter's Heart*.

Alianor True holds undergraduate and graduate degrees, respectively, from Cornell University and the University of Michigan, Ann Arbor. For the last five years she has worked summers as a seasonal ranger at such locations as Grand Canyon National Park, Sequoia National Park, the BLM lands of Nevada, and Big Cypress National Preserve. Her first book, *Wildfire,* was published by The Island Press in Spring 2001.

Glenn Vanstrum is a cardiac anesthesiologist in San Diego, California. An avid underwater photographer, he has participated in scuba-diving expeditions around the world, from the Arctic to the tropics. He has published widely in popular magazines and book collections, including previous contributions to the *American Nature Writing* series. He is currently writing a book about his many outdoor adventures in faraway places, to be published by Oxford University Press.

Gretchen Yost is a graduate, in philosophy, from the University of Oregon, Eugene. For the past three years she has lived in a cabin near Bondurant, Wyoming, working summers as a wilderness ranger in the Wind River Mountains. Her writing has appeared in journals and books, including *Wildfire* and the *American Nature Writing* series. She is currently editing a collection of writings by park rangers in the United States and Canada, as well as writing a book about her experiences in the Wind River Mountains.

Tom Zydler is a native of Poland, where he worked as an English teacher. For a number of years now he has lived on his boat near Fort Lauderdale, Florida, while pursuing a career as a landscape and wildlife photographer and natural history writer. His forthcoming book on barrier islands will be published by John Fielder's Westcliffe Publications in Colorado.

PERMISSIONS